The Stone Gospel

A ghost story

Derek E Pearson

First published 2018
Published by GB Publishing.org

Cover Design © 2018 Paul Collett

GBP

GB Publishing.org
www.gbpublishing.co.uk

For Sue, who listens and smiles when it's good, for Lynne MacDiarmid who's dancing mind raises sparks, and for my brother Tony who ran out of time too soon.

Acknowledgements
As always with thanks to George Boughton and the GB Publishing team who hear my ramblings with interest and empathy, no matter what strange paths I lead them down. And to Wills for his editing and input.

CONTENT

When the sky is grey as an elephant's hide
And salt breeze blows cold from the sea.
I walk ancient paths on the castle's side,
Press my feet where the time-worn bones reside.
And the roots of the Earth remember me.

Men of iron gouged its shoulders from the chalk and the clay,
Not for Queens nor for wizards as some fools will tell.
It was raised in one night as his throne for the day
When the Devil was crowned, and the damned had their say.
And these paths led us all straight to Hell.

[1]

The child looked up from his play by the inflated paddling pool, which was striped bright blue and acid yellow. The day was hot and still with just the occasional breath of a breeze, barely enough to ruffle his thick mop of chestnut hair. He squinted in concentration. Jerome was a six-year-old who liked to concentrate fully on any task at hand. He took play as seriously as helping his mother in the kitchen or reading one of the books she considered too old for him; books supplied by his doting grandmother.

He would also spend long hours folded over his drawings, eyes focused and mouth stretched into a thin line. Unlike most other children he wouldn't draw on anything other than good white cartridge paper, and he used yellow and black liveried, Staedtler HB sketching pencils, which he always kept sharpened to a fine point. The drawings Jerome produced were highly detailed and precocious – and had proved a bone of contention between his parents and the teachers at his school.

The school was an excellent institution with a solid reputation for preparing its students for the rigours of secondary education. It was housed in a fine Georgian building near the top of the hill around which the town had been built. And, although it was practically in the shadow of the town's fourteenth century cathedral, its philosophy was rigorously secular. Children, it said, are sponges for absorbing information if it is presented to them properly, but they are also free spirits who should be given a degree of independence to experiment and enjoy life. Otherwise, without that period of release, they might react like overstretched elastic bands and something essential might snap.

Games, play, and the art room were designed to be those periods of release, when the children could run free, compete with their peers, and unleash their creative juices. Paint and coloured clay (both of a brand easily washable from clothes) were the materials of choice in the art room, and the walls usually reflected whichever TV programme was most popular that week. *Doctor Who* might proliferate for a few days, or *Bob the Builder*. Later *Thomas the Tank Engine* might take pride of place; or *Dennis the Menace* in his striped jersey with his snarling mutt *Gnasher* at his side. Mum and dad were perennials of course, as were houses, pet animals and sunlit gardens with trees like green lollipops on brown sticks.

1

The paint was laid on thick, sometimes interspersed with coloured paper gummed down with a glue stick. The thin, blue plastic aprons the children wore while practicing their art had been pulled off a large roll the teacher kept in the cupboard. These were scrunched up and thrown in the big bin in the corner of the room at the end of a lesson, all of them a sticky mess. All except one. Jerome's spotless apron was invariably carefully folded up and handed to his teacher, who knew to keep it safely in a drawer until the next session. His obsessive pencil drawings were widely admired, but stood out starkly amid the brightly coloured, butterfly chaos of the gallery created by his classmates.

No matter what subject the class had been given Jerome always drew people, and his work had a startling effect on the viewer. White-eyed and electrifying his figures seemed to float across his page, and no two looked the same. While he worked he would look up and squint into empty space, as if he was studying his subject. His teachers would wonder what was going through the mind of the isolated little boy, completely absorbed in his own world while sitting in the middle of a boisterous class full of clatter and laughter.

In games, he would apply himself to whichever task he was given with humourless determination. His games instructor compared herself to a wild animal tamer for the hour of her class, especially when friendly childish rivalry might spill over into spite, or blatant cheating took place under her exasperated gaze. She had a whistle and an authoritative voice but claimed she would be better equipped with a chair and a whip. She adored children, she said, but why were so many of them so dead set on proving Darwin wrong? The monkey might have come down out of the trees and learned how to put on its own shoes, but it was still a little monkey when fuelled by sugar and mischief.

And then there was Jerome Talbot, his small, severe face already firmly stamped with the ghost of the handsome man he would become. He was slender, smaller than most, and elfin, his narrow, dark-eyed face intent under a mop of unruly hair. He never ran wild or shrieked like the others. When he ran it was always from wherever she told him to run from, and when he stopped it was always wherever she had told him to run to.

If precision ever became an Olympic sport, she thought, *he would easily win the gold medal.*

The school's headteacher was a woman who detested hearing any of her staff voicing negative attitudes towards the students. She considered such attitudes as a demonstration of severe limitations in the person voicing them and might quietly indicate that their career would be better served elsewhere. Out of her earshot some teachers put forward the opinion that Jerome was, 'too far up his own tight little arse to be normal'. They talked about the symptoms of Asperger's Syndrome, wondered what his home life was like, and during the next parent/teacher evening his house leader cautiously pumped his parents for any explanation that might disclose why the little boy was *always* so serious.

Mike Talbot, the father, believed his son was just a very clever boy who was taking the world a little seriously for the moment. Mike was one of those relentlessly jovial men who constantly apologised for flirting, and described Stephanie, his wife, as 'the long-suffering Mrs T', without realising how accurate that description had become.

'One day,' he explained, 'you'll be telling people about the time you had a Nobel Prize winner in your class and you'll say, "He was a quiet child, but you could see the genius shining in his eyes". Or he'll be making a statement from the front step of number ten Downing Street and you'll think, "Thank God, an honest man at last". Jerome's a bit quiet just now, so what? He's got a lot to think about. He's just putting his brain in order, you wait and see.'

Stephanie, 'Never Steph' thank you, it sounds too, you know, biological' was not so sure. 'Do you think he's all right?' she asked with a note of concern in her voice. 'Is he, you know, autistic or something on the spectrum?' She dropped her voice a register when asking this.

No, she was assured, Jerome *is* very bright and fully aware of his surroundings. There were no indicators for anything like that, and anyway, their son was in the top ten per cent of his year. He was outstanding in all his classes and his behaviour and attitude to learning were exceptional. He took his studies incredibly seriously for a six-year-old – perhaps a little *too* seriously. What, the form leader wondered, did he do to lighten up? What made him laugh at home? Was he ever silly or play the fool? Had anything ever happened to him when he was younger? What was he like at Christmas and on his birthday?

Stephanie looked askance at Mike and he shrugged.

'What? He's a kid, what do you think he does? He opens his presents and he reads them, watches them, draws on them, or plays with them. These days he mostly tries them on. He's at that age, growth spurts, you know? Needs new clothes all the time. Nothing fits for more than five minutes and he grows out of them. Costs a fortune, we'd need a second mortgage, but thank

God for his Nanny and Granddad. They love to buy him stuff; usually from charity shops but good quality all the same.'

Stephanie defended her parents, 'No, Mike, that's not fair. Jerome's uniform didn't come out of a charity shop; they got that in John Lewis. Anyway, something did happen when he was younger, Miss is right. Don't you remember what happened when he had that really bad chest infection when he was three?'

Mike nodded, 'Oh yeah. Poor little mite was very ill, wasn't he? Temperature nearly blew the end clean off the thermometer.'

'Mike, come on, he nearly died! He got pneumonia. He had that fever for four days and the doctor wanted to take him to hospital, but he was too sick to move. I thought Dr Varma was going to move in, he's a saint that man.'

They remembered the pale wasted figure of their son in his cot, and how close it had been to becoming his deathbed.

Then Mike grinned at the pretty young teacher across the table.

'Still, all's well that ends well, as they say. He's all right now, never had a day's sickness since, not even a cold. Got all his illness out of the way at once, didn't he? It's out of his system and all over and done with now.'

'Mike, do you remember how he would talk to himself when he was unconscious? You said it was like he was talking to someone and waiting for the answers. It was really odd.'

'Oh, yeah, his little face was all frowning. What was he talking about?'

'Going on a journey or something. I know he was only three, but his English was already pretty good by then. Wait, no, you didn't hear him at the end. You had gone to bed and were sound asleep that last morning. Exhausted you said. But I heard him at the end. "All right", he said clear as a bell, "I'll stay for now." I can hear him like it was only yesterday, "I'll stay for now," he said, and his fever broke. A week later he was off the antibiotics and back on his feet, his chest as clear as a spring breeze.

'Thing is, before then he was always such a happy, smiley kid, you know? He'd giggle at anything, even his dad acting the fool, and seeing *that* would wipe the smile off the Mona Lisa, trust me. After that he became so serious. It was like he'd gone to sleep as one person and woken up as someone else. He's still lovely, and I love him to bits, believe me, but I miss that sweet little laugh of his, I do. It was so innocent, like he didn't have a care in the world.' She sighed, 'Hearing him laugh would brighten my day no matter how rotten things were, and, you know something? Sometimes, I wonder where it went? And will it ever come back?'

Almost a month later Jerome looked up from the plastic fishing boats he was carefully arranging in patterns around his paddling pool. He squinted into the dappled shadows under the trees and then smiled in greeting. His mother was in the kitchen where she could see him playing on the lawn in the far corner of the garden. She was thinking that the apple and pear trees under which he was playing would have a good crop this year. She would have some to share for the school's Harvest Festival in September. Mike was hopeless in the garden, but it was Stephanie's pride and joy. It looked wonderful in the summer, and after the recent mixture of rain and sunny days the flower beds had excelled themselves. She unloaded the washing machine and filled her laundry basket. It was forecast to be another bright and breezy day, perfect for airing the sheets. She'd hang out the laundry and then make Jerome some lunch, share an omelette with him perhaps, or cook a few fish fingers and baked beans.

It was only once she'd carried her basket out to the washing line that she looked across at the paddling pool. His little boats floated in the still water, slowly drifting out of the tight circle he had formed them into, but of her son there was no sign.

An hour later Mike was on his way home from the office and the police had been supplied with a description of Jerome and the clothes he was wearing. A policewoman was talking with Stephanie and plying her with tea. The officer had introduced herself as Rose, and she had helped Stephanie hang out her washing while giving the distraught mother time to talk.

Stephanie was desperate for Rose to understand that she was a good and caring mum. She wasn't one of those parents who let their kid's just wander off. She had only turned away for a second, she said, and anyway the gate had a child-lock on it. Even Mike had trouble with it. Jerome couldn't have got out, he couldn't! And he wasn't the sort to wander off. He was a good boy, quiet and polite. Happy with his own company, not demanding, you know?

Rose nodded her understanding but kept a careful eye on Mrs Talbot. She'd seen people collapse with shock when something like this had happened, and Stephanie's lips were turning white. They finished pegging out the laundry and returned to the kitchen where Rose made more mugs of tea. She was wondering if she could leave Mrs Talbot alone long enough to go empty her straining bladder when the doorbell rang.

Stephanie leapt to her feet, 'That'll be Mike at last. Thank God.'

Before Rose could stop her, the woman had bolted to the door. Rose heard Stephanie muttering wildly to herself while she struggled clumsily with the lock. She was on the point of going to help when she heard a terrible shriek from the hallway that almost made her drop her tea. She hustled to the front door and was confronted by Stephanie loudly weeping while hugging the life from a small boy whom Rose instantly recognised as fitting his mother's description. It was Jerome.

On the doorstep stood an evidently alarmed, middle-aged man. He looked from Stephanie to Rose. His eyes widened at the sight of a uniformed police officer and he began to stutter. Rose barked,

'Stay right there, please, sir. I'll be straight back.' She rushed to the Talbot's downstairs toilet.

Minutes later, and much relieved, Rose called dispatch to let her colleagues know the missing boy had turned up, returned by one Mr Charlie Croker the sexton of the cathedral.

'The little chap was in the Lady Chapel,' he'd explained. 'I had to go in there and put out some extra seats for a special service later and I heard him. He was chatting with the statue of the Virgin as if he knew her and waiting as if she was answering his questions.'

He lowered his voice so that only Rose could hear him, 'We used to have a parishioner do that, old Mrs Grantly. She had dementia, but our young friend here seems a little too young for that. When I said hello the lad stood up and told me he would "just be a minute", if that was okay with me, thanks very much. Then he finished his conversation and told the Virgin goodbye.

'Then, bright as a button, he told me his name and where he lived. I told him to wait for me and organised one of my colleagues to put the chairs out while I brought him home. I thought he was a bit young to be out on his own, you see, but he told me he had come out with the Lady.

'Then he took my hand like a good boy and thanked me for taking him home. So polite, which is a bit of a surprise these days. The things some kids say. Shocking. I blame the parents...'

Rose took Croker's details and thanked him for bringing Jerome back. She told him that someone would be in touch for a more detailed statement in the next few days. The sexton was obviously innocent of any wrongdoing. He had found the errant child and returned him to his mum. He was a good man.

She saw him to the door and he departed, just in time to leap out of the path of a dark blue Vauxhall Insignia as it barrelled up the drive. Mike Talbot fell out of his car and hurried to Rose's side, ignoring the man climbing out of his flower borders. Croker glared at his back and stalked away, muttering furiously.

'Is there any news about Jerome? I came as fast as I could. Where's Stephanie? Is she okay? Oh, I hope she's all right. It would kill her if anything happens to that boy, and there are some sick bastards out there. Shit! You know something? I've probably been clocked by every speed camera between here and the office, can you do something about that? I'm Mike Talbot, Jerome's father, by the way. Nice to meet you, officer...?'

'Call me Rose. Everything's all right, Mr Talbot. Your wife's in the kitchen with Jerome. That chap you nearly ran over just now, Mr Croker, he just brought him home. He's safe and well. He was up at the cathedral...'

Talbot roared, 'He's *home*? But I've lost an entire afternoon's pay to get here. What do you mean, he's home? What's going on? Has Stephanie been panicking about nothing again?'

Rose pulled the door to behind her and stepped forward, speaking quietly yet firmly. She had taken an instant dislike to the blustering, red-faced bully in front of her and had to fight hard against her rising antipathy.

'Mr Talbot, might I suggest you calm down. Your wife's had a rough time since your son disappeared. I know, I've been with her for most of it. Be grateful Jerome met somebody like Mr Croker or his situation might have been a lot worse.

'The question is not why or how he's back home, but how he got out past a child-proof gate lock in the first place? And why did he go up to the cathedral? There's a trained specialist on his way here now who will want to have a little chat with Jerome, and then maybe we'll get some answers. So, I'd thank-you to show a little more sensitivity when you talk with your wife, please, Mr Talbot.'

The man drew a ragged breath and his shoulders slumped, 'Yes, sorry. Stupid of me. Of course, you're right.'

Rose calmed herself with a deep breath and nodded. 'Thank-you, Mr Talbot. Good, that's much better. Your wife and son are waiting for you.'

The man scuttled past her, but not without first pausing to give her figure an appreciative and lingering appraisal. She couldn't believe the heat in his eyes. She wanted to slap him so much that her fingers tingled with anticipation and she had to clench them into balled fists.

'Creep,' she muttered under her breath. She thought he must have heard something because he looked back over his shoulder, and then she realised he was just checking out her butt. Her flesh crawled.

And Stephanie married that creep? She wondered. *She seems like such a nice, sensible woman. And she's had a child with him? No wonder the kid's shaking all his screws loose.*

She heard Talbot's voice booming from the kitchen with false heartiness.

'Sensitivity, I said,' muttered Rose, 'I must look it up when I get home to see if there is a new definition. I'm obviously missing something. Must really mean "act like a total wanker".'

She heard a car pull up on the road and a minute later a tall man stepped onto the drive. She smiled a greeting. Jerome was in good hands.

Sharif Mohammed was nearly always stopped at customs when returning from his holidays abroad. From his full, silky beard to his noble, hawk-like features and coffee-coloured complexion, Mohammed fit just about every physical profile ever written for Islamist terrorists by the so-called popular press.

He was aware of it. He knew he might appear intimidating to some people, right up to the moment they became the focus for his large, liquid chocolate eyes, and they found nothing but intelligence and gentle compassion there.

He didn't even resent his regular delays at UK airports. When the border officials saw what was in his files they always treated him with great respect and would fast track him through customs.

Dr Mohammed was a noted celebrity in his chosen field of child psychology. His ability to see through to the heart of his patients' problems had become legendary. Some even referred to him as the 'child whisperer'. His services were often required by police forces throughout the world.

He grinned with genuine warmth. 'Rose, it's good to see you looking so well. You were quite ill, I believe?'

'Sharif, yes, great to see you too.' Rose grinned back. 'And yes, I was ill. Glandular fever. I was completely wasted for a few months but now I'm back on the beat and better than ever.'

'Good, good.' He took her hands in his, held them out away from her sides and scrutinised her body. Rose mentally compared the way Mohammed clinically examined her with the way Talbot had ogled her figure. To the former she was a professional colleague and a person to be respected, to the latter she was little more than tits and ass in a police uniform, an outfit which probably made her more enticing.

Mohammed shook his head and pursed his lips. 'You've always been a healthy, slim woman but you need to get some meat back on those beautiful bones. That fever must have burned you like a candle. Come to the house and let's prepare a feast for you. Maryam would love to see you and we really enjoy cooking for good company. Now then, to work. Who have you got for me? Dispatch was a little vague.'

Rose outlined the situation, keeping her voice low but clear. Mohammed listened intently with his eyes downcast and unfocused, nodding at salient points during her discourse. When she had finished he asked if he might see the gate lock. Rose accompanied him, she was curious to see it herself.

It was an expensive model constructed from steel and robust blue plastic. Mohammed studied it for a few moments before he said, 'Ah, yes, I see.' He took the handle and squeezed it, turned it, then pushed it down and pulled it to one side. The jaws of the lock yawned wide and he lifted the latch. He swung the gate open a little way, it moved with well-oiled silence, then carefully closed it again.

He glanced at Rose. 'Do you think the boy could have opened this on his own?'

'No, his mother tells me even his dad has trouble with it. Anyway, Jerome couldn't reach that handle. As you'll see he's not very tall for his age – and he's only six. No, not a chance.'

'Very well. Good.' His eyes scanned the neat garden as if he wanted to preserve it in his memory for closer study later. 'So then, shall we meet young master Jerome Talbot and see what he has to say? Please, Rose, after you.'

[3]

Talbot's voice was still booming loudly when they entered the hallway, but it faltered and died when first Rose and then Mohammed walked into the kitchen. Talbot's mouth remained slackly open as if halfway through an unfinished word. His wife's eyes widened in surprise. Jerome looked up from his place on his mother's lap and examined first Rose and then the tall psychiatrist with intense curiosity. Mohammed smiled at him, and after a few seconds Jerome smiled back.

Rose made the introductions. Talbot stepped forward to shake hands with the newcomer, then quickly stepped back to his place, hovering beside Stephanie and his son. Mohammed leaned down to shake hands with both mother and child, giving each a chance to consider his eyes and make their judgement.

He had already dismissed the father as being incidental to his visit, but he could tell that the bonds between mother and son were deep. He spoke gently, aware that his deep, steady voice was one of his most effective tools for gaining a person's confidence.

He didn't think of his subjects as *cases*, in fact he didn't even think of them as patients. Each was a precious person, a unique character with individual challenges, a person who must be brought out into the light and given the opportunity to shine.

This concept of bringing people into the light underpinned his entire methodology. His colleagues mostly preferred to shine a forensic searchlight onto their cases, and they might choose to make considered judgements from a pre-emptive library of attributes and conditions. They would become frustrated with the way Mohammed refused to bandy stock phrases with them, telling them instead that he was just taking a gentle walk with his young friends. He wanted to understand them, come to terms with their unique language, while also trying to understand how their personality and sub-personality's landscape was populated.

'I try to bring them to a place where they can enjoy the sunshine,' he would explain, 'and perhaps from there we can help them gather the courage they need to see back into the darkness and find out what caused their problems.'

To one parent who wondered aloud how long the treatment process might take, the psychiatrist answered with the name of the thesis he had written for his Doctorate, *The sun needs no minute hand*. He then explained further,

11

saying that his treatment plan was to allow the child to come to a good place in their own time and in their own way, and that sometimes there were no clear signposts to point the way.

'I can't force them to get well or take their hands and lead them somewhere better. To do that will only mean we've taken their problems to a different place, not resolved them. I help them draw back the curtains or open the door to the light, but it's them who must tell me what they see. They must take that all important first step towards truth.'

Some of the more hidebound traditionalists in the field considered Mohammed's work to be 'new-age yap crap' but even they couldn't ignore his success rate, nor the vanishingly small percentage of relapses among his patients. Most children treated by Dr Sharif Mohammed got better and stayed that way.

He was happy to share notes about how he did what he did, and willingly allowed others to observe his methods – so long as they remained quiet. There were, he declared, no secrets when the minds of children were at stake.

However, no-one could work out what he was doing that was different. He talked to the patient and gave them room to say their piece. Perhaps, they said, it was simply that he was a little more patient. Mohammed's wife Maryam was certain her theory about his methods was the correct one.

'He's got his Doctorate and he spent years in postgraduate study. He can talk about theoretical treatments, behavioural disciplines, and case studies with the best of them, but that's all just the icing on his cake.

'It makes him legitimate and credible, but the children don't know or care about any of that, why should they? Sharif loves the child for who they are, and he allows them to love themselves in return. He accepts everything, expects nothing from them but honesty, and he always tells them the truth.

'Children instinctively know they can trust him and they react accordingly. They think of him as their particular friend, a special pair of ears they can talk to without judgement or censure. They almost forget he's there when they pour out their fears and secrets, but how does he do it?

'He's a man just more than six-foot-four tall, a powerful guy, but he becomes almost invisible while they talk with him. It's a gift, but how can you teach it? I guess he must have been born with it.'

Jerome quizzically examined Mohammed as if trying to remember where he'd seen him before, and the psychiatrist returned his gaze. The boy had big, luminous blue eyes that were filled with a soft, lambent light. They were the focusing point for a narrow, elfin face under a shock of unruly chestnut hair.

Mohammed thought Jerome would photograph well, and would almost certainly grow up to be heart-breakingly handsome – if he was allowed to.

Talbot coughed loudly. His eyes were rapidly tracking from his son to the tall man who seemed to have effortlessly dominated the kitchen. Mohammed drew attention like a magnet, and with a twinge of acute jealousy Talbot noticed the smiling interest building on his wife's face.

'So, what do we do now?' he asked. 'Do we just stand around looking at each other like idiots or do we find out who abducted our son? What happens next?'

Mohammed smiled at him. 'Yes, of course. You're a man of action, I can tell, Mr Talbot. A man of fire and energy. I bet your colleagues admire you as the "man who gets things done". I too admire such attributes.' His face radiated an expression of guileless honesty and his words set Talbot to a blushing attempt at modest rebuttal.

Mohammed nodded, 'We should be very grateful if you could lend that energy towards assisting Officer Platts in trying to find out how Jerome got through the garden gate? A gate which has such a solid, child-proof lock. I would find it difficult to open such a device myself. Did Jerome climb over it do you think? There must be clues somewhere, and two pairs of eyes are so much better than one. Meanwhile Jerome and I will have a little chat to see what he remembers. And his mum can help us, if she would be so kind. Is that all right with you, Jerome?'

The boy nodded as if he had been hypnotised. Mohammed nodded back and smiled gently showing white teeth. Stephanie smiled too, as did Talbot. A happy gang all ready to work well together.

Only Rose remained aloof from the sudden Mexican wave of happy expressions that swept the room. She knew why Mohammed wanted the father out of the way, the man was an interfering jerk, but now she had been stuck with the creep and would have to keep him 'entertained' for as long as possible. With a sense of mounting nausea, she became very aware that the man's eyes had swivelled in her direction. They didn't remain on her face for long. After a few seconds, they began tracking eagerly southwards.

'Duty calls,' she sighed, and led him out.

At that very moment, the sun was momentarily blotted out by a small but dense cloud and the kitchen became dark as a cellar. Then the sun shone once more, brilliantly illuminating Stephanie and Jerome from behind with a halo of golden light. They glowed, and Mohammed was briefly reminded of another iconic and familiar grouping.

13

He asked permission to join them at the kitchen table, sat down, and then spent a few quiet moments examining them. He could clearly discern the facial resemblance between the two, despite the son's chestnut colouring and the mother's golden hue.

Time and parental stress had pencilled faint, dark lines around Stephanie's eyes, but had failed to eliminate her luminous beauty. Mohammed closed his eyes for a moment, emptying his mind of all judgement and presumption. Then he opened them, bringing himself fully into an acutely observant awareness of the here and now.

His breathing had become deep and regular while he entered an almost meditative state. One of his uncles was a Sufi teacher and ever since he was small Mohammed had been taught how to enhance his senses to better appreciate the greatness of God's work. That ability aided him now.

When he opened his eyes once more he saw how Jerome and his mother glowed in the light. He saw anxiety, tiredness, frustration, anger, and love chasing each other across the woman's face. He saw curiosity, love, coolness, and independence stamped on the boy's. And something else. Something else shaped Jerome's expression. *What?* Time to start the conversation.

'Jerome,' he asked. 'How did you manage to open the gate?'

The boy shrugged in his mother's arms, his hands loosely held together in his lap. He seemed physically relaxed, but something sat tense and watchful behind those glowing eyes.

'Did *you* open the gate?'

Jerome shook his head. An emphatic negative.

'Did it open itself?'

The boy shook his head but flashed an arch smile. In a soft, piping yet musical voice, he said, 'That would be silly. The gate isn't like a supermarket door.'

Mohammed agreed, 'No, no, you're right, it isn't. So how did it open to let you out?'

Jerome rolled his eyes as if the answer was patently obvious.

He said, 'The *Lady* opened it of course. She knows how. She knows lots of things. More than Daddy, I bet she even knows more than you.'

[4]

Stephanie's head came up and she flicked a questioning glance at the psychiatrist. She mouthed the word, 'Lady?' Mohammed gently shook his head, but the boy caught the motion.

'She did,' he protested. 'She said she had something to show me, but I had to go with her to see it. *She* opened the gate, I promise.'

'What does she look like?'

Jerome shrugged again.

'Is she pretty like mummy?'

The boy thought about this then shook his head.

'She's old.'

Mohammed pointed at himself. 'Old like me?' He was in his mid-thirties and looked a little younger. Jerome giggled, it seemed a strange sound to come from his serious, narrow face. There was little humour in it.

'No, not like you, silly. She's really old.'

'So, is she old like a tree?'

'Are trees old?'

'Some are, yes. Hundreds of years old.'

'Older. Old like the castle.'

The Queen's Mount, also known as Merlin's Castle, was an Iron Age fort just outside the town and the other side of the recently completed bypass. It lowered over the freshly metalled dual carriageway like a crouching beast preparing to spring on an unwelcome interloper. It was one of Jerome's favourite places, especially when the 'sky was grey like an elephant's hide and salt breeze blows cold from the sea' as a local poet once described it.

'How old's the castle? Do you know?'

'Old as the moon, the Lady says.'

'You talk to her?'

'She tells me things. Secrets.'

'What kind of secrets?'

'If I told you they wouldn't be secrets anymore, would they?'

'True.' Mohammed grinned ruefully. 'Can you give me a clue?'

The boy looked sly and leaned forward, his eyes blazed.

'Root and bone, chalk and stone,

Mix the mud with a new-born's blood.

Build it high and dig it deep,

16

Within its walls my secrets keep,
Until the King once again takes his throne.'

Jerome's voice had taken on a dry, scratchy quality, and, Mohammed noticed, his long fingers had curled into claws as if gnarled by age and rheumatism. His mother looked shocked.

'Jerome, where did you hear that? It's horrible. You wait until I see your teachers, I'll give them a proper talking to. Letting a six-year-old read things like that. What are modern schools coming to?'

Mohammed asked, 'Did you hear that at school?'

Jerome answered in his own voice, 'I write it on paper and draw over it, so they can't see, but the words are still there.' His voice changed again, 'Hidden words have dreadful power, kine shall perish, and milk will sour. Men's bones shall cover the ground like a tomb, and barren shall be the goodwife's womb. Look to the past and you shall see, the proof of my work in your history.'

And he cackled like a hag.

Stephanie shook him. 'What are you doing?' She stared at Mohammed. 'He's never acted like this before. What have you done to him?'

The psychiatrist nodded. He said, 'Is she here now, Jerome. Is she here with us? The Lady?'

Jerome smiled and tilted his head to one side. The temperature in the room had dropped noticeably, to the point that their breath was steaming from their mouths. Outside the sun shone on the garden and flowers blazed bright in the borders. In the kitchen, winter chill rimed the table with frost. The boy looked at his mother and hissed at her. 'Shall I tell you the tale of the pretty whore who opened her legs to the handsome Moor...'

Stephanie slapped him hard enough to raise the shape of her hand on his cheek. He jolted as if waking from a daydream and tears stung his eyes, but he didn't weep. He blinked rapidly, and his mouth worked while he fought back the sobs.

'Mummy, what? Mummy, I'm sorry.'

She hugged him hard. 'Mummy's sorry too, my love, mummy's sorry too. What made you say such mean things? What were you saying? You made mummy upset, you mustn't do that.'

Mohammed interjected, 'Jerome, I'm sorry, but do you know what a whore is?'

The boy knuckled tears from his cheeks, 'No, what is it?'

'Nothing important. And what is a Moor?'

'I know that, it's a place in the countryside. We've been to Dartmoor. I liked it. You could see very far, and there were ponies.'

'That's good, Jerome. Very good. Did you know that in the old days people used to call people like me, Moors?'

'No, why?'

'The past is an interesting place and people did things differently there, but I prefer the way things are now. Why did the Lady take you to the cathedral? I wouldn't have thought she liked it much.'

'She didn't. She got angry when I ran in there. She wanted me to go to the stone, but I wouldn't. I ran away from her into the big church and she didn't want to come in, but she stood near the door and shouted at me to come out.'

The chill had vanished from the kitchen, but a cold shiver ran down Stephanie's spine. 'What stone is that, love?'

'You know, the old stone in the graveyard. The big stone with no words on it. It fell over next to the other one and now it looks like a letter 'L'. It's covered in ivy. The stone, mummy, in the trees near the blackberry bush.'

'*Old Harry's* couch? Yes, I know. Why did she want you to go there?'

'She didn't say, it was a secret. But I didn't like it.'

Mohammed asked, 'Why not?'

The boy sniffed away the last of his tears. 'It was buzzing, like bees, like bees whispering.'

'Whispering?'

'Yes. It was like singing, but it was creepy. It gave me goosebumps. I didn't like it.'

Mohammed said, 'You went to the Lady Chapel. Why there?'

Jerome shook his head, 'She's not the Lady. She's pretty, she laughs. She's a mummy like my mummy, not like the Lady at all. She's young, like mummy, but she has brown eyes like Mrs Murray in the art class at school. I like Mrs Murray, but she's not as pretty as Maryam.'

Rose and Talbot walked through the back door into the kitchen and hesitated, as if the air had an intimate taint to it and they suddenly felt unwelcome.

Talbot said, 'Nothing, not so much as a footprint. The ground's too dry for anything to show up. Officer Platt tells me there are experts who could come over and look, but I say one expert's enough for one day and it's time for Jerome to have his tea. Are we done? What's wrong with the boy? He's got a face like a spanked arse.'

18

Mohammed got to his feet. 'We've had a lovely talk. You have a very bright and imaginative son, Mr Talbot, I'm sure he takes after you. He'll make you very proud one day. I'd love to chat with him some more if that's okay with you. I need to talk with some people and make sure of my facts.'

He fetched out his wallet and drew out two business cards that he handed to Jerome's parents.

'If you need me call me on my mobile, don't worry about the time. And if I may, could I come back and see Jerome in a few days' time? Say, Friday at 11am? I'll bring the cakes if you bring the tea, deal?'

Talbot huffed, 'I'll be at work but I'm sure Stephanie won't mind.' He looked at the card. 'Welton-on-Wyckes? Nice, proper little village. Slice of *Ye Olde England*. We've looked there, haven't we love.'

His wife just blinked at him, said nothing. He showed the visitors to the door.

'Been nice working with you, Officer Platt, hope we can do it again sometime. And thanks for your help with the boy, Mr, ah, Mohammed, see, I remember names. Need to in my job.'

They shook hands and then Rose and Mohammed were outside on the doorstep. Rose said, 'What now?'

Mohammed answered, 'Do you fancy a look at the cathedral?'

19

[5]

Rose asked, 'So then, what did you think of Jerome?'

They made an incongruous couple as they walked together down the quiet, tree-lined road. They headed towards the big roundabout at the bottom of the road from which they would descend the steps down to the canal towpath that would take them under the busy A road before bringing them back up into the older part of the town and then the cathedral. The tall, bearded, brown man and the attractive blonde police officer drew curious glances from the few people who saw them together.

He replied, 'First I'll ask you a question. What did you think of the family? First impressions are very important.'

Rose breathed out hard. 'I can tell you the father's a total lecher. Can you believe he even pretended to stumble so he could try to cop a feel of my arse while we were out in the garden? He got sucked in there, I moved out of the way and he fell on his face.' She grinned at the memory.

'Mother's been beaten into submission, poor woman. She loves her son to bits, that's obvious, but life hasn't turned out the way she thought it would, and she doesn't have a clue what to do about it. In her heart, she knows what Talbot's like and uses up all her energy trying not to see it. Bastard's probably been unfaithful, likely done it more than once. He might even pay for it, I've seen the sort before. Sex is his way of dominating something he's never really understood, the female of the species. I feel sorry for Stephanie, I do. Jerome's everything to her, and he's devoted to his mum, but there's something there I can't quite put my finger on. It's not that there's something lacking or missing between them, it's just that they don't seem to be on the same page. It's as if something's conflicted and creating a barrier between them... Sorry, listen to me. That must sound like the worst kind of amateur psychobabble to you. I'll shut up.'

Mohammed said nothing until they had descended the steps and walked under the wide A road then followed the path out onto a narrow street of beautiful Georgian houses and converted warehouses that fronted the canal. Unlike the Talbots' road this one was lined with parked cars and the pavement was too narrow for them to walk together side-by-side.

'You're very astute, Rose, and you have a clear eye. I agree with you about the father. He spent so much time looking hard at your body that I expect he raised bruises, however I doubt he pays for sex. He's an emotional miser, but paying for it? No, that would be an admission of defeat.'

The number of people using the pavement increased as they neared the shops and cafés that surrounded the cathedral square, so they ceased their conversation until they had threaded a path through the crowds and entered the relative calm of the Cathedral Close. The fine building at the heart of several acres of grass, gravestones and woodlands had originally been founded in the early twelfth century but had been treated as an ongoing project ever since. It still had some exquisite gothic touches but more austere Jacobean and less imposing Victorian restorations and 'improvements' has almost swamped its original beauty.

Rose indicated the architecture. 'You've got to love the old girl. She's like a Hollywood star who's had so many facelifts you can barely recognise her. And she's not even the queen of this particular castle; there's a much older incumbent.'

She pointed to a copse of trees beyond the eastern length of the cathedral.

'Just there was a Saxon chapel. It was built to sanctify and defend the original settlement from a much older place of worship, for which they say the Queen's Mount was the centre.'

'You studied the town's history?'

'I'm a local. I grew up with it. As a kid, we were taken on walks from here and along the invisible path that links the Close to the Mount. There was an uproar when the council allowed the bypass to be built straight through the old path. People dressed up as Druids and chained themselves to the excavators, it all got very messy.'

'Invisible path? Really?'

'From the little Sisters. There's only two of them left now, which is a shame. Let me show you.'

She led Mohammed around the copse to the south side of the cathedral where an imposing graveyard sloped away to a wall and a dense, shadowed treeline in the distance. Clumps of trees broke up the landscape and wild summer flowers peppered the lawns, but even in the bright sunshine the land had a subdued air about it. Grave markers clawed the air at many crazy angles. The headstones were old, and their inscriptions worn away to barely discernible markings. Rose led the way to a circular group of mighty and crook-backed yew trees and bent low to duck under the branches and reach their centre. Mohammed had to crouch lower and nearly caught his beard in the yews' inquisitive branches.

In the centre of the circle was an ivy-covered L-shaped mound. The ground was littered with used condoms and their packets, but that did little to detract from the ancient power of the massive stones confronting them.

Rose tilted her fine head to one side. 'Looks like they're still being used for fertility rituals on a regular basis, doesn't it? At least the kids are being careful. The trees need trimming back a-ways. There used to be room to dance around the Sisters when I was little, and one teacher, Mrs Barker, she would play her guitar. It all seemed very innocent to us, but I think old 'barking' Barker thought she was respecting the original spirit of the place. Archaeology proved her wrong though. There used to be six standing stones in a circle about where the yews are now, and a seventh lay flat in the centre. The standing sister was moved by some bloke in the eighteenth century to prove something or other, I can't remember what, but I'm sure the fallen stone is where it always was. It hasn't moved since before the Roman's came. It's rooted to the ground.'

'What do you think it was used for?'

'I don't really know. But some folk say it was for sacrifice, human sacrifice.'

'Does the school still bring its pupils here?'

'I don't know. I'd be surprised if they didn't. This is a patch of Iron Age history right on their doorstep. And there's the invisible path, which is magical for a kid.'

'More magical than a sacred circle of used condoms?' asked Mohammed.

'Yeah, I think I'll have a word about that at an assembly. The kids will find out about sex soon enough, we don't want them getting curious about used condoms before they need to. Probably health risks anyway.'

'I think you're right. So, where's this path?'

Rose chuckled, 'It's invisible, haven't you been listening? Come on, let me show you how to see it.'

She began by leading Mohammed anti-clockwise around the fallen sister and then she pointed at a clotted tangle of ivy.

'You wouldn't know it, but it starts in here.' She made a disapproving sound. 'This really isn't good enough. Look there, someone thinks this is a toilet. Disgusting.'

Mohammed leaned closer to examine the offending article, which drew another disapproving sound from his companion.

He looked up, 'No, Rose. No, you're wrong. That's a pile of entrails on the stone, not fresh but fairly recent. Someone has disembowelled a small creature and left its guts as an offering.'

'Someone? Don't you mean a fox? We get a few around here and they're bold as brass.'

'Good point, why hasn't a fox eaten that? Probably be a real tasty treat after all the leftover pizza and burgers they're used to. Why is that still there? It should have been snapped up before now.'

'No, I mean a fox left that. Sharif, you're not saying a person did that?'

'Yes, Rose, I am. That's not how a fox would leave its kill, too neat. A human did that, and it looks ritualistic to me. Look around you, can you see feathers or fur? If that was an animal kill, there would be traces.'

'Great, marvellous. Fucking great. Damn, hell, and shit! That means this is a crime scene. I'll have to call it in. Sorry, Sharif, you're a witness. We'll have to clear the scene. Follow me.'

Mohammed waited by the circle of yews while Rose got in touch with dispatch. It was clear that whoever she was talking to was far from pleased. When she rejoined him she found him rubbing his eyes and blinking.

She asked, 'You okay?'

He said, 'Must have something in my eyes. I kept seeing a shadow moving in the corner of my eyes but when I looked it was gone. Weird.'

Rose looked abruptly to her left. 'That's strange, I just saw something too. Must be an effect of the light through the trees, branches moving in the breeze.'

Mohammed lifted a few blades of grass and dropped them. They fell straight down. 'What breeze?' he said.

'While we wait,' said Rose, 'let me show you that invisible path. We'll have a few minutes. The sergeant just reminded me I'd called bang in the middle of the change of shift and unless there's a clear and present risk to life, limb or the Prime Minister they'll get that sorted first.' She shrugged. 'And they won't rush for the Prime Minister. It's all very British and it works, most of the time.'

She came to Mohammed's shoulder and took his arm. 'Come to the side a bit, a bit more, a bit more, that's it. Stop there. Now, do this.'

She showed him how to hold his hands flat and make a small square frame with his fingers and thumbs, then she told him to hold it up before his face.

'Now, look through that towards the gate in the wall, that one, down there in the west wall, see it?'

Mohammed did as she told him. The game seemed a little childish, but he could feel Rose's excitement at showing him something he didn't know. There was the gate neatly framed.

'Okay, right, I see it. What now?'

She chuckled again, 'Okay, great. Now, can you see the Queen's Mount on the horizon? You need to see them at the same time.'

He raised his hands slightly. 'Yes, I can. I can... Oh, my word!'

Rose almost jumped with glee, 'You see it? You see the invisible path?'

He could almost hear the voice of the little girl who had first been shown the secret of the invisible path years before. She was proud of her shared secret, and with good reason.

In the little frame created by his hands Mohammed saw the gate, which had curiously high side pillars. Two miles or more beyond the gate and just on the borders of the town was the man-made hill called the Queen's Mount. Between the gate and the Mount stretched a straight line of roads and clearings. Not a single tree blocked the line, not a building barred the path.

Rose chattered at his side. 'The path runs exactly due west from here, straight as an arrow. It starts at the Sisters and stops at the Mount. At the solstices, the sun would have risen directly behind us and shone down that path. Some people say that the Sisters would have been arranged to frame the rising sun and direct its light along the path. That would have looked awesome. People dress up and come here at mid-summer and mid-winter. Some make up Druid prayers, some quote Elvish from *Lord of the Rings*, it's quite a theatre. One guy once turned up dressed as a Jedi Knight and he had one of the swords, one of the early lightsabers like Alec Guinness used. He didn't say anything, he just stood there and let the sunlight catch the blade and it glowed just like in the first film.

This other bloke was dressed like a Klingon and he tried to read a poem to the sun in fluent Klingon, you know? Poor sod. He was nearly lynched, but I don't know why. He was only doing the same as the others, wearing a costume and speaking in a made-up language.'

She shrugged. 'Nobody really knows what Druids' language sounded like. The Romans killed them all off claiming they practiced dark arts and human sacrifice. Present-day Druids muddle together a stew of tree hugging, new-age crap, astrology, and a bit of old Wicca, and they run around beating each other on the buttocks with rowan twigs. So long as it keeps them happy why not? What *was* that?'

Mohammed saw it too, a flicker of darkness amongst the gravestones. For no reason, he suddenly felt cold fingers grip at his heart. There was a threat in this lonely place, even in the middle of the afternoon on a still, bright, sunny day. Something tweaked at his mind and he lifted his hands up before his eyes once more, made the frame and gazed along the invisible path. *How was that possible?* he wondered. The line it drew was black as charcoal. It was as if the rest of the town basked in sunshine while the path to the Mount was bathed in eternal night, except one place. He could just make out the white crossbar of the bypass at the end of the path, like the tip of a billiard cue. Or the end of a wizard's wand.

'If any officer can find me something to do in the middle of the summer holidays it'll be Rose Platt. Hi, Sharif. I see she's roped you in too. She's got a talent for involving others in her mischief has our Rose. Gah, it's too hot for messing about in an environment suit. Okay, where's the body?'

The raw steak coloured face of Crime Scene Officer (CSO) and pathologist Sandy Hines was the only flesh visible on her body. The rest of her was covered by her *Tyvek* suit and hood with its elasticated gusset, her outfit completed by booties and gloves. Her comfortable figure was not flattered by her attire, and Mohammed wondered whether her beefy colouring was due to the day's heat or her short temper and high blood pressure. A young uniformed officer named Phil Coombe was at Hines' heel. He called out, 'Hiya, Rose. You, all right? Hello, Sharif, nice to see you. Lovely day for it.'

The eerie, chill sense of menace that had touched Mohammed's mood lifted at the sound of the new arrivals' voices and he welcomed them with a smile.

'Hi, Sandy, hi, Phil. Sorry, but this one's down to me. I found the remains. Rose was showing me the Sisters and I saw the entrails. They're in there on the fallen stone. I thought it might possibly be ritualistic, an offering perhaps.'

Hines shook her head. 'Nothing surprises me anymore. Righto, I'll take a look. Phil, please, let me have my case.' She donned her glasses and mask. Her voice became muffled. 'You lot stay here. I'll not be long. Talk amongst yourselves if you must but not too loudly, genius at work. I need to concentrate.'

The pathologist ducked down into the shadows at the heart of the group of yew trees. Coombe leaned over to Mohammed and in a loud whisper asked, 'Has Rose been giving you the tour of her private parts? Ow!' He ducked out of the way before his colleague could deliver another slap to the back of his head.

'Ow, no, I didn't mean anything by that. It's just banter. I meant the tour of the town's secret paths and byways. My Carole still loves coming up here with me and looking down the famous invisible path. We've walked it you know, from here to that stupid bypass. There's a bridge but it's well off to one side. The Council was going to put it in the path's straight line but there was a major petition to stop them. It would have ruined the line to have a stupid bridge at the end, they didn't get it.'

From the circle of yew trees, a voice boomed. 'I can still hear you out there, you know. What do you understand me to mean when I say keep it QUIET! Now shut up! And I mean you, Phil.'

Coombe blushed to the roots of his close-cropped hair. 'Sorry!' he yelled back.

'SHUT UP!'

Rose whispered, 'You spend a lot of time with Sandy?'

Coombe made a zipping motion across his lips but nodded energetically.

Rose looked sympathetic, 'Tough luck, we've all been there. Don't worry, it'll be someone else's turn soon.'

Mohammed felt his gaze drawn once more towards the distant Mount. Without the little frame of his hands the black path stretching towards it wasn't very obvious, but it was there. He felt as if his feet were planted in a black stream darkened by time and wondered why the town Council hadn't made more of a fuss about such a noteworthy feature. He was reminded of the uninterrupted viewpoint that stretched from the medieval 'Henry's Mound' in London's Richmond Park to the dome of St Paul's cathedral, some ten miles distant. That view was protected by statute, but it was the people of the town who protected this ancient path. The bypass proved that the voice of the people was sometimes not loud enough. And this path was older, much older, than the avenue to St Paul's. He wondered what had been here when it was carved from the clay and chalk, when the Sisters were raised, and the Mount created.

Rose stood at his shoulder, 'Old parish records called the fort "The Queen's Mound". Throws a different complexion on the place, don't you think? Maybe used condoms are more fitting. Who knows, this might have been the centre for a sex cult rather than a place of human sacrifice.'

Hines emerged from the yews, pulling at her mask, and stripping the hood from her sweat soaked auburn hair. She looked grave and storm clouds gathered in her green eyes.

'What day is it?'

Coombe answered, 'Friday.'

Hines barked at him, 'I know it's fucking Friday, you mewling fuckwit. What's the date?'

Rose said, 'Ninth August, five fifty-six pm.'

'Thanks. Righto.' Hines breathed deeply and shuddered. 'Right. Call it in, get a full forensic team here. Those remains are human. We're looking at murder.'

[7]

The grating sound of Jerome's pencil was getting on Stephanie's nerves. Even through the living room wall it sounded like tiny claws scratching at the plaster. It needled into her brain and felt as if something was scouring tiny metal teeth along her bones. The boy had eaten his fish fingers and drunk his milk in silence, and then asked if he might do some drawing. She had wondered aloud if he might want to watch television instead. The *Clangers* would be on soon, she told him, and *In the Night Garden* shortly after that. The appeal of either escaped her but she knew her son liked them. No, he had answered, thank-you, mummy, but may I do some drawing?

She shrugged and smiled and told him yes; but reminded him it was bedtime at seven because tomorrow was another big day and he must get his sleep. She kissed his cool cheek and told him she loved him. He hugged her neck, kissed her mouth, told her he loved her too, and then ran off to get his paper, sharpener, and pencils.

Half an hour later she desperately wanted to snatch the pencil from his busy fingers and snap it in front of his eyes. That or burst into tears. The events of that day had frayed her nerves to tatters, starting with Jerome's strange disappearance and then his return with the man from the cathedral. His eerie interview with that tall Muslim man, Dr Sharif something, what was his surname? Mohammed? Yes, that was it. Her mind buzzed with too many questions about how Jerome had got through the gate, about the strange Lady he described, the nasty little poems her son had quoted. And she had *slapped* him. She had never slapped her son before, never. It was unthinkable.

Scratch, scratch, scratch... The sound ground on and on. And it was only six thirty-five. She sipped at her naughty glass of white wine.

Mike had left her to it. Told her he was off to the golf club for a bit of sane, adult company. He would get something to eat while he was out. He had looked at her with his snide smile and told her that, anyway, she would be happier spending some more prime time with the only man who counted in her life, wouldn't she?

She had sarcastically thanked his departing back for all his support and he had rounded on her. In a threatening snarl, he reminded her that her panic about the little prince taking a walk had cost him an afternoon's commission, and that *she* brought precious little money into the house. That part wasn't fair, and he knew it. She had paid the deposit from her own savings, she had halved the mortgage with part of her inheritance after her widowed mother died. And she freelanced for the local paper during term time. They could never have afforded their home without her money. Not for the first time she calculated whether she could afford to support the house and Jerome on her own. It would be tight, but she could do it.

She contemplated a future without her husband. Apart from his snoring and farting during the night would her life be so very different? And then she remembered the way he had eyed up that nice policewoman, Rose. He had looked at her as if she was a plate of pie and chips and he was starving. Only he wouldn't want sex with a plate of pie and chips. A quiet voice at the back of her mind told her that the way Mike smelled when he came home sometimes was from more than eyeing a woman up, much more. She had recognised the sweet scent of *White Linen* on his skin, barely disguised by the beer on his breath. It was a scent she never wore. She sighed feeling exhausted with her life and pushed the thought away. Then she drank some more wine. *Easy does it, Stephanie. One drunk in the family is enough.*

Scratch, scratch, scratch... She glanced at her watch. Six fifty, time to go and slow down the future Rembrandt. She pulled her fingers through her blonde hair and went to pour the rest of her wine back into the bottle. She would put it back in the fridge and have another glass with her meal later. She stood up and yawned. A shadow fell across her, as if something had blocked the early evening sun. She glanced back towards the window overlooking the garden, the one through which she had watched Jerome at play so many hours before. What met her gaze turned her blood to ice water in her veins. A woman stood there glaring at her from the other side of the glass, her lips parted to expose powerful looking brown teeth in a humourless sneer. Her haughty face bore a fierce expression of proud malice.

A quiet, piping voice at Stephanie's elbow said, 'That's the Lady.'

She screamed.

...

Mohammed rang his wife and told her that he was going to be delayed on police business and that she should start dinner without him. She demurred, reminding him that it was his favourite fish supper and that anyway it was all prepared, so it would only take minutes to put on the table when he got in. She would nibble a carrot until he came home, then nibble one of his earlobes as an appetiser.

'If it's nice and sweaty. I need the salt'.

He lowered his voice to opine that she should think herself lucky to have a husband whose earlobes were so appetising, but that he could think of several parts of her anatomy that were much tastier, even without salt. Hines interrupted his banter by calling his name from the freshly placed scene of crime tape she was examining.

'Gotta go, see you soon. Love you.'

'Loveyoubye.' She snapped the words out so fast they collided with each other.

Mohammed had never believed he would ever meet a woman like Maryam. He'd had a few girlfriends before meeting her, and some of his relationships had even been quite serious, but none of them held a candle to his beautiful, vivacious wife. He looked across at the beet-coloured face of the pathologist and hoped she wanted to tell him he could go home if he wanted to. He badly needed his wife in his arms. It had been a strange and long day and he wanted to take advantage of Maryam's sharp intelligence, see if she could help him understand some of what had happened with Jerome Talbot. He pocketed his phone and strode to Hines' side.

She didn't say he could leave, of course she didn't. Instead she asked him if he would go to the station with officer Platts and provide a formal signed witness statement.

She finished, 'And then the pair of you can go home. Is your car handy?'

He explained that he'd left his car at the Talbot house, but it was only a few minutes' walk from the Cathedral Close, and if Rose didn't mind he'd drive her to the station. Rose didn't mind.

The pair were soon back at the canalside underpass and then onto the Talbot's street. Mohammed had fished his key fob from his pocket and aimed it at his Mazda 6 when they both heard Stephanie's scream of fear. Mohammed didn't hesitate. He pounded up the drive and vaulted over the tall garden gate like the athlete he had been in his youth, adrenaline coursing through his body. Rose was still wrestling with the child-proof lock when he reached the back of the house and ran straight into an area of freezing mist. He had seen *something* there, something coherent, like a well-defined shadow. And then he had heard a snarl of fury and he was drenched in a pall of icy dew. He shivered uncontrollably until the day's heavy warmth returned to his limbs.

Rose skittered into the back garden and almost collided with him. She recoiled from the wall of cold mist that surrounded him, and then looked around. Through the kitchen window she could just make out Stephanie Talbot. She was down on her knees sobbing, her shoulders jerking, and her head bowed. Beside her stood Jerome. He was gazing at Mohammed with a strange expression on his face, part relief and part disappointment. He was ignoring her. Rose tried the door into the kitchen and found it locked, she rattled the handle. Stephanie looked up with terror etched onto her features, but when she saw Rose she leapt to her feet and hustled to unlock the door. She threw it open and almost fell onto Rose's shoulders, barely able to breathe through her sobs.

Jerome never took his eyes from Mohammed, tracking him as he walked around to the back door and entered the kitchen. He walked up to the tall man and took his hand, as if they were going to walk somewhere together. Mohammed hunkered down until his eyes were at the same level as the boy's.

'The Lady was here? The one who took you for a walk?'

Jerome nodded. 'Yes,' he said. 'She wanted to show me her baby.'

[8]

Maryam was a pragmatist and she was used to schedules getting thrown into disarray by her husband. Dinner was going to be a little late and, she had learned, they would be joined two unexpected guests. One had already eaten but might like a pudding, ice-cream would be perfect, and the other hadn't eaten yet. They would also be staying the night in the spare back room. Mohammed had sweetened the pill a little by asking if all the above was okay and apologising for the short notice. She knew he wouldn't have done any of it without a good reason, and she could hear the stress in his voice.

She asked, 'Is this something to do with that police business you're involved with?'

'Yes, partly, but something else too. Something odd that frankly I don't understand. It's Mrs Talbot and Jerome her son, the people I interviewed earlier today. Mrs Talbot has been scared out of her wits by something pretty freaky, and the boy is acting like that kid Damien from *The Omen*. I've got the impression they need protecting but I don't know what from. I don't know if they need a shrink or a shaman, but I do know they need help if only for one night. Is this really okay with you?'

'It's okay, of course it's okay. I trust your instincts, Boots, always have... Sounds like one of the creepy ones. Will we need to borrow a crucifix from someone? Should I order a bucket of Holy water?'

Mohammed felt relieved. She had used his pet name, which meant that mentally she was already standing by his shoulder, and ready to face whatever came their way.

'Based on what I've experienced so far a thick jumper and an umbrella would be more useful. Look, I'm at the police station and I should be about another ten minutes before I'm done here. I'll be home in half an hour. Does that give you enough time?'

'Plenty, see you soon, love, and concentrate on your driving.'

'Hey, would I take risks when I've got your fish curry to look forward to? Don't you worry, I'll drive like I've got *Miss Daisy* in the back of the car, my mouth's watering already. See you soon.'

When Maryam welcomed Stephanie into her house her first impression was that the woman looked like a survivor from a plane crash. She had a survivor's defeated, deflated look. Her eyes were unfocussed, and she seemed dazed. All she was missing was the blanket around her shoulders.

The boy was elf-like, small, and slender. He had a quizzical, intelligent face and large blue eyes that searched Maryam's face as if trying to judge what he should think of her. He was holding Mohammed's hand as if they were old friends. *Mo's magic strikes again,* she thought.

Her husband had an almost supernatural gift for dealing with children, it was a pity they didn't have any of their own. God knows they'd tried hard enough. She told him the sex would have been too much of a bother if they didn't enjoy it so much, with anyone else it would just be a pain in the arse.

'That would mean you were confused,' he quipped, which earned him a punch on the arm. A friendly punch.

She looked at him now, arriving home with his lost sheep in tow, and she felt herself to be on the brink of understanding why he was the way he was. There was that quality he brought to the troubled mind, the calming oils he poured onto troubled waters just by his presence. He would have made a great Imam.

Mohammed introduced her to their guests. Stephanie accepted a welcoming hug, but Jerome held out his right hand for a sturdy yet brief shake. His left remained firmly clasped around Mohammed's big fist. Maryam ushered everyone into the living-room. The sun was low in the sky and she looked out of the tall bay window. She drank in the vision of the quiet village bathed in the radiance of sunset before she pulled the floor length curtains together and switched on the room's uplighters.

When she turned back to her guests she noticed that Jerome had relinquished her husband's hand and now sat at his mother's side on the two-seater leather sofa. He had taken a large satchel from his back and placed it on the floor by his feet as if he wanted to forget it, but his eyes were continuously drawn to it as if by magnets. Mohammed suggested they might enjoy a drink before dinner and Stephanie shook herself and apologised. She reached into the bag she had brought with her and handed up two bottles of decent white wine, one already open with barely a glass consumed.

'Sorry this one's open,' she said, 'but they were both cold when I put them in the bag. I had a glass from it a bit earlier, before... before... you know. It would just go to waste.'

Mohammed told her she shouldn't have and tried to refuse but Stephanie insisted. Jerome accepted the offer of a coconut water and pineapple/mango juice concoction that seemed the most harmless of the drinks Mohammed found in the kitchen. He took the two bottles out of the room and returned a few minutes later with a tray on which sat three glasses of wine and a tumbler of yellow liquid. He had also poured some roasted nuts into one bowl and some Bombay mix into another. Breadsticks jutted up from a glass tumbler. He wanted to make the impromptu dinner party seem as normal as possible after the strange day. He handed out the drinks but left the snacks on the tray, so people could help themselves.

'Cheers, then,' he said raising his glass. 'Over the teeth and round the gums, look out tummy, here it comes.'

He sipped and winked at Jerome who was chuckling into his glass of juice.

The boy repeated, 'Look out tummy, here it comes.' And he swallowed a mouthful. 'It's nice,' he said.

'The wine's excellent too,' said Maryam. 'It's very kind of you to think of it.'

Stephanie shook her head. 'After everything you've done? Don't be daft. It's the least I could do.'

Maryam looked at the clock on the mantle shelf. 'I'd better go put dinner out. Jerome, would you like to try some fish curry? I made it myself.'

The boy looked up at his mother. She shrugged and said, 'It's up to you.'

He smiled and looked back at Maryam. 'Yes, please.'

She grinned at him, 'Good choice. Come through in five minutes.'

She hustled out, her glass in her hand. Stephanie watched her leave then turned to Mohammed. 'Have I got time to put our things in the room?'

'Of course. Jerome, do you want to see the room?'

The small boy shook his head. 'No, thank-you.'

'Then wait here and we'll be right down. Do you want to wash your hands before dinner?'

Jerome looked at his hands. 'I washed them before,' he said.

'Good, that's fine. We'll just be a minute.'

Mohammed led Stephanie up the stairs to the spare room at the back of the house. The two single divans could be pushed together to form a double if needed, but they were normally occupied by Maryam's teenage nephews when her sister and brother-in-law made one of their frequent and enjoyable forays into 'the sticks'.

Stephanie gazed around the clean, neat room, and sighed. 'When I woke up this morning I didn't think I'd be sleeping in a strange house tonight, or that I would make such good friends so quickly. You've no idea what this means to us, honestly. If you hadn't, if you... I don't know what I would have done.'

From downstairs they heard Maryam call, 'Ready!'

'Come on,' smiled the tall man. 'Let's go eat.'

He led Stephanie down to the dining room where Maryam was laying out plates and cutlery, then said, 'I'll get Jerome.'

He crossed the hall to the living-room, and with a shock saw that it was empty.

'Jerome,' he called. 'Jerome, where are you?'

Then he saw two shadows against the curtain across the bay window and quickly strode over to pull them apart. Jerome stood alone staring out at the night. His eyes looked almost black and insect-like in the sodium glare of the street lights. He smiled eerily at the tall man at his side, his fine skin pulled tight across his delicately boned features. For just a moment Mohammed gathered the intense illusion that he was looking down at a living skull. And that was when the glass of the bay window resounded as if a fierce gust of wind had struck it – or a pair of furious fists. Mohammed jumped and stared out into his front garden. He caught the dissipating shreds of darkness that might have been a human figure. *She knows he's here*, he thought. *And she's letting me know she knows.* Aloud he said, 'Come on, Jerome, dinner.' And with a hand on the boy's shoulder he steered him away from the window, pulling the curtains to as they went.

The boy looked back over his shoulder at the freshly drawn curtains. He chuckled to himself, a low, sly sound. He picked up his satchel as they walked past the sofa then looked up at Mohammed and grinned like a deaths-head once more. In a strange, hissing voice he said, 'Time for dinner.'

In the dining room Stephanie and Maryam were swapping recipes while they dished out the food. The slight, willowy blonde had relaxed in Maryam's company and regained a semblance of the woman Mohammed thought she must have been before finding herself thrown headlong into an unfamiliar and sinister world. A world that had first opened to her when her son had gone missing that afternoon. Mohammed had only known her as a disturbed and anxious mother, but in her more relaxed state he found her bright and charming. She couldn't compete in looks with the dark and mercurial beauty of his wife, but he fully understood what had probably drawn Mike Talbot to her in the early days.

Stephanie had that fragile, porcelain beauty that would compel some men to seek to protect her, and others to dominate and oppress her. Talbot was clearly of the latter persuasion. What Mohammed didn't understand is what had compelled Talbot to seek out female company elsewhere when he had such a fine woman at home. That was as much a mystery as whatever was happening to the couple's increasingly unearthly son.

And where was Talbot? Stephanie had rung her husband's mobile to let him know where she was staying for the night, but the message she got in return told her the number was currently unavailable. She then rang the golf club to pass on a message, only to be told that he wasn't there and hadn't been seen all day. Mohammed had tried not to hear the tired resignation in her voice when she thanked the club receptionist and hung up.

She had left a note on the living room table before she locked up the house and climbed into the back of Mohammed's car with Jerome. Her son had scanned his home and the surrounding area as if expecting to see something, or someone, waiting there. While he searched he hummed a little tune Mohammed didn't recognise. Its rhythm sounded earthy and potent.

He asked, 'Hey, Jerome, I like the song. What is it?'

The boy stopped humming. 'What song?'

And then Jerome became silent. In another child that might have seemed like sullen behaviour, but there was nothing churlish about the boy's expression. More an expectant watchfulness and an increased sense of arch mischief. He was patiently waiting for the punchline to be delivered, the trap to be sprung, the surprise guest to finally join the party.

And now it was nearly two hours later, and the air almost crackled with anticipation around the boy's head. Even while he spooned food into his mouth a smile quivered at the corners of his lips. Mohammed decided to open the conversation a little.

'That Lady you went for a walk with, was she a Queen?'

Jerome chewed ruminatively for a moment, then shook his head. 'No, *she* told Queens what to do. And Kings. They asked her advice and whatever she said they listened and they always did what she said. She's very smart. That was why she got her babies.'

'Babies? She had babies? She was a mother?'

'No, she was never a mother, not like that. People gave her their babies, so she could tell them about the future before a battle or before they did something important. This is nice fish. Please, may I have some more?'

Maryam jolted as if waking from a reverie. 'Of course, let me have your plate. Do you want some more rice too?'

'Ooh, please.'

'Coming right up.'

Mohammed waited until the child had received his refilled plate with a thank-you, then he continued his line of enquiry.

'So, how can a baby help someone see the future? I don't understand.'

Jerome licked his lips free of sauce. 'The Lady would send them to the happy place then she would look into their hearts.'

'Happy place?'

'Yes, the happy place. I nearly went there once when I was ill, didn't I Mummy.'

Stephanie looked up from her plate in confusion. 'What happy place? What do you mean, when you were ill? When was that?'

Jerome shook his head at his mother's stupidity. 'Oh, mummy, don't be so silly. When I was very ill, and the doctor came around all the time, remember? I was so hot I felt freezing cold and I nearly went to the happy place; but they told me it was too soon, and they wouldn't let me go in.'

Mohammed asked, 'Sorry, Jerome, but who's "they"?'

"The shiny, nice people at the gate. They wouldn't let me in. They sent me home to Mummy.'

Stephanie choked and held a hand to her mouth. 'Oh, my God, oh, my God. He's talking about the time he nearly died. He had pneumonia and he nearly died. That's the happy place? Death!'

Jerome smiled, 'This is yummy. Can we have this at home, please, Mummy?'

Stephanie looked as if she wanted to either scream or burst into tears but couldn't make up her mind which to do first. She opened her mouth as if to speak but no sound came out. Maryam came to her rescue.

'I'll give mummy the recipe. Is mummy a good cook?'

'She makes fish fingers. I like them too. And omelette.'

Mohammed chewed at his subject like a terrier. 'Jerome, please, what happened to the babies? I mean, what really happened?'

'I told you, silly. They were sent to the happy place and the Lady read their hearts. Their insides was all left on the table as a special present for the Lady and the rest of them was burned up to ashes and put in a pot and the pot was put in the ground under the table with some flowers. The people would sing a song while they did it. The babies were special, like me.'

'And did the Lady have a name?'

The boy chuckled, 'She had lots. The Romans called her Andrasta, but the people called her Agrona before the Romans came. The Romans didn't like her much and they said the people were cannonballs, which frightened them.'

'Do you mean *cannibals*?'

'S'what I said. Cannonballs. I've finished now, may I please do some drawing?'

Stephanie recovered her power of speech. 'First wash your face and hands and then you can draw for a bit. It's late as it is but I guess you can stay up another hour, but then we go to bed, okay?'

'Okay.' They watched his slight form climb down from the chair, pick up his satchel and head for the door. He turned, 'Where shall I wash? And I really need a wee. Sorry.'

Mohammed put down his knife and fork. 'I'll show you. I'm finished too.'

When they were alone Stephanie slumped in her chair and shook her head.

'He's always been an imaginative child but never like this. Nothing like this. Where's he getting all this stuff about the Romans and babies? And cannibals? He's only six for God's sake. He should be talking about *Peppa Pig*, *Olaf the Snowman* and *Thomas the Tank Engine*. Who is this Lady? What did he call her?'

'Agrona, I think.'

'You ever heard of her?'

'No. New one on me.'

'And you're a smart woman. Where would a six-year-old boy come up with a name like that?'

'I don't know. Wait here a second.'

Maryam was true to her word. In a matter of seconds, she returned to the dining room with a smart tablet in a black leather case. Stephanie had started clearing the dishes and had topped up their glasses of wine. She said, 'I'll help you with the washing-up.'

'No, the machine can do that. Let me take those into the kitchen while this warms up.'

A minute later she was back. Stephanie heard the smooth sound of the dishwasher from the kitchen. Everything seemed so normal, so mundane, but she knew the sense of normality was treacherous. She swallowed hard. Maryam placed a gentle hand on hers. She said, 'How are you feeling?'

Stephanie tried to smile but her face crumpled. 'I feel like I was walking on what I thought was a perfectly solid lawn and then suddenly discovered I was on quicksand and it's sucking me down fast.'

'What about Mike?'

'What *about* Mike? Where is he? What good is a father and husband who disappears when you need him most? Sharif wouldn't do that to you, would he?'

Maryam decided to change the subject. No, Sharif wouldn't do that, but this was no time to be comparing husbands, it might make Stephanie feel worse. She fired up her search engine and tapped in the Lady's name. It took her a few attempts to get the spelling right. Agrona.

The women gazed at the brief paragraph displayed on the screen.

Agrona: Warrior goddess of the ancient Briton's, when the land was called Prydain and before the Roman invasion. Goddess of war, worshipped by the Iceni. It is said her worshippers practiced human sacrifice and even cannibalism. Later called Andrasta by the Romano-Celts, it is believed Boudicca, the famous British warrior queen, prayed to her before attacking the Romans. See pre-Roman Britain and the Welsh god Aeron who derived his name from her.

Maryam breathed deep. 'I think we've found her,' she said.

[10]

Mohammed watched Jerome at work with deep fascination. He had heard of automatic writing and had even been involved with some experimental attempts to contact the dead when he was a student, Ouija, and the like. He had thought them all very suspect. As a Muslim, he was not meant to countenance such things, but then he was also not meant to drink alcohol. He sipped at his glass. He considered himself an enlightened man and treated the Quran as a fine book of great thoughts, and a wonderful work of literature, but he also thought of it as a guide book not a rule book. Many, if not most, of his Christian friends felt the same way about their holy book. And yet, now he was watching something remarkable happen, and neither his faith nor his training as a psychiatrist could help him explain what he was seeing. While he watched the image under Jerome's swirling hand had developed like a photograph on old-fashioned film.

The boy drew as if his life depended on it, only stopping the strange looping path of his pencil across his page to sharpen its point. His hand moved quickly without losing any of its absolute control over its medium.

Mohammed watched to see if Jerome ever blinked, watched until his own eyes watered in sympathy. The sheer concentration on display was hypnotic and exciting, and if he hadn't seen it happen with his own eyes he would never have believed such a young hand could create such a mature work. He wondered if Jerome might be the victim of a form of Savant Syndrome but considered it unlikely. He lacked all the primary indicators. So, what was he doing? Was he channelling an external force? Was he in contact with a talent from another spiritual plane? How was he doing this?

Mohammed thought about the portraits he had seen by the troubled twentieth century Swiss artist Giacometti and saw similarities in the texture and scrambled linear finesse of Jerome's work. The Swiss had been a sophisticated and innovative artist, a perfectionist who described portraiture as trying to find an acceptable way to get across the bridge of his sitter's nose, and yet created something as visually solid as rock in the vibrating cloud of his laser sharp lines. A cloud becoming solid, that was where Mohammed's wandering mind was taking him. That was what Jerome's drawing looked like... a phantom slowly becoming real. The ethereal form was gaining weight and definition while he watched. Only the eyes remained white and hollow as if lit from within.

Jerome's hand moved his pencil like a high-speed machine, but his body remained still. His breathing was light and gentle almost as if he was deeply asleep, and yet his eyes flickered across the page, devouring the image as it formed. When he spoke Mohammed jumped slightly, it was so unexpected.

In a dreamy, piping voice, and without interrupting his drawing, the boy said, 'Your wife is a lovely cook. Can we come for dinner again?'

Mohammed nodded, 'I'm sure that'll be fine. Maryam always cooks enough for surprise guests, and I'm greedy enough to eat it all. You would help me with my tubby waistline if you were to eat some of it too.'

'You aren't fat. You're nice.'

'Thank-you. I like you too. That's a brilliant drawing.'

'The pencil has to be sharp or it's no good. My art teacher thinks I'm weird. She wants me to paint houses and trees and flowers with poster paint like all the others. I don't want to.'

'Why not?'

'They're boring. The others just muck about anyway. They all paint the same house. Whose house has a door in the middle and four windows, one in each corner? Our house has the door on the left, yours is on the side. Houses are all shapes and sizes. Why don't they draw what they see?'

'Is that what you do?'

'Yes. Making stuff up is rubbish. Why would you want to do that? It's like telling lies.'

'So, that drawing you're doing now. Where can you see her?'

Mohammed could plainly see the figure was that of a woman.

'She's the Lady. I'm mostly remembering her, but I can see her face in the mirror on that wall.' He pointed over Mohammed's shoulder.

Mohammed turned to look in the mirror and baleful, white eyes glared back at him. It was only for a second, and then she was gone like dry autumn leaves blown away in the wind. Suddenly, Jerome stopped drawing, pulled the page from his pad, and began tearing the work into shreds.

Mohammed protested, 'Why are you doing that? It was really good. *Really* good. You should have kept that.'

Jerome kept tearing until the only part of the page left intact was a scrap containing the furious eyes. He shook his head.

'Words and drawings have special powers if they're true. But you must finish what you're doing, or you shut the door and it all goes away. *She* went away so I couldn't finish the drawing, and that meant it was just a rubbish sheet of paper with scribble on it. Why would anyone want to keep that? It's silly.'

'What door? I don't understand.'

'*The* door. The door between here and there, between now and then, between her and me. And her and you. You want to know about her, don't you? The Lady. She wants to know about you. You touched her in the garden, didn't you? She wants to know how you did that. She thinks you're special too, like me.'

'Does she want to send me to the happy place?'

Jerome chuckled slyly. 'I only said that to frighten mummy.'

'So, there is no happy place?'

'Oh, yes, there is, but not everyone's happy there. Some people are very sad, and some are very scared.'

'How do you know?'

'I went as far as the gate and I looked inside. I heard the voices. Lots of people missed being at home. I heard babies crying. Some people were laughing. Some were just talking. It was like being in the tea place in *M & S*, you know? You hear all sorts.'

Then he chuckled throatily and spoke with the crone's dry voice once more. 'Here comes the ram to butt his horn. Oh, dear. The husband so forlorn.'

Before Mohammed could ask him what he meant the doorbell rang.

'Knock, knock,' said Jerome, with an odd, gloating smile. 'Knock, knock. With the scent of a woman on his hungry old cock.'

Mohammed looked at his watch. It was almost ten o'clock. He called out, 'I'll get it.' To Jerome he said, 'I'll just be a second.' The boy nodded, still smiling.

Mohammed unlocked the front door and swung it wide. The outside light hadn't come on, but he very quickly recognised the shadowed silhouette of Mike Talbot. He could smell him too. The raw reek of alcohol stained the air. The man was unsteady on his feet. Mohammed wondered how he hadn't fallen down. Talbot belched. 'I've come for my missus. She's here.'

Mohammed nodded, 'Yes, she's here with Jerome. Did you drive here or get a cab?'

'What's it to do with you? I've come for my missus, get her out here.'

'Don't you think you should come in and get a coffee or something? I don't think you should be driving, Mike.'

43

'Don't you fucking "Mike" me. I'm Mister Talbot to you. I don't know you! *We* don't know you. Will you send my missus out here or do I have to come in and get her? Left a fucking note, did she?' He shouted, 'Oi, Stephanie, get your arse out here, NOW!'

Talbot stepped into the light of the hallway and Mohammed saw the unfocused rage on his alcohol bloated face. He looked like a scarlet toad about to explode with fury. He looked like an angry schoolboy. When he spoke, hot spittle spat from his clenched lips. Every word emitted the stench of beer and spirits into Mohammed's face. The man was dangerously drunk.

He ranted, tears streaming from his reddened eyes, 'Come in my house and tell me what to do, *in my own house*! You and that blonde plod tart. I'm not having it, you hear me. Fucking cheek! Who do you think you are? What makes you so fucking special? You wipe your arse the same as me, what makes you so high and mighty?'

'Please, Mr Talbot, keep your voice down.'

'There you are, see! There you are again, telling me what to do. That's it! I've had enough of you, mister high and fucking mighty!'

And Talbot threw the first punch with all his strength.

[11]

It would also be his last. Mohammed had no difficulty evading the flailing fist, but things went very wrong for his attacker. Talbot had put every ounce of his drunken fury into the strike. This man had taken away his woman, this man had taken away his son. This man had come into Talbot's house and treated him like shit in front of Stephanie and that slapper of a copper. Time he got what was coming to him. Talbot lashed out with murderous intent, but instead of pounding flesh and bone his blow met empty air. Mohammed had simply stepped out of the way.

The drunken man fell full length to the floor in an uncontrolled stumble, swearing all the while. He landed hard on the polished wooden boards, knocking the wind from his body and bruising his face. Then he retched painfully, spasms wracking his body. Mohammed could see that Talbot's nose had begun bleeding and shook his head with a mixture of pity and disgust. Then he became very aware of the two women standing together in the dining room doorway, and of another, slight figure gazing out from the living room while clutching his satchel to his narrow chest.

Mohammed addressed the boy. 'I'm sorry, Jerome. I'm sorry you had to see that. I'll help him up.'

'No, it's all right. He tried to hit you and you didn't do anything. He tried to hit you and fell over. He's drunk like a skunk and he smells like one too.'

Stephanie said, 'That's enough, don't forget he's still your dad. Don't be so rude.'

She was breathing in deep, measured breaths. Mohammed could see how hard it was for her to contain her frustration.

He said, 'He can sleep it off here in the other spare room. He's not fit to drive.'

From the floor a voice wailed, 'Stephanie, Stephanie, love, I want to go home. I want to sleep in my own bed.'

Through clenched teeth his wife replied, 'Why didn't you just stay put and sleep it off while you were there? You had to come here and ruin a lovely evening...' She bent down and fished through his pockets for his car keys. She found them in his trouser pocket and withdrew them. She sniffed her hand and grimaced. 'Ah, nice, he's pissed himself too. That's just great.'

Jerome said, 'Daddy's wee-weed on himself like a little boy. He should wear a nappy like a baby.'

'Jerome, enough. Don't make things worse.' Stephanie regarded her hosts. 'I'm really sorry about this, really sorry. It made a lovely change to have a civilised evening for once. Mike should wear a tee shirt that says, "Instant arsehole, just add alcohol". He's all right really. The problem is that booze doesn't agree with him, but he keeps trying to convince himself that it does. He says that's what real men, like him, do. And he *drove* here like that? What if he'd run someone over on the way here?' She sighed, her voice cracking. 'I'd better get him home...'

Maryam opened her mouth to speak but Stephanie held her hand up and shook her head. 'No, thanks, really. But I can't let him stay here. I'd better get him home. I'll just fetch our bag.'

Jerome watched his mother climb the stairs, then turned to Mohammed.

'Can I stay here? Daddy won't mind.' He frowned at the prone figure at his feet. 'He won't care.'

Mohammed looked down into the earnest, narrow face and wondered what the child's life must be like. He wondered what it was about the boy that had first attracted the malevolent spirit he called the 'Lady'. Unhappiness with life had whipped his mother into a state of exhaustion and evident despair. That evening he had seen the faintest glimmer of the light that must have once attracted men to her like moths to a flame, but now that flame was all but snuffed out.

Jerome had become the foundation on which she balanced her precarious grip on life and normality. His father was not much help. Too self-absorbed, little more than an empty space even when he was in the room. It was obvious that Jerome had no strong male parental model to whom he could turn in his hour of need. Was that what had brought him onto the Lady's radar? Had the spirit latched onto and fed from that hollow space in the child's heart, like a vampire bat drawn to an open wound? Mohammed knew from experience how the stink of loneliness and despair pollutes too many houses, and he had seen how it hovers like a shroud on the shoulders of the friendless. It must be a pungent signal to the sensitive nose. A quiet, hopeful voice diverted his thoughts.

'Can I stay? Please?'

Mohammed recognised the scratchy note of pleading in the question.

'Of course not, Jerome, don't be daft.' Stephanie bustled back down the stairs and broke the tension. 'You can carry the bag for mummy, there's a good boy. Sharif, you've done so much already, but, could I ask you to help me with Mike? I couldn't manage on my own.'

'If you're sure you won't stay...'

'Best not. I'm embarrassed enough as it is...'

The man on the floor broke wind loudly and unpleasantly. The sulphur stench filled the hallway. Stephanie blinked and wrinkled her nose, pursing her lips as if reluctant to breathe.

'I'm so sorry. Can we get him to the car? Please.'

Barely five minutes later Maryam heard a car engine start and then fade away into the distance. Her husband came back into the house with his arms held away from his sides. He regarded her ruefully.

'My fault for bringing them here. Sorry, Sprog, what a mess, and I've got urine and blood on my hands and down my clothes.'

'Stay right there.' Maryam hurried into the kitchen and returned a few seconds later with a five-gallon bucket, a bottle of antiseptic cleaning spray and a cloth. She had pulled on a pair of rubber gloves and had donned an apron.

'Come on, out of my way, and don't touch anything.'

She rapidly cleaned the front door, concentrating on any of the surfaces Talbot might have touched. Then she closed and bolted it. She turned to her husband.

'Okay, Boots. Get naked and put your clothes in the bucket, then get your raggedy ass up into the shower and wash that man right outta your hair.'

He reached out to her with a grin and she shrieked at him, 'Don't you come near me with another man's piss on your hands. I can still smell his farts. How does she put up with that? Now, go on, clothes in the bucket and get yourself sanitary.'

'Yes, ma'am. I hear you.' Mohammed peeled of his shoes and socks then his shirt and jeans. He stood before her barefoot in his boxers, Maryam smiled wickedly.

'I don't make no purchase without getting a good look at the merchandise. I said "naked" mister. Let's do the job properly.'

By the time her husband rejoined her in the kitchen Maryam had washed the floor in the hallway and started a load of laundry. The dishwasher was still humming. She had a mug of coffee before her and a half-full cafetiere on the table. She poured a mug for him and splashed cold milk into it.

He wrapped his dressing gown around his legs and sat down next to her.

'Can I kiss you now?'

'I've got coffee breath.'

'I'll suffer in silence.'

They embraced and kissed tenderly. Then they sat watching the laundry in the machine. Mohammed asked, 'Did you take the money out of my jean's pocket.'

Maryam sat up, her eyes and mouth flew open.

'I didn't look. I never thought... you never carry money around at home.'

'No, I don't, you're right. Don't worry, I'm joking.'

She punched him on the arm.

'Don't joke,' she said. 'Not after tonight. *That* is not the way to end a dinner party. Say, do you think they got home okay?'

'Yeah. Stephanie put a towel she always uses on the driver's seat. We dumped Mike in the back, and Jerome sat up front with his mum. She shouldn't have really. She'd had some wine and the child car seat wasn't the best. They'll be home by now. That towel really bugged me, this sort of thing must be a regular event.'

'How will she get him indoors?'

'Wake him up and help him walk to the door, I guess. Or leave him to sleep it off in the car.' He shrugged, 'Look, we offered to let them stay and she said no. We offered again, and she still said no. What else can we do? We're a long way from Samaria and anyway I reckon we did everything we could. Even the best Samaritan has to admit defeat sometimes. I don't get soaked in urine for just anyone, you know.'

They watched the washing machine for a few seconds, Mohammed sighed.

'I've seen this one. Everything's repeats these days. I ask you, what do we pay the licence fee for anyway?'

Maryam took his arm and put it around her shoulder. 'I've got to stay up until it's done so I can put the clothes on the dryer. You go to bed, I'll see you in a few minutes.'

'What, and miss the car chase? That's the best bit and it's right at the end. Anyway, you've primed me with strong coffee and warm lips. How can I sleep with all that going on in my body? I'll wait up with you.' He squeezed her shoulder. 'It tires me out, you know? I see so much in my line of work: marriages that don't work; marriages that should never have happened; people poisoned in toxic partnerships. The kids suffer, and the parents wonder why they bounce off the rails and misbehave sometimes. Who can blame them? Look at Jerome. He's got his Lady, and, you know something? He's so convincing he's got me seeing her too! I'm meant to be the calm professional and now *I'm* seeing ghosts in the mirrors and I'm walking through ectoplasm in their back garden in broad daylight. Who you gonna call?'

'You're seeing *what*?' This is too much. Sounds as if to me you have been streaming re-runs of *Supernatural*.

By the time he'd finished telling her about his day the laundry was finished but remained unnoticed in the silent machine.

Maryam looked deadly serious, 'I'm telling you, Sharif, I've heard about this sort of thing before. Poltergeist activity around a disturbed youth is a recorded fact. Jerome isn't attracting this spirit Lady of his, he's *causing* it. Promise me you'll be careful. People get hurt by this stuff and you're too important to me to be one of them. Promise me? I mean it.'

'Don't you worry, Sprog. I'll wear wolfbane and a bulb of garlic around my neck. I'll be careful, I promise.' He kissed her tenderly. 'So, what happens if we leave that laundry in the machine and go straight to bed?'

'Let's find out.'

They left the kitchen arm-in-arm, then moments later Maryam flew back in and opened the washing machine door. She heaved out the laundry and dumped it in the waiting basket, then she started folding it over the dryer. Mohammed watched her from the doorway.

She muttered, 'I'm sorry but it will smell if I leave it in the machine. I can't do it, I just can't.'

'I love you, you know,' he said.

She grinned back at him over her shoulder, 'You just remember that when the nasty ghost Lady offers to take *you* for a walk, little boy. You just remember that, okay!'

'Come on, no-one can see us, I promise. It's just you and me. It'll be okay.'

'No, look. There's police tape all over the place.'

'We can duck right under it. Come on, don't be a coward.'

'No, Rich, please. I'm scared. It feels wrong. There's something wrong. Let's go, please.'

The blocky cathedral looked like a brightly illuminated golden Christmas cake floating at the heart its night darkened grounds. The lights and sounds of the town seemed held at a distant remove. Silence reigned. Nothing stirred among the gravestones or in the clumps of trees, not an animal or a bird. There was no breath of wind. The branches of trees reached like petrified arms towards a star speckled, cloudless sky. They seemed ghostlike in the cathedral's reflected radiance. The Cathedral Close could almost have been mistaken for a still photograph, almost, except for a small and easily missed area close to the sister stones.

Two shadowed figures were pressed close together in the lee of the circle of yew trees, darkness within darkness. The young man wore smart canvas pants and a sloppy tee shirt that suited his slender frame. The girl was dressed revealingly in heels and a short skirt, her midriff bared and her full breasts barely contained by her plunging halter neck crop-top. She had dressed to impress for her second date with Rich Ewell and her attire had worked its magic all too well.

They had started the evening with a few drinks at *The Swan*, a popular pub where the barman liked to welcome young, good looking girls onto his premises, rightly believing they were good for business.

Chloe Payne ticked a lot of boxes on the barman's checklist. She was tall, leggy, and showed a lot of cleavage. He thought her pretty face was a little overdone under her tousled mass of blonde hair – her eyeshadow was almost Goth – but lots of girls wore too much makeup these days.

And anyway, he mused, why worry about the mantelpiece when the fireplace looked so welcoming? If he had known her age the leering barman would have been outraged to the core of his suburban English soul. Despite her mature appearance Chloe was not yet fifteen and Rich Ewell was nineteen, almost twenty.

Ewell knew how young she was. He had first met her in the park when she was on her way home from school. She was in the neat green blazer and grey skirt, white blouse, and black tights of her school uniform. Her face was free of cosmetics and from the neck up she looked her age, but there was no mistaking the promise of her ripening body.

Ewell was an old hand at grooming. He knew how to use social media to get into a girl's private moments and see what appealed to them most. He kept notes. He also knew how to appeal to a girl's burgeoning vanity. He told them boys their age were immature. They were drooling sex trolls, knuckle dragging morons. They deserved better, and he could provide everything they needed. And more.

On their first date, he had taken Chloe for a meal at the tapas bar. She had never been there before and thought it was all very sophisticated. Ewell talked her through the menu and ordered on her behalf. They drank soft drinks and talked about movies and music. He walked her home, and when they reached a quiet street he pulled her into a shadowed corner and kissed her, hard. She had opened her inexperienced mouth to his tongue and hadn't pulled away when he pressed his urgent erection against her groin.

Things seemed very promising. The second date would prove the real deal. There was no suggestion of food this time. When Chloe asked what and where they would be eating, he told her they would grab something later. That night they would take a romantic tour of the town; but first he suggested they have a drink. Ewell didn't want food in her belly that might slow the effects of the alcohol. If she was good, he would buy her a burger and fries later.

She had never drunk white rum before and Ewell had quickly poured three doubles into her, the potent spirit disguised by a sugary sports drink. She was a little unbalanced and leaned closely against him when Ewell eventually steered her out into the night.

The barman drank in the girl's fine curves like a connoisseur. He noticed she had no visible panty line under her tight little skirt. That meant she was wearing a string or a thong. Or less. The barman's mouth watered at the thought, his porn-fuelled imagination visualising her firm golden flesh.

'Lucky bugger,' he muttered. 'Go on. Give her one for me. Give her two.'

From *The Swan* to the Cathedral Close took just a few minutes. All the way Ewell had his arm around Chloe, his discreet thumb stroking the soft skin of her bare stomach. Firm yet yielding flesh.

The big gate into the close was padlocked at sundown, but he knew there was a wrought iron kissing gate by the old willow around the corner. That was never locked. Inside the grounds and in the shadow of the willow he

51

kissed her, and she opened her mouth to him. He ran his hand up her thigh and traced the curve of her naked buttock with tender fingers, stroking her. She might as well have not bothered with the string she was wearing. He pressed his finger between her legs and felt her moist heat. She was ready for him. He pushed his finger into her and tried to move aside the thin strip of fabric.

She gasped, wriggled, and pulled away. 'Please, not yet. Not here. It's not proper. Someone might see us.'

He shushed her and took her hand, pressing it against the front of his pants where his thickened penis stood proud.

'Feel that,' he said. 'You did that. The woman in you did that. So, what are you going to do about it? Are you a prick teaser? Is that it? Are you one of those girls who lead a man on and then stop at the last minute? Are you going to act like a little girl now? Do you want to run home to mummy? Go on then. Run away, little girl. But don't expect me to run after you.'

Chloe writhed in mental anguish. She didn't want to let Ewell down, he had been nice to her. He had made her feel like an adult, treated her as an equal. But things were going too fast for her and her head felt numb. The alcohol was affecting her balance. The ground wouldn't stay still, and nausea threatened to overwhelm her. She decided.

She murmured, 'No, Rich. No, I'm not a prick teaser, really. But not here. Anyone could come along and see us. There must be somewhere else.'

'There is. Come on. Take my hand and I'll show you.'

And he had led her round the cathedral to the circle of yew trees. As they approached she wondered what was laced around the trees, and then she realised and pulled up short. The sight of the police tape had an immediate sobering effect on the girl. Suddenly she had realised she was alone in the dark with a man who, in truth, she barely knew. It was their second date and he was trying to force her into a place where a crime had been committed as if it was a room in a four-star hotel. She reeled back.

'No, come on, let's go please. Look, something's happened here. We shouldn't be here. I want to go, please.'

Ewell hadn't expected the tape either but was too excited to let it stop him now. He hissed at her. 'Look, you knew what you were getting into. Stop messing me about. That's nothing to worry about, it just guarantees our privacy.'

He unzipped his pants and pulled out his erect penis. It looked almost luminous in the shadowed light. He stroked it.

'You did this to me and you're going to help me deal with it. Come on. Chloe, you know it's only fair. Or do I tell all your friends what you're really like? A little cock teaser. Come on, at least touch it. It won't bite.'

She reached out a trembling hand and put her fingers around the tumescent flesh. It was the first time she had seen an erection, first time she had touched one. It felt hot and hard against her hand and leapt slightly at her touch, like a small independent animal. It felt like a hot tube of flesh covered wood.

Ewell groaned, and his knees buckled slightly. He thrust his hips at her and reached for her shoulders, pulling her down.

'Use your mouth. Put it in your mouth and lick it like a lollypop. Suck it, there's my good girl.' He groaned again.

That was the final straw. Chloe pulled free of his grasp and ran back towards the kissing gate. She had thought he was nice, but now she knew he was a disgusting creature who wanted her to do vile things. Fear lent flight to her heels and she paused just long enough to pull off her shoes, so she could run faster. She thought she could hear him running after her, slavering like a wild beast. That hot, hard thing of his became bigger and more terrifying in her imagination. She whimpered in fright. When he caught her he would rape her, how could she have been so stupid?

Ewell stood by the shadowed circle of trees and watched her run away with a sneer on his fine features. His hand was gripped around his member as if it was the handle of a knife. He was a predator but prided himself that he was not a rapist. He knew when to stop. Where was the pleasure in forcibly taking something when so many girls happily gave it away? The true joy was in the conquest, she had to want it too. If that silly tart wanted to hang on to her stupid fucking virginity let her. Fuck her. *Or rather,* he thought, *don't.*

He chuckled. It didn't help him deal with his immediate situation though, did it? He had been so close. He had touched her there, he had felt her through the stupid little string she was wearing under that belt of a skirt. Why would a girl dress like that if she didn't want to go all the way? Just looking at her a man had his eyes on the prize. She might as well have been fucking naked!

He groaned with frustrated lust. *Enough.* He ducked under the police tape and entered the circle of yew trees, his hand still stroking his erection. He would have her one way or the other that night. It would have been better if she'd been there with him at the time, but hey, he knew how to have a great time on his own. He'd had plenty of practice.

53

Ewell had a fertile imagination, which he could reinforce with memories of girls who hadn't run away at the last minute. Girls who had let him do everything he wanted with them. Everything and everywhere. And sometimes more than once.

He shut his eyes and remembered soft mouths and warm bodies, pert little breasts, and open legs. He remembered hips in his hands and the tears of pleasure the girls had shed. The odd little whimpers of orgasm that sounded like involuntary cries of pain. His hand ministered to his needs and he quickly came onto the ivy-covered stones he had so often used as a bed. Jets of hot salty semen splashed onto the mottled rock.

He heard a subtle sound behind him, a quiet laugh of delight, and he looked around expecting to see Chloe returned to him. He knew she would change his mind. He smiled. The fact that he had just pleasured himself didn't matter. There was always a second round in the chamber.

And then he saw he was wrong. Badly wrong.

Several metres from the yews Chloe hesitated. She had crept back because she wanted to say sorry. She was surprised when Ewell hadn't chased her or hurt her and wondered if she had misunderstood the man's intentions. Maybe she could do something to help him after all. She didn't have to go all the way. Or put it in her mouth. He wouldn't make her do that.

Then as she neared the yew trees she had realised he was gone. She looked around as if expecting to see him smiling at her from somewhere in the shadows. He would be glad to see her the way he always was. He would make her feel wanted. Make her feel like a grown woman.

Then a crunching, tearing sound erupted from within the circle of trees, it was terrifying in its abruptness as was the howling shriek from a man in agony. His scream got higher and higher and was interspersed with rasping gasps and desperate, pleas for mercy. The sounds ended in a bubbling gurgle as if mid-scream he had been dumped head first into a bucket of icy water.

Chloe froze in terror. And then a scratchy laugh came from behind the police tape and the yews' branches began to twitch and move as if something was forcing its way out of the trees and towards her. Chloe turned and ran as if wild beasts pursued her. She didn't stop until she was pounding on her home's front door.

Her parents were shaken by her appearance, her clothes, and her evident state of panic. Her father brought a basin for her when she was violently sick. When she was finally calm she told them what had happened. Her father listened and regarded his little girl with bleak concentration until she had finished her tale. She had left nothing out, or almost nothing. He looked sideways at his wife who gazed back at him with murder in her blazing eyes. He nodded. 'I'd better ring the police.'

[13]

'Morning, Rose.'

'Morning, Sarge. Quiet night?'

The desk sergeant yawned hugely, stood up and arced his back before rubbing his hands over his grey crew-cut.

He said, 'You're having a laugh, aren't you? Didn't you see the local news this morning?'

'No, why?'

'There's been another murder in the Cathedral Close. Nasty business too. Local Romeo got himself ripped up like a paper bag. Bits of him have been scattered about like leftovers from a dog's dinner. SOCO are still doing the jigsaw puzzle. Rather them than me, I fancy having me breakfast after I leave here.'

'Bloody hell, really? What's Hines saying about it?'

'Nothing, yet. She's not made it in yet, night watch took the call. Just what you want in the middle of the night. Bloody business.'

Rose gazed at him. 'Whereabouts in the Close?'

'Where they found the baby's guts, on and around those old stones. Oh, right, yes. That was you wasn't it. You found the guts. Well, now our killer's traded up. He's gone from ripping out a baby's belly to ripping up a wanker's body.' He made a motion with his hands, as if he was tearing sheets of paper.

'Not like you to speak ill of the dead, Sarge.'

'No, I mean it, literally. They found traces of semen at the site. Some of the blood spatter was over the semen, so he must have just finished the deed when he was attacked. Nice of his killer to wait.'

Rose pulled a face. 'Anything else I should know?'

'Wait and see. DCI Sutton's pulled in the local CID. They're in her office with her going over whatever we know, which is naff all, of course. You shouldn't need to worry about it. I doubt they'll bring you in.'

'I dunno, Sarge. I dunno. I got involved with an odd little case of suspected abduction yesterday. A six-year-old boy claimed a woman told him she had something to show him. She led him up to the cathedral and she wanted to take him to the stones, but he ran away into the cathedral itself.

'The sexton found him in the Lady Chapel having a chat with a statue of the Blessed Virgin Mary. Boy said she was talking back to him. The sexton took him home, but the kid's been acting weird ever since. Dr Sharif Mohammed was called in for the interview. You know him?'

'Yeah, he's a good bloke, sound as a pound. Sounds to me like that kid's just trying for a bit of attention, don't you think? They can be like that at six. Lovely age, but, you know, a bit random. They haven't settled down to any particular direction yet, always full of surprises. They keep you on your toes, you'll find out one day.'

It was a brave person who would bandy baby talk with Sergeant Roger Fowler, proud father of four and doting grandfather of six. Rose decided to just nod her head and bite back her doubts about Jerome. She wondered if the stones would have already claimed a third victim if Jerome hadn't bailed out at the last moment.

She said, 'I guess you're right, Sarge.'

Then she padded off to put her bag in her locker and fetch her kit for the day. She still thought the heavy-duty locks on the lockers looked like overkill. Not for the first time she thought they would be better suited to padlocking a super-tanker to a small tropical island, but they were there for a good reason. They were the direct result of the theft of officers' property when an 'all hands' call had seen the station left empty one winter's evening a few years before.

Tired and battered officers had returned from a run-in with a dangerous band of travellers and found that everything of value had been lifted from their crowbarred lockers. Everything not stolen had been ruined and strewn across the locker room floor. One of the thieves had also defecated onto a pile of clothing then used some of it as toilet paper. It was both disgusting and embarrassing. The local press had a field day, headlines included, 'Cops and Robbers', 'Nick of Crime'

Rose hadn't been on duty that day, but she sympathised with the officers who had. The thieves had not yet been caught, but there would be a good drink for the officers who finally tracked the bastards down. A damn good drink.

'Morning, Rose. Have you got a minute?'

DCI Sutton stood in the doorway in her familiar attitude that said, 'come with me' and would brook no argument.

Rose nodded, 'After you, Chief.'

She was led to Sutton's office where she was introduced to a brace of officers from Worthing CID; DS Mayfield and DI Cremer. Both men looked as if they had been cast from the same mould, built for size instead of comfort. For some reason, she was reminded of the locks in the locker room. They were oversized in a square-built, chunky way. There was not a single ounce of fat on either man, and, although seated comfortably, they vibrated with a tense stillness, like bowstrings waiting to be plucked.

Cremer spoke first, and his voice was a surprise, light and pleasant to the ear. She had expected growling monosyllables. She detected a gentle Scottish lilt to his diction. Rose decided to like Cremer until further notice.

'Good to meet you, Rose.'

He stood and held out his firm, dry hand for her to shake. Mayfield did the same. Once they were all safely seated Cremer continued.

'We'd like some local insight on this Ewell case and the Chief thought you the best candidate for informed guide. You grew up here and went to school next to the cathedral. You know the history of the area. Did you know Rich Ewell?'

'Not personally, but I've heard of him. Word says he's a ripe piece of shit who likes his girls young, too young, but there's never been a formal complaint against him. There's no suggestion of rape, but we keep an eye on him all the same. He's the assistant manager of the deli in the square and lives in the flat above it. Good looking guy in an obvious way, you know...' Rose realised she was talking about the man in the present tense. 'At least, he was.'

Cremer leaned forward. 'Do you think one of his girls' families might have had reason to kill him? Revenge killing?'

'No, sir. This is Sussex not Columbia. Someone might give him a good kicking or take a cricket bat to his bones but nothing else. Okay, look, I guess if he did the naughty with a local farmer's daughter he might end up looking down the business end of a twelve bore. But I hear he died in a very bad way, I mean, I hear the man was ripped to shreds. Is that true? How could someone do that?'

'There's a witness to the killing. A schoolgirl called Chloe Payne was with Ewell in the Close. It seems he had gone a bit too far, got a bit too intimate with her, and she legged it. She says he had got excited, pulled his penis out and tried to get her to give him a blow job. Chloe is fourteen, by the way, and virgo intacta, which should make her a protected species if it wasn't for sticky items like Rich Ewell. As you say, he was a prime piece of work.

'Anyway, it seems she reconsidered and decided to go back for a chat – or something. The logic of that escapes me, but who can fathom the mind of a fourteen-year-old girl?'

58

Rose shook her head in frustration, 'I remember girls like that at school. I must have been a nightmare for the boys at school, I was more interested in hockey than anything they had in their trousers. Enough tried it on; that hockey stick came in handy I can tell you. How could she be so daft as to go back?'

Cremer took a deep breath. 'Who knows? She was telling the attending officer all this in front of her parents, so we can presume she held a fair amount back. The officer says she was dressed like a King's Cross Saturday night special. Total tart, arse hanging out of her micro-skirt and boobs out to here. Ewell would have found plenty of places to park his bike. He must have thought he was onto a sure thing. The dress she went out in was in her shoulder bag, so we presume she must have changed in a public toilet before she met him. Her dad said she wouldn't have been allowed through the door looking the way she did when she got home. Her folks seem to be good people.'

Rose tilted her head and narrowed her eyes, 'Predators like Ewell are drawn to girls like that. I think they must be able to smell them from miles away. So, then, he's been murdered. How did he die?'

Cremer held her blue gaze with his grey stare. 'You already said it. He was torn limb from limb and then the pieces were ripped apart. And somebody did it with their bare hands, there are no knife marks. On the evidence so far, we're looking for a bona fide monster.'

[14]

Mohammed took a long pull on his coffee. His mouth was still full when his mobile phone rang. He didn't recognise the number, but he swiped 'accept' and put it to his ear. He was still trying to swallow his drink without choking himself when an urgent voice said, 'Hello, hello... is that you Dr Mohammed? Hello? Are you there?'

He placed the voice instantly. 'Hello, Mrs Talbot. Sorry, I had a mouth full of coffee. How are you? How's your husband?'

'Still asleep and snoring like a pneumatic drill. Thank God, we've got a big enough sofa, so I could shut the door on him and get some sleep myself. I just wanted to say thank-you for a lovely meal last night, and to apologise again for Mike. He has mood swings, and when the booze takes him he's a pain. So sorry, I wish you hadn't seen that, I really do. Sorry... Yes, darling, what is it? Dr Mohammed... I don't know. I'll ask. Hello again, Doctor, Jerome would like a word with you, is that okay?'

'Sure, yes, thanks.'

There was a pause, then, 'Hello, Dr Mohammed?'

'Good morning, Jerome. Please, call me Sharif. What can I do for you? How are you? Are you, all right?'

'Sharif?'

There was a period of silence as if the boy was pondering the new word. Chewing it over. Mohammed waited, then heard a deep breath, almost a sigh.

'Can I call you, Dr instead? Please, is that okay?'

Mohammed smiled, 'If you like. Do you mean like *Doctor Who*?'

Another pause. 'No. No, not really. She hasn't got a beard like you.'

Mohammed disguised a chuckle as a short cough.

'So then, Jerome, what can I do for you?'

'I've done you a drawing. This one's finished. Do you want to come and get it? I did it last night while daddy was snoring, and mummy was crying downstairs...'

Stephanie's voice broke in, 'That's enough, Jerome. The doctor doesn't want to hear all that. Go and finish your breakfast. The doctor's a busy man, he can't run around after you all day.'

The boy protested, 'But, mummy, I did him a drawing. It's in my room.'

'Go and eat your breakfast, there's a good boy.'

'But, mummy...'

'Now, please, Jerome.'

Mohammed listened to the exchange with interest. He noted how Stephanie was deliberately using the boy's name now she wanted him to do something, instead of the terms of endearment with which she had first greeted him. Then her voice came loudly on the phone and he realised she had reclaimed the handset.

'Sorry, Doctor we've got to go. I can hear Mike upstairs. He'll want his breakfast. I'll call you.'

'Stephanie, look, I'd like to see Jerome's drawing.'

'I'll call you. We've got to go, okay? I'll call you. Bye.'

She hung up before he could say anything else.

'Who was that?' Maryam swept into the kitchen in a cloud of soapy perfume. 'And the bathroom's free for you. I left the stuff down.'

Mohammed marvelled at his wife's ability to leap from one subject to another in the same sentence. Personally, he always had to complete a thought before moving on. Maryam seemed able to focus on several points at once. He had once showed her a clip he used in his perception classes. There were two teams of five players each, one dressed in black the other in white. He had asked her to count how often the white team passed a basketball to each other.

At the end of the sequence he said, 'Well?'

'Thirteen, but what was that thing with the moondancing bear?'

It was true, a man dressed as a bear had sashayed onto the scene and moondanced through the weaving players. Ninety per cent of viewers would be so focused on counting the times the ball was passed the bear would go unnoticed, but not Maryam. She was a phenomenon. He rose to his feet and drained his coffee.

'That was Stephanie. She wanted to say thanks for last night and apologise for Mike again. Jerome says he's finished a drawing for me which is interesting. He says he did it while his dad was snoring in bed and his mum was crying downstairs on the sofa. Stephanie shut him up, and then said she had to go because Mike was waking up and moving around. No, she said "we" had to go.'

'Did she sound scared?'

'No, not scared as such. Just urgent.' He echoed her words. 'More "we've got to go" like that.'

'You think she didn't want Mike to know she was talking to you?'

'It's a thought. She let Jerome talk to me. Wouldn't he tell his dad?'

'I don't know. Mum and son seem very close. I've only seen the dad pissed out of his box so I'm no judge. You've seen them together when he's sober. Do they get on do you think?'

Mohammed searched his memory. 'I think Mike is a passing visitor in his own house, a familiar stranger as it were. I could be wrong, but I see that relationship as a divorce waiting to happen. Mike's playing around with other women and I think Stephanie knows it.

'Jerome said something when Mike was knocking on the door last night. He was using an alternative voice that sounded like an old woman, what was it? Something like "Here comes the husband so forlorn", then "knock, knock, knock, knock, with the scent of a woman on his hungry old cock". I'm sure that was it, or close enough.'

'The little boy said that? And it rhymed? Wow. You didn't tell me that.'

'Yeah, strange, huh?'

'Freaking weird if you ask me. Look, go have your shower. Thank God, it's the weekend, there's no rush. I'll catch a bit of news while you're up there.'

She kissed him briefly on the lips. 'Be careful.'

He kissed her in return, 'You're the one who slipped on the soap.'

'Got a nice bruise on my arse to prove it.'

'Lucky bruise. It's a nice arse.'

'Get on with you.'

When he joined her in the living room forty minutes later her mouth was set in a thin line and she wore an expression he seldom saw on her face, one of bitterness and anger.

'What is it?'

She pointed at the TV. 'You know something? Sometimes I'm glad we don't have children. I know you work with them, but if we had our own children I'd live in a state of permanent terror. Read that.'

She had the local headlines on the screen and had clicked on the murder of Rich Ewell. Mohammed read about a nineteen-year-old man's dismembered body being found in the Cathedral Close late the night before. The only witness to his killing being his girlfriend, a local girl who was a student at St Catherine's on the hill. But couldn't be named for legal reasons. He turned from the screen to his wife's bitter face.

'Murder, nasty business.'

'Murder? Sounds to me like he deserved it. Look, he was nineteen and she'd only scraped into year 10. She's got to be, what, fourteen? What's she doing with a nineteen-year-old bloke in the Close in the middle of the night?

And what does a nineteen-year-old man want with a schoolgirl all alone in the dark? D'you think he was showing her his butterfly collection? He was after just one thing and it wasn't her witty conversation. What if that girl was our daughter? Would you be happy about it? What were her parents thinking? Why was that little girl out so late?'

Mohammed fought his strong instinct to shrug. He knew that when Maryam got the bit between her teeth she would worry at something until she had torn the stuffing out of it. He remembered a meal they had once enjoyed in a top-end Indian restaurant in Piccadilly. Maryam wouldn't rest until she had the recipe and could exactly replicate the dish at home. Obviously, this case had piqued her interest in the same way and now she wanted to know more.

His landline phone rang, and he almost ran to answer it. Minutes later he returned to the living room with a light in his eyes.

'Talk of the Devil. That was the local police. They want me to go to the station to interview Chloe Payne about the murder of her boyfriend.'

'Chloe Payne? Is that the girl's name?'

'Yes. Oh, and you were right, she's all of sweet fourteen.'

[15]

When Mohammed entered the station, Rose was already waiting for him by the inner door next to the enquiry window. She had them both buzzed in and took him straight through into the station's bright offices. Some of the people who knew him shouted greetings.

Rose grinned apologetically, 'Sorry we're keeping you so busy, Sharif. Is this okay with Maryam, calling you out on a Saturday like this? I know she prefers to keep her weekends sacred.'

'No problem, really. This case took her fancy when she read about it on the red button this morning. She wonders what a nineteen-year-old man was doing out late at night with a fourteen-year-old girl. She was more into that side of it than the murder angle, she seriously hates the idea of kids being corrupted by predation. What about the victim? The news said he had been dismembered and the poor girl witnessed it. What happened?'

'Sorry, Sharif. If you don't mind, I'd prefer not to say anything yet. I'm sure you agree it would be best if you talk to Chloe without any preconceptions? We need you to bring a fresh eye to this one. CID's got its fingers all over it but so far, they're stumped – and pathology isn't being much help either, at least not yet. Would you mind if I ask you talk to her with a completely open mind?'

'No worries, happy to. And anyway, it's the only mind I've got. Let's see what she has to say.'

'Great, thanks. I'll be with you during the interview but don't worry, I know the rules. I'll keep mum and blend into the background. Her parents are quite happy for you to talk with her without one of them in the room. They've signed the waiver and given their permission. They agree with us that she'll probably say more if they aren't there to hear it. They seem to be good people. Nice, normal people, you know? This whole thing has got them really worried'

'Okay. Oh, one thing, is Chloe an only child?'

'Yes, and that's the end of your questions until later, okay? Right, here we are.'

The station had four interview rooms. Three were for suspects and their legal representatives if required, the fourth was for victims. There was also a medical examination suite for cases of suspected rape. That was down on the lower floor next to the pathology and forensics lab.

Chloe had been taken to the victim's room. Subject to what she told Mohammed she might also be invited to visit the medical examination suite.

Rose opened the door onto a sunlit, cream coloured room containing a hot drinks dispenser, water cooler, four comfortable chairs and a low, round coffee table. A slender girl with long blonde hair and tired looking blue eyes looked up from the magazine she was reading.

She put the magazine on the table, stood up and smoothed her medium length skirt against her thighs, then pulled her hair back over her shoulders. Her movements were coltish, and she seemed unaware that while manipulating her hair she had pressed her full breasts forward against the fabric of her blouse in a very provocative way.

Mohammed quickly saw why Chloe had become the target for a manipulative sexual predator. For all her physical maturity she had the facial expressions and awkwardness of someone much younger. In her school uniform she would be one of the ultimate fantasy figures for men with certain sexual preferences. She might as well have 'victim' tattooed on her forehead.

Chloe regarded the tall, dark, bearded stranger with alarm at first and flicked a glance at Rose as if she was asking her what she meant by bringing this strange man into the room. Then Mohammed smiled gently and asked her to please take a seat. His voice calmed her, and she smiled back.

Maryam had often voiced her opinion that if Mohammed had ever decided to walk the deviant route, especially with young girls, he would have become the most successful predator in history.

'They melt when you smile at them,' she said. 'They're putty in your hands. It's a good thing you're a good man or I'd personally round up the pitchfork and lynch mob and stretch you from the highest tree, you hear me?'

Rose introduced him and sat to one side, Mohammed shook Chloe's hand and then pulled his chair round so that he was sitting sideways to her, far enough away not to be threatening but close enough to study her face and read her expression and body language. What she did and how she behaved could be as important as what she said. He thought of it as physical leakage.

He closed his eyes and inhaled deeply. He noticed Chloe's fresh floral scent with spicy undertones and recognised *L'air Du Temps*. The perfume was too sophisticated for such a young girl. She had probably raided her mother's supply. Otherwise she smelt clean, much like his wife had done straight from the shower.

He opened his eyes again and emptied his mind of all preconceptions. Chloe would take him on a journey if he allowed her, she must act as his guide. He loosely clasped his hands in his lap. The girl followed suit, passively mimicking him. He tilted his head to one side slightly and smiled again. She returned the smile.

'Chloe, it's very nice to meet you.'

'It's nice to meet you, too, Doctor.'

'Please, call me Sharif. We won't stand on ceremony here.'

'Sharif, yes. Okay.'

'So then, Chloe, Rose tells me you had a scary time of it last night. Take your time and, please, tell me what happened. Tell me everything from when you first met Mr Ewell last night to when you, ah, when you went home.'

Chloe started with changing her clothes in the garden shed. She had borrowed her date outfit from a friend whom she described as being 'a bit shorter and a bit less curvy'. The same friend would have provided her with an alibi for the evening, if she needed it.

Ewell had agreed to meet her by the path through the trees on the canal side of the big roundabout. The sun was still up when they met but the man had looked her over with real appreciation in his eyes. He had called her a hot babe, asked her if her skirt had been sprayed on. Then he said he liked her just as much in her school uniform, but the pub landlord might have something to say about it if he had tried to buy her a drink while she was dressed like a schoolgirl. Unless he thought she was a stripper.

Then he kissed her on the mouth and pressed his tongue between her teeth. He showed her how to do it back. It made her feel strange. He ran his hands all over her and pressed against her. Her skin felt hot and cold at the same time. She could feel his thing through his pants. It was hard.

And then he had said, 'Enough for now. Let's go for a drink.' And he had taken her to The Swan. Chloe told Mohammed everything. How she had felt dizzy when they left the pub. How Ewell had taken her to the kissing gate, how he had touched her under her skirt, what he had said. She told them about him exposing himself to her, getting her to touch it. How he had told her to put it in her mouth. And then she had run away.

She spoke dully as if remembering the words from a TV programme she didn't truly understand. Her tired eyes gazed at the centre of Mohammed's chest and only her lips moved. The memory of the previous night held her in its grip and she described it as if hoping she could somehow talk her way out of it, but she couldn't. She was finding it hard to believe what had happened to her, hard to believe she had allowed him to do those things to her.

And then she explained why she had gone back, that she had been telling herself that she would not go all the way. She was just going to help him get comfortable. Give him a handjob, that was all.

All the time she was explaining this she was shaking her head as if even she didn't believe what she was saying. As if subconsciously she knew full well what would have happened when Ewell got her back in his clutches, but her conscious mind fought to deny it.

Mohammed felt the heat of Rose's anger fill the room, but the young officer kept her peace as she had promised. And then Chloe started to quiver in her chair as if she was shivering from a chill, and she stuttered out her memory of the sounds Ewell made while he died. She told how the branches of the trees moved while whatever had killed him pushed its way out towards her, the noises it made.

'If I had waited to see what it was,' she said, raising her eyes to look into Mohammed's, 'I think I would have died last night, wouldn't I?'

Mohammed nodded. 'Yes,' he said, 'I think you're right.'

[16]

Chloe's father was sitting on a bench in the walled ornamental garden to one side of the police station grounds. The garden had been a gift from a grateful and wealthy couple who had been burgled back in the nineteen seventies and had had their stolen goods returned within the month. Rose knew the couple had rapidly followed each other to the grave during the noughties and each had received a respectful police escort during their funerals. With the police force in its present impoverished state she wondered if such a thing would be possible now; either solving the crime so quickly or finding enough spare officers to provide an escort for the dead.

Mr Payne folded his daughter into his arms and looked from Rose to Mohammed. He said nothing, but the question was plain on his squarely handsome face. *Will my little girl be all right?*

Mohammed said, 'Chloe has been a great help, Mr Payne. She's an intelligent and honest young woman who knows she has committed an error of judgement. There's no harm done. Ewell was used to dealing with girls who had a lot less backbone. Chloe knew when things were going too far, and she bailed out. She's learned a lesson about men that will serve her well in the future.'

He dug out a business card and handed it to the father.

'If Chloe feels she needs to talk some more, please, give me a call. It will be an informal chat and I'll enjoy it. I think Chloe got a lot off her mind today, she's done brilliantly well.'

He reached out and shook the girl's hand and then her father's. Rose led them away. When they reached the gate in the garden wall Chloe turned and mouthed 'thank-you'. Then they were gone.

Mohammed sat on the vacant bench and gazed sightlessly at the rose bushes planted in the centre of the garden, immersed in thought. Then he lifted his eyes to the cathedral, perched high enough on its hill to peer over the garden wall. He wondered what had torn a grown man to shreds up there, and whether it was somehow connected to Jerome's eerie Lady. Once more he wondered how close Jerome had come to death the previous day, and what might have happened if Chloe had waited to see what came out of that circle of trees.

He jumped when Rose said, 'Penny for them?' She smiled ruefully. 'Sorry, I didn't mean to startle you. You were miles away. Thinking about Chloe?'

68

'Yes,' he admitted. 'Chloe, Jerome, Ewell and that poor disembowelled child. Have you heard any more about that, by the way?'

'You're joking. We're still waiting for Sandy Hines to set her seal on that one and she hasn't come in yet. Actually, she's running late.'

'Well, it is Saturday.'

'No such thing as the weekend in pathology, but I suppose she might have something else to do before she gets here. It's too easy to forget that people *are* people and have lives of their own.'

A furious bellow erupted from beyond the garden wall. Rose screwed up her face and rolled her eyes.

'Subtle isn't she. Sounds like she's hauling poor old Phil over the coals again. Hey, Sharif, can I get you a coffee before you go back to civilisation? I mean a real coffee in Boothroyd's tearoom. I wouldn't mind a chat away from the madhouse.'

'It would be a pleasure, yes, but please, this one's on me.'

'Don't get sexist on me, Sharif. I can afford a coffee for a friend and still pay the mortgage.' She treated him to a warm smile. 'Anyway, who else gives good psychotherapy for the price of an Americano? Come on.'

They found a table in the corner of the tearoom where they could talk without being overheard. The crisply white aproned waitress took their order and returned shortly afterwards with polished silver coffeepots, a cow-shaped silver creamer, and delicate porcelain cups and saucers. Rose had followed Mohammed's lead in ordering a toasted tea cake which they thickly larded with salty butter. They chewed and sipped appreciatively. Neither made a sound until their plates were clean and they had each poured another cup of richly flavoured coffee. Rose picked crumbs off her plate with a fingertip. Mohammed studied her, waiting for her to start talking. Her bright blue eyes glowed in her beautiful face when she returned his gaze.

'Sharif, what do you think's going on in the cathedral grounds.'

'In what way?'

'In every way. Jerome, Chloe, Ewell, and the baby bowels on the stones. It's like something's woken up and declared war on the town. I've been on the force here for five years and I think I'm a good copper. I've seen just about everything that one human being can do to another, usually through drink or drugs, but I've never heard of anything like what happened to Ewell. I would have understood if the dirty little bastard had been stabbed, I might even think he deserved it, but he was ripped to bits. It's like something from a horror film got hold of him...'

69

Rose sipped at her coffee and then she spoke in a hoarse whisper.

'Well then, what did it? Everyone at the station is carrying on as if nothing strange is happening but I'm getting freaked out. This isn't a case of shoplifting or someone getting hit by a drunk driver, this is murder! People are getting slaughtered, babies and adults, and I can't help but think that the Sisters are part of it.'

'How?'

'I don't know. But think about it. You found the bowels on the fallen Sister. Ewell was killed there. Jerome said the Lady tried to take him there. Chloe said something was pushing out through the circle of trees towards her, but she doesn't know what. And why isn't she more scared? I'd be shitting myself. And Jerome, he's acting like the kid from *The Exorcist*. I tell you...' She held up her right thumb and forefinger, almost touching. 'I tell you, I am *this close* to giving old Mrs Mayhew a visit.'

'Who's she?'

'You don't know Florence Mayhew? To most people she's the local loony. She says she's a witch and claims to be a genuine Druid. She's been caught naked at midnight up on the Queen's Mount in the middle of winter when most people are tucked up warm in bed. She used to be a poet of sorts, came from wealthy stock. Never did a day's work in her life. Claims she's from an ancient British bloodline that predates King Arthur, even before Stonehenge if you believe her...'

She paused and smiled. 'You *must* have heard of Florence Mayhew. She's a celebrity. I remember one May Day she blessed the maypole on the green by hitching her skirts up and rubbing her private lady bits against it. Raw and scrawny as a plucked chicken under those skirts she was. Never shaved her legs – or anything else. Freaked out a class of year nine girls all set for the dance, but Old Flo' claimed she was recovering the sexual rites of spring and what she called the rituals of a woman's moon blood. She had to be in her late fifties when she did that. She's famous.'

'Sounds worth a visit for the novelty value alone. Why don't we? She might help shed some light on old town legends and such. I'd like to know more about the Sisters and the secret path to the Mount. Show me where she lives, and I'll ask her. Should we take flowers?'

'Branches of rowan wrapped in holly and ivy might be more like it, cut with the blade of a silver knife. Let me pay for the coffee and I'll take you to her. No need to bother with the car, fifteen minutes on foot and we're there.'

'How well do you know her?'

Rose grinned broadly. 'I was one of those kids that day at the maypole. I decided that her showing us where her gynaecologist shone his lamp was one hell of an introduction, and I've stayed in touch ever since. Oh, by the way, you know I said she's a loony?'

'Yes.'

'Forget it. She's smart as a knife and twice as sharp. Give me five minutes to get the bill and I'll introduce you.'

[17]

The house was set back from the road and surrounded by mature trees and hedges. It was completely screened from prying eyes and melodious with wind chimes and the cooling sound of a fountain, which Mohammed could hear but not see.

Rose led him along a curved flagged path. They disturbed a host of bright butterflies that filled the air with colour. The garden was heavy with age and would be described as natural rather than neat, but it was obviously well-tended by an expert hand.

When the house came into view Mohammed came to a stop to appreciate the view. It was beautiful. He guessed it was Tudor and it reclined in the heart of its lushly green lawns and borders as if in genteel repose under its carefully trimmed thatch. Unlike some half-timbered Tudor cottages that had been restored – or built from scratch – by fanatic Victorians and that ever since have resembled stark black and white copies of the originals, this house was gentle on the eye.

Its palette was a feast of honey and cream dappled with green shadows. Honeysuckle had taken possession of most of its facings and its wooden framed, leaded windows peered through its blossoms with the welcoming twinkle of an elderly and beloved relative's eye.

Mohammed sighed, 'I want to come here for my holidays. Maryam would love this place, it's gorgeous.'

Rose agreed, 'I've been visiting Flo' since I was Chloe's age, younger. I love this house, and she's got badgers, hedgehogs, foxes, and deer in her garden. She's a one-woman conservation trust, and so what if she chooses to run around without her knickers on? Come on, let's see if she's in.'

The entrance door was strongly constructed from age-blackened oak and studded with pyramidical nail-heads. It stood under its own ornamental eaves and two stone steps led up to it. There was a worn boot scraper to the right-hand side. Mohammed found himself suffering from a severe case of déjà vu.

He said, 'I've been here in my dreams. This place is perfect. It's everything I've always loved about English architecture, this and Westminster Abbey and St Paul's. I feel I can breathe here.'

Rose nodded. 'Flo's physic garden is a revelation. She makes a great cup of fresh herbal tea that would wake up a dead man. Her wild mushroom soup and home-made bread is worth a Michelin star. Enough chat, let's let her know we're here.'

She reached up and tugged on a chain almost hidden in the honeysuckle. A bell tinkled merrily inside the house. Rose bounced on her heels and checked her watch.

'She's normally in around now. She might be in the garden. Wait here a second...'

She rounded the shoulder of the house and disappeared from view. Mohammed heard her calling out, 'Hello, Flo'? You've got visitors, love. Flo' you out here? Hello?'

She reappeared. 'No sign. She might be having a nap, but I doubt it. She's normally got more energy than a ten-year-old kid with a sugar rush.'

Rose reached up and knocked hard on the door. It swung open.

'That's odd. Flo' knows about the troubles we've had with burglars just lately. She wouldn't leave the door open like this.'

She pushed it wide and stepped into a long dark hallway with a wooden stairway at the far end. The floor was rush matted over large, cream, and burgundy flagstones, which had been shaped and grooved by the passage of countless feet over long centuries.

'Flo'? Hello? It's Rose. Can I come in? Hello? What am I saying? We're here. We're in.'

Three doors led off the hallway. Rose opened the one to her left, Mohammed at her shoulder. It led into a combined study and laboratory with glass distillation equipment covering a long table and shelves of books against the wall. Herbs hung to dry from hooks driven into the ceiling beams. Mohammed recognised the scents of some of the herbs, sage, rosemary, and lavender were there. Bay leaves and parsley, he knew, and mint, coriander, chilli, and basil, but others were strange to him.

He asked, 'Is she an apothecary?'

Rose shook her head, 'No, I told you. She's a witch. She told me all about the old herbs and some of the fungi she uses to make what she calls hedge recipes, along with tree bark. Never had a day's sickness in her life. When I suffered from bad period cramps she knocked me up a tonic that worked a lot better than Paracetamol. Flo's a genius with all this stuff. But where is she?'

They crossed to the single door across the hallway. This opened onto a comfortable living room. Most of the furniture was wooden and might have been as old as the cottage. A table running down its centre could easily sit ten or more diners. Benches were pushed in at its sides and high backed, hand carved chairs at either end. A large china bowl sat in its centre which was filled with aromatic lavender. More books lined the walls.

A group of well-stuffed armchairs were clustered around an inglenook fireplace and more herbs hung in bunches from hooks there. The only nods to modernity in the room were some reading lamps, a black lacquered uplighter, and a large radio/CD player with a turntable for old-fashioned vinyl records on top, all placed in a glass-faced unit in the far corner.

Mohammed noticed a fine portrait hanging in a prime spot on one of the walls. It was nicely framed under glass. There were also simply framed line drawings in ink and pencil, some on the walls and others on the shelves. He realised that they were all portraits of the same woman. The artist patently adored his subject, creating sympathetic works of great vivacity and beauty.

Rose followed his gaze, 'She was lovely in her day. I think these were done by one of her lovers back in the sixties. Flo' knew them all back then. She says she met Aleister Crowley when she was a youngster and thought he was a complete fraud even then. Flo' was born in nineteen thirty-one and the Great Beast died in nineteen forty-seven in Hastings. No reason to think she was lying about meeting him. In fact, I don't think Flo' ever told a lie.'

Mohammed studied the portrait, a watercolour finished with gouache. The vitality and energy of the subject shone from every brushstroke. He noticed that the young woman's face had a flushed and excited look. The portrait was charged with erotic power. Her erect nipples were plainly visible under the filmy blouse, but there was nothing trite or tacky about the work. The artist was obviously extremely talented. He looked for a signature and found it painted in neat calligraphy on the lower left corner of the work. M. Fraser. R.A.

'Flo' calls this one the *Titty Tweaker*.' Rose was at his elbow.

'I can see why.'

'She says Millicent was looking for a very particular effect, as if the sitter had either just made love or was just about to.'

'Millicent? A woman painted this? It's wonderful.'

Rose nodded, her eyes bright. 'Millie Fraser, Royal Academy. I don't know the complete story about Flo' and her, but they were an item back in the sixties. I think Millie introduced Flo' to a number of distractions. They got into the London set; Rolling Stones, Mary Quant, Terence Stamp, David Bailey, you know "The Beautiful People". She has an album full of signed photographs and even I recognise most of them. Flo' says that beauty is not about gender it's about the heart, and that you should only go to bed with people you trust. Doesn't matter what sex they are.'

Mohammed nodded at that. 'Sounds like a wise woman.'

'She is, but where is she today?'

They left the living room and crossed over to the last door leading from the hallway.

'This is the kitchen,' explained Rose. 'For Flo' the kitchen is the heart of the home. I've often sat in here over a cup of tea while she relived what she called her glory days. I think she's got a few more years of glory left. You'll see.'

She pushed open the door and the smell of decay instantly assailed their nostrils. A figure lay stretched out on the floor in front of the kitchen range, black blood pooled around her head and shoulders.

They had found Florence Mayhew.

[18]

'Suicide? Flo' Mayhew? You're joking! She was full of life.'

'Full of cancer more like. And eight decades of that home-made wine and apple spirits has left her liver looking like a string vest. She had a year left, tops, and the last few weeks of her life would have been tough. Really tough. She knew it too. I've read the last few entries in her notebook. There's some odd stuff in there but she knew. It's obvious.'

Sandy Hines pushed a stubby fingered hand through her short cap of hair and scowled at Rose.

'It was almost ritualistic. She did it with that razor sharp little sickle she used to cut her herbs. A silver sickle, mind. Solid silver blade. No old rubbish for Miss Florence Mayhew.

Rose absorbed the information with stunned disbelief.

'I didn't know... she used what? Look, are you sure?

Hines let Rose's unintended slur on her forensic abilities pass but raised a warning eyebrow.

She continued, 'I'm sure, trust me. She cut her own throat and she did a very fine job of it too, slicing through everything useful including the jugular and the carotid. Death would have been almost instantaneous and probably painless. She did a neat job, and it's not exactly something you can practice for is it?

Rose had thanked the pathologist and made to leave when the woman called her back.

'She was a friend of yours?'

'Yes, Sandy. Yes, yes, I like to think I am, or was.' Her shoulders slumped a little. 'I don't know why I'm surprised. All the time I've known her Flo's always made her own choices, chosen her own path, you know? She wouldn't surrender to anything, and she wouldn't let cancer dictate to her. Cancer or anything else. She'd go her own way. She always did.'

Something pricked at Rose's eyes and she swiped at her nose with the back of her hand. It had been a terrible shock to find Flo like that, but at least she had been found by a friend and not some random stranger following their nose to a decomposing corpse. Rose would need time to accept the truth of Flo's death, and the shocking manner of her passing.

Rose smiled weakly, 'Yes... She was unique, special, you know? It was a privilege to know her, and she wouldn't suffer fools, not Flo'. She made me feel special too. Oh, listen to me wittering on. Sorry, Sandy. I'll let you get on. I bet you've heard this sort of thing a thousand times. Thanks for letting me know, anyway, and I'll get out of your way. Thanks.'

'Wait a second.'

Hines hustled over to a plastic storage box and peeled up its lid. She drew out a cloth covered notebook with multi-coloured self-adhesive bookmarks peppered through its pages. She handed it to Rose.

'Don't lose it. And if you find anything interesting in there let me know. It's that notebook I was telling you about, Ms Mayhew's final thoughts. If we need it as evidence for the inquest you'll have to surrender it, but until then I'm sure she wouldn't mind a friend reading it. She didn't hide the book, she left it out in plain view. I think she intended what's in there to be read, and a good friend will be a lot more simpatico than a grumpy old pathologist.'

Hines tapped the book's cover. 'You know there was no note? That's unusual in cases like this. So, there might be something in there, if you can read the writing.'

Rose smiled thinly. 'I know her writing. I've known it for years. And she's shown me this book before. Have you got the others?'

'Others? No, no we haven't. At least there were no more at the house. Oh, here, there's something else. Take a look at this. Any idea what this is?'

Hines pulled on latex gloves and opened the steel door to a chilled evidence locker at the back of her pathology lab where biological samples were kept. She came out with a pot large enough to contain a mature shrub. It looked heavy. Hines placed the pot on the ground and lifted out a spherical object wrapped in a colourful fabric that was bright and exquisitely patterned. Rose lightly fingered the fabric, it felt like silk.

Hines placed the object on her workbench and unwrapped it. Rose recoiled.

Under the bright LED lamps of the pathology lab the freshly disclosed ball-shaped object looked mottled and oddly translucent, infused with a grey-green light throughout its flecked mass. To Rose it looked like an immense eyeball.

At its centre was a dark core that Rose found profoundly disturbing, from which stretched out a single thick vein of inky matter that spread out on the surface of the ball to create a bluish green 'pupil'. Rose had the unsettling sensation that the thing was looking back at her. She craned forward for a better look, filled with morbid fascination. She reached out a hand to touch it but withdrew her fingers before they made contact. Hines had worn gloves and the thing had been wrapped. Best not to tempt fate.

'What is that thing? Where did you find it?'

'To answer your first question, your guess is as good as mine. We're going to have it scanned and undergo the usual barrage of tests as soon as we can get the time, but we don't get priority these days. It might take days, but we'll have a better idea what it is once we know what it's made of. I don't want to cut it up until I know at least that much.

'As to where we found it, it was wrapped in the shawl and placed in that pot, just exactly the way you saw it just now.'

Hines hefted the pot. Its walls looked thick and its outer surface was dark red. Its interior was black and seemed coated with greasy soot. Even to Rose's untutored eye it looked ancient.

Hines continued, 'Pamela Clarkson from the local museum, you know her? Okay, she looked at all this and thinks the shawl's Egyptian. She says it could be at least a thousand years old, which is incredible considering it's in such good condition.' She plucked at her blouse. 'This is silk, I bet it won't last a tenth of that.'

She rolled the pot in her hands. Rose could see what looked like rope patterns embossed into its surface. Hines placed the pot next to the strange eyeball.

She said, 'The pot is Iron Age or older. Kirsten says it's been coiled then smoothed flat with a tool, I don't know, antler or bone or whatever. The black is probably cooking grease while the red is the colour of the clay with something added to make it darker. See those patterns like impressed rope? Kirsten got very excited about those. She says this type of pot is normally found in shards, you know, pieces, and has to be reconstructed. This one is intact. It's like your friend Flo could step into a time machine and collect whatever she wanted from whenever she liked. Pristine artefacts, hundreds, and thousands of years old. Rare as hen's teeth.'

'Where did you find the pot?'

'In Ms Mayhew's herb drying and distilling room. That's an amazing place. That whole house should be under a protection order as a museum dedicated to the ancient apothecary's art.'

'Witch.'

'What did you say?'

'Flo'. She was a witch; and she said she was a Druid too. Nothing so masculine as an apothecary.'

'Fair enough,' said Hines. 'Right. Well, if that's the case,' she raised the pot, 'if that's the case I reckon we've got her witch's cauldron.'

[19]

Small, black-headed gulls strutted around Rose like articled solicitors' clerks in court, grey wings folded flat against proud backs. They wore the black summer cowl on their heads, which would be replaced in autumn by little black earmuffs like tiny headphones on white skulls. Their bright, black lacquered eyes glinted like jewels, eager to seek out a scrap of bread, a tasty treat, or any crap their industrial grade digestion could manage.

Rose watched them without really seeing. Her mind was a sucking mass of conflicting emotions. She had lost a friend to suicide but had learned that the same friend was already afflicted by a terrible disease that would have taken her away in agony after a year.

Hines had said that Flo's end had been swift and painless, and she might even have swallowed an herbal soporific before making that cruel cut in her kitchen. Rose wondered what medicinal leaves Flo had chosen. Were they common or garden herbs such as might be in any hedgerow?

And why use the silver sickle when she had ultra-sharp kitchen knives, perfect for an even cleaner cut? And why in the kitchen? Why spill her life onto the cold, stone flagged floor? She loved her kitchen, true, but did she have to die there? Was there a message there, in that narrow body on that cold floor?

She idly watched one gull tuck its head into its shoulders, fluff out its plumage, and hiss aggressively at the cluster of birds around it. All of them scattered with offended shrieks of complaint before settling once more into their lawyerly strut. Was that the behaviour of an alpha bird, or was it suffering from painful wind? Aggression or indigestion?

Who knew what the shrieks, calls and behaviour of gulls really meant? How could anyone lay claim to anything other than a guess? And Flo' in her kitchen. Was killing herself there a message? Or did she simply have everything to hand and decided it was time?

But, she would have been much more comfortable in her bed, on a chair, or in a tub of warm water. Why spill her life onto that unyielding stone floor? Was there something that made the stones special? Something about the stones themselves? Rose felt as if she was teetering on the edge of something vast, as if she held a thread in her hand and all she needed do was tug hard at it and watch the curtain hiding the big secret unravel before her and everything would become clear. But she couldn't quite get the right grip, there was something, something... but what? Something about the stones. What?

She looked around the familiar landscape. Ever since she was a pre-teenager she had come to this park to think things through. She was one of five children who lived in a small semi-detached house on the fringes of a social housing estate. The house had been crowded and loud with argument and laughter. The park was a peaceful haven where she could concentrate on homework, read a book, think through her relationships, and get away from the noisy bosom of her family. It was still her preferred venue when she had mental knots to unpick.

If she emptied her mind, she thought, perhaps the answer she sought would bob to the surface. She breathed gently and became the calm centre for her eyes and ears. She allowed perception to replace thought, and imagined tension flowing out of her into the green spaces and up into the blue sky textured with fair weather cloud.

The park was down by the canal. Sometimes she saw boats putter past as if they were cruising along the undulating lawns. To her right was a deep hollow that had once been an outdoor amphitheatre but had more recently been the place where the Round Table would build a giant bonfire for its fireworks display on the Saturday night nearest to the fifth of November.

To her left was a fenced-in playground with its colourful swings, slides and climbing frames, a place where adventurous toddlers and younger children could burn off their energy before bedtime. Elsewhere groups of mature trees clustered together like gossipy neighbours, as if discussing the changes they had seen over long decades. And perhaps, she wondered, they mourned the friends they had lost over the years. A human life would be a mere blink of an eye to such long-lived spirits. Flo' had spoken to the trees. She claimed they answered, if one knew how to listen.

Other than the gulls few people flocked there. Mostly she saw children who had dragged themselves away from computer games, social media, and TV long enough to get some fresh air and meet friends face-to-face instead of online. Parents pushed buggies along the paths in vain attempts to calm their caterwauling infants. They would meet and chat with other parents, swapping baby tales. The babies would become silent when they saw each other. They would gaze into each other's eyes, perhaps realising that they were not unique, that there were other precious bundles people loved and fretted over. And they would share silent and profound communications, perhaps smile at the oddness of it all, this new thing called life. And then wave to each other in sympathetic greeting to another new traveller in the world.

The park was tame, perhaps even bland, but it suited Rose's mood. There was too much turmoil in her mind to accept anything more dramatic. She wanted a blank page on which to write her thoughts and untangle the rebus of Flo's death. Again, and again she came back to the image of Flo's blood on the stone floor. Why use the silver sickle? Hines had said the death looked ritualistic. Was it? Silver blades held power. What if Flo's suicide was about more than escaping the living nightmare of cancer and cirrhosis? What if... What?

Her hands hurt. She looked down. Flo's notebook was clutched tightly in her fingers. It was still unread. Rose's thumbs pressed down hard as if squeezing the pages of the book together to stop her friend's words leaking out.

She didn't know how she felt about reading the book. Previously she had only ever dipped into it by invitation. She felt odd at the idea of turning these densely written pages without Flo at her side pointing out the pertinent passages.

She clearly heard the familiar cultured voice in her mind's ear. It was as if her friend had joined her on the bench.

'You see here, my dear Rose. I try to explain, no, describe, how nature works as a palimpsest. You need to learn how to read the messages from the goddess in the layers. They are quite clear to the aware eye – but as you know, not every open eye can see.'

She would laugh and smile a smile worthy of the Mona Lisa. Her eyes glinted with mischief.

'A true woman can see the messages, but how many human females can claim to be true women? They are daughters of Eve, not followers of Lilith. To become a true woman, we must first accept the inner goddess, but most females prefer to accept the inner drudge, and choose worthless labels to hang around their necks: daughter, girlfriend, wife, cook, mother...' She took Rose's hand, 'Police officer.' Rose felt the phantom pressure of Flo's strong brown fingers.

'Release the goddess and there will be nothing you can't do. Nothing. Look, read this passage, that one there. And don't go reading the whole book, not yet. You'll know when it's time for that, soon enough.'

You'll know when. The notebook felt heavier than its size might allow, a solid weight pressing down on her flesh. She gazed at it once more and saw how her fingers were whitened against its blue cloth cover.

Flo' laughed at the world and its mundane follies. Did she laugh at her cancer? Did she treat it as a message from the goddess? A sign? What did she say about death that time? What was it? Rose lifted her hands from the book and kneaded the pins and needles from her fingers while rummaging through her mental archives. What was it? Oh yes.

'Don't treat that faker, Death, so seriously. He'll have your bones mouldering in the clay when you should be walking in glory. And you do walk in glory my dear. You do.'

And like the touch of a falling feather Flo's lips had brushed Rose's cheek. The touch was light as air yet charged with meaning. Rose had felt electricity course through her skin.

'Kaffe kasita kafela,' whispered Flo', 'non filius, publius, omnibus, suis.'

They had been good friends, thought Rose. Perhaps now was soon enough. Perhaps now was a good time.

She opened the book and began to read.

[20]

Render fine clay sanguine with my blood,
Then fire the pot in rowan wood.
Make it sing loud the gospel of stone.
Take teeth and blood, flesh, and bone,
Breast and breath, hair, and heart,
Leave nothing, take the smallest part.
Take them, take them all!
Slice the brain and grind it small.
In the clay protect them,
In sacred fluid serve them.

Spice it with my flesh, I still abide.
Bind tight the krater's outer side.
Take black tallow wax and seal it well,
Trap the spirit within its shell.
At midnight crossroads bury them deep,
And bring woe to those who disturb my sleep.

Under this was written in pencil, *natural gelatine?*
On the next page, also without a heading, Flo' had written:

I wore Spring so sweetly,
Bore Summer so well.
Autumn gold gilded me,
But now Winter's spell
Mocks youthful vanity,
Demands my life's toll.

Cruel frost burns my hair grey,
Arctic chill stills my breath.
Daylight dims and I welcome the day
That brings that sweetest gift – death

Mohammed reread the pages and chewed thoughtfully at his lower lip.
Rose regarded him expectantly.

84

He sighed. 'What do you want me to say? The first poem looks like part of a recipe for human in aspic, the next is about ageing and death. Shakespeare did it shorter and better "sans teeth, sans eyes, sans everything". It's not a suicide note. She's asking for the gift of death not choosing to take her own life. It doesn't say suicide anywhere, just "I'm old and fed up with it". Do you see that too?'

Rose didn't answer, she was already dialling her mobile phone.

'Hi, Phil. Is Sandy there? Right, yes, I'll hold, thanks.' There was a brief pause during which Rose looked at Mohammed with raised eyebrows.

'Yes, hello? Yes, Dr Hines, you said that if I found anything in that book I should call you. That notebook you gave me? Yes, that one. I'm here with Dr Mohammed and he's been reading it with me. That's right, Sharif...

She looked up, 'Sandy says hi.'

He smiled, 'Please, say hi back.'

Rose did, then continued, 'The thing is, Sharif says he thinks one of the passages looks like a recipe for what he described as "human in aspic". He...'

She listened, her jaw working. 'Okay, right, I see. You have, right. Thanks, Sandy. Yes, I will. Thanks again.'

She clipped her phone back to her stab vest.

'Sandy says you're right. That weird ball of stuff I told you about turns out to be cremated human remains and paper ash suspended in a mixture of clarified fat and some kind of gelatine. Preliminary findings of course, but she thinks she now knows where the baby remains on the stone Sister came from.'

Mohammed took a deep breath and wiped a large hand across his face as if trying to rub away the image he had just been given.

He said, 'You've seen this ball of fat and ashes. What does it look like?'

Rose estimated its diameter with her hands. 'It's about that big and it looks like a giant eyeball or really big frogspawn. It looked...' She hesitated, then shrugged. 'You know how everything you've never eaten before is meant to taste like chicken? Well, I guess everything you've never seen before is meant to look like something else, something you'll recognise. This thing doesn't. It looks like what it is, an abomination. It made me feel cold just looking at it, and it doesn't look as if someone made it. No, it looks organic, more like someone grew it.'

She shuddered, 'I expected it to move. It's crazy but I wouldn't have been surprised if the jelly stuff had split and something horrible crawled out. Shit! Sorry, I'm not making much sense, am I?'

85

Mohammed grinned, 'You're doing okay trying to describe something you don't understand. Sounds weird enough. I'd like to see this ball of yours, do you think Sandy would let me? I know I'm only a curious outsider. And could I keep this book for the evening? I'd like to see what else is in there.'

Rose screwed up her face. 'I'll ask if you can see the ball, but I'm afraid I can't let the book out of my hands. It might be evidence and Sandy asked, no, she *ordered* me to hang on to it. It mustn't leave my sight. But if you have the time you can read a bit more with me – here, look at this.'

She flicked through the book searching for the right page. 'Here you go, what do you think of this?'

Mohammed read:

No craft of man must cross the secret path
To do so will seal the town's fate.
Her hand shall rend the bitter half,
And scatter its parts across the gate.
Bridge the breach, repair the way,
Take life for life, the town must pay,
Until the path returns to its true state
And the sun shines clear at break of day.

'I've seen parts of this book before,' explained Rose. 'But Flo' never showed me any of this stuff.'

'Is it recent do you think?'

'I don't know, I don't think so. It's quite early in the book.'

'Okay, what's the last entry?'

'I haven't looked.'

She thumbed through the tightly written pages until she arrived at blank lines.

'Here we are...' She read aloud:

"The Witch and the Moor,
Are trying to gauge,
The words that they saw,
On an alien page.
Sorry, my Rose,
For these lines that rhyme.
I would write them in prose,

But, I haven't the time."

"The Witch and the Moor" she says. She means us.'
'How could she?'
'She's put my name in there, see. But how could she know we would be reading this together? It's impossible, isn't it?'
'If she does mean me it's very interesting,' said Mohammed thoughtfully. 'Only one other person has ever called me a Moor, and that was very recently.'
'Who?'
'Jerome. Jerome Talbot.'

[21]

All the next day Jerome was agitated. His mother kept trying to make him watch TV, but he was too excited to settle in front of the box. Pictures were pouring into his head and he had to get them out onto the page as fast as he could.

He was sharpening his pencil every few minutes, filling a bowl with narrow wood shavings. The smell of graphite was thick in the air. He had used up an entire pad of paper and then a second. Every page held an image of the Lady and at first glance every drawing was identical, but each harboured subtle differences.

Woven into the drawings were words Jerome didn't understand, but they were important. They quickly became lost in the web of lines his spider fingers wove, but they still held power. And the drawings moved.

When Jerome flicked through his pages the Lady's arms and hands moved, performing a complex dance that created lines of scarlet magic in the air above his paper. But they did nothing yet, the gestures were incomplete, and he had run out of drawing paper.

He pestered his mother for more drawing pads, begging until she was on the point of tears. He didn't want lunch, he didn't want a drink, and he didn't want television. He wanted to draw. He didn't throw a tantrum – he was never so crude – but he was flatly adamant. He had to draw, he must draw, and he needed paper to draw on. His mother had to get some.

The exhausted woman capitulated and took him into town, holding his hand tightly all the way. He pulled at her arm like a puppy on the leash, eager to run. Every moment spent away from his drawing was a moment wasted, and the Lady didn't want to wait.

Jerome couldn't see the frightened expression on his mother's face. It would have meant nothing to him if he had. His entire being had become absorbed by his need to draw, draw, and then draw some more. Draw until the pictures stopped coming and he would be done at last. The Lady had given him a special job to do, he wouldn't let her down. He couldn't.

At first Stephanie had protested when he picked up five drawing pads and placed them in a pile on the stationer's counter. In the face of his silent expectation she told him the money would have to come out of his Christmas presents. He had already had his birthday. She insisted she meant it this time.

Jerome said nothing, he just nodded and jiggled from one foot to the other. His eyes were blank, and his fingers twitched like little pink animals, eager to return to their task.

Back at the house he resumed his work, his tongue protruding from his compressed lips. He didn't hear his mother speaking on the telephone, almost weeping with fear and concern. He didn't hear her relieved expressions of thanks. He didn't hear the car pull up on the road outside, or his mother answer the chimes at the front door. He didn't look up when a tall shadow fell across him where he knelt on the living room floor, furiously drawing, and continuously sharpening his pencils until they were too short to use. The bowl of shavings also held a small collection of discarded stubs.

'Hello, Jerome,' said Mohammed. 'I've come for that drawing you promised me. Is it one of these?'

The psychiatrist bent to pick up the neat stack of drawings and the boy lashed out at his hand with the point of his pencil.

'No!' he barked. 'These are mine. Don't touch them, they're in order.'

Mohammed watched the red blood well up in the deep wound Jerome had inflicted to the back of his hand. The boy was already sharpening another pencil's point to his satisfaction before continuing his onslaught on his drawing pads.

The psychiatrist had never been stabbed with a pencil before. He wrapped his hand in a tissue and decided to clean the wound with disinfectant and bandage it properly later.

'Then which one is mine? Is it here?'

The boy said nothing. He leapt to his feet and almost ran from the room. Mohammed heard him pounding up the stairs. He took the opportunity to study some of the drawings without disturbing their order. They all seemed identical, full length drawings of a dark woman. He flicked through them and was startled to see the woman's arms and hands move smoothly.

He replaced them when he heard Jerome scurrying down the stairs. The boy burst back into the room and looked suspiciously from the tall man to his growing stack of drawings.

'Did you touch anything? Did you move anything?'

'No, Jerome. I didn't move anything. You asked me not to.'

Mollified, the boy held out a sheet of paper on which Mohammed discerned a densely drawn portrait. It was quite fine. Mohammed thought back to his art history and music lessons and stories of the six-year-old Wolfgang Amadeus Mozart playing his own compositions on the piano for the amusement of the Viennese aristocracy – while blindfolded. Picasso was a noted academician by the age of twelve. Would Jerome grow up to be a fine artist? Would he too be remembered as a prodigy in the years to come?

'What did you do to your hand?'

Perturbed, Mohammed looked at the boy's face. He saw genuine concern written there. Jerome pointed at the wound his pencil had inflicted.

'It's bleeding, look. Mummy's got a plaster. Come on.'

Stephanie was in the kitchen, her preferred bolthole when the world conspired to upset her or became too strange to bear. She was cleaning the cooker, an overdue task but also a job that would help take her mind away from whatever her son was doing in the living room.

When Jerome and Mohammed came into the room she bolted upright like a startled animal. She literally quivered with shock and darted looks from one to the other. She emitted a guttural noise as if clearing her throat. Mohammed wondered how close to the edge she was. He didn't agree with handing out tranquilisers on a wholesale basis, but if ever a woman needed help he was looking at her now.

'Mummy, the doctor hurt his hand. Have you got a plaster for him, please?'

Stephanie studied her son as if he was a lit firework about to explode, then across to the bloody tissue wrapped around Mohammed's hand.

'What happened?'

Mohammed shrugged. 'I caught it on a thorn.'

'Wait here, Doctor, I'd better clean it first. We don't want it to get infected.'

Jerome said, 'Mummy, can I have some milk, please?'

'Of course, love. Drink it in here, please. We don't want to spill it on the carpet, do we?'

Jerome was sitting at the table with a half empty glass and a cream moustache by the time Stephanie returned with the first aid kit. She turned on the overhead light and donned a pair of glasses before addressing Mohammed's wound.

She fetched out a small bottle of clear blue disinfectant and began cleaning the cut with a pad of cotton wool. She squinted closely at the upwelling blood.

'I think some of the thorn is still in there. Let's get that out first.'

She fetched out a pair of tweezers and concentrated on pulling out the black point she had seen without hurting her patient. It took two tries; the object was slippery with blood.

'Ah, got it.' She placed the thing on the tissue Mohammed had been holding against his hand, then cleaned and dressed the cut. All the while her eyes flicked back to the black and impossibly regular cone she had extracted. A broken pencil point. She raised her eyes to his face and then swivelled them at Jerome. He returned an imperceptible nod.

He said, 'Thank-you, Mrs Talbot. That's much better. Jerome was busy when I came in and he didn't want his work disturbed, but he's given me a lovely drawing, look.'

Stephanie nodded at yet another of the interminable stream of drawings completed by her son since his disappearance, all the same subject. The Lady.

'Yes, it's lovely.'

She realised Mohammed was staring at the drawing as if he was seeing it properly for the first time under the bright kitchen lights.

She said, 'What is it?'

He replied, 'I don't believe it. I know this woman. I've seen portraits in her house. It's Florence Mayhew the way she looked fifty years ago.'

[22]

The sun set after another hot and fine summer's day in the town. It turned the sky above the Queen's Mount a fiery red and the line of the secret path burned bright from the Cathedral Close to the bypass. As it approached the bypass the path became dark and looked sick somehow, as if infected by contact with the invasive dual carriageway. Rose and Mohammed stood in the gateway of the Close, the silent and shadowed circle of yew trees on the rise behind them, still wrapped in blue and white police tape.

They could feel the presence of the stones at the centre of the trees like a living energy, as if the stones were watching and waiting for them to draw near enough to be caught.

Rose whispered, 'Are you sure you want to do this?'

Mohammed nodded, 'Yes, if you're okay with it too. I don't know how, but I think everything strange that's happening relates to this path from the Sisters to the Mount. Jerome Talbot is drawing Florence Mayhew as a young woman, and he says he can see her, his mysterious Lady. We presume Mayhew turned up the day after she cut her own throat and she tried to bring him here. He escaped, but she's still affecting him somehow.'

He pointed down the glowing path. 'Why is this the only road in the whole town that glows like that? What makes it special? And why does it wink out before it reaches the bypass.'

He gestured back towards the trees.

'Until recently the Sisters were just a useful place for couples to get a little privacy, but now a baby has been sacrificed on the stones and Ewell was killed there. What does it mean? How is it connected to Mayhew's suicide?'

Rose looked back over her shoulder.

'Should we start from the Sisters? That would be the right way.'

'Do you really want to?'

'No, I just thought... But no, no I really don't.'

'Thinking of Ewell?'

'Yeah, him and the baby. You know something? No babies have been reported missing yet. Isn't that strange? You know? You'd think someone would be missing their child and report it to the police. Isn't that odd?'

'Do they know how old it was yet?'

'The victim was cremated after some of its collagen was used to make gelatine and create the ball of jelly that contains it. According to Sandy the

92

jelly also contains several organic preservatives, including vinegar, salt, and lemon juice. She compares it to an egg and says the jelly is rich in nutrients, though what sort of yolk is composed of cremated baby and paper ash? It seems crazy to me.'

She shuddered and pulled both hands through her hair and stood silently for a moment, her eyes shut, and her face pointed upwards towards the purpling sky. Mohammed regarded her and felt a tug of guilty desire. She looked exquisitely beautiful in the evening light, and something in her body called to him. He could smell the perfumed heat of her skin on the warm air.

He clamped a lid on his building emotions, reminding himself that the one and only woman he loved had kissed him goodnight after dinner and trusted him to be alone at night with a gorgeous policewoman because she knew he would never let her down like that. Never.

He walked through the gate and took his first steps on the secret path. Somewhere behind him he heard a sardonic chuckle, as if someone had seen straight through his civilised shell and discovered the beast lurking within.

The laughter said, 'Who are you trying to kid? If you thought you had a chance you'd be on her like a street corner dog. The stones are empty, why not ask her? Go on, she'd be flattered.'

He walked further down the path then turned back. Rose was regarding him with an impish expression, her eyes full of mischief. She chuckled, but it didn't sound like her. It was an insinuating sound, full of promise.

She said, 'Judging by the number of used condoms around the Sisters I bet more couples walked up the path towards the yew trees than used them as the starting point to walk away. What do you think?'

God, suddenly she was everything he desired in a woman. Her smile broadened, and she breathed in deeply, accentuating her curves under her white tee shirt. She was off duty and out of uniform. Her tee shirt was tucked into black jeggings and she was wearing black Converse boots with white socks. She was slender, slimmer than Maryam, but every inch of her was pure female. He stepped towards her, almost reaching out, then stopped.

'Come on, Rose,' he said. 'We're here to walk the path. We can count condoms another day. Let's go. Yes?'

That earned him a disappointed pout. Then Rose laughed, and it was her own laugh once more, genuine, and lively. The shadow of mischief passed from her as it had never existed.

'Yeah, let's go. It's late enough as it is. I don't want Maryam thinking I'm keeping her husband out all night. Lead on Macduff, I'm right behind you.'

It was just over a three-mile walk. Rose had parked her car where they could find it near the bypass and Mohammed had driven them both to the Cathedral Close. It was downhill most of the way. The entire trip, including Rose driving him back to his vehicle, should take no more than an hour. They had each planned to be home before midnight.

Mohammed marvelled at the silence on the path. Almost to prove to himself that he hadn't become suddenly deaf he said aloud, 'Isn't it quiet.'

Rose agreed, 'Yes, apart from that music. Must be kids practicing. I bet their parents love it at this time of night. It's nearly all drums.'

Mohammed cocked an ear to the darkness. He couldn't hear any music.

'You must have extraordinarily acute hearing,' he said, 'I can't hear anything at all.'

She grinned at him, 'You're joking right? That's really quite loud. Brrump-a-bump-a-bump-a-brrump. Bump-ta-ta-ta-taaa-brrump. It's like some kind of rock marching music. You must be able to hear it. Listen, there... hear those horns? You can't miss it.'

He strained his ears and suddenly he *could* hear something, but it wasn't drums. It was a choir singing a series of high notes, ethereal and beautiful. Walking beside him Rose was making drumming sounds to reflect the sounds she was hearing, while he was hearing angels.

The music got louder.

Rose raised her voice, 'There'll be complaints about this. I'm surprised people aren't out banging on doors.'

'Yes, but which door would you bang on? Where's the music coming from? It seems to be all around us.'

The houses along the path were dark, and the orange glow from the street lamps seemed muted, barely reaching as far as the road's surface. The sun had gone from the sky. Ahead of them was the silver worm of the dual carriageway, looking further away than two miles. Behind them the cathedral had vanished into the night. They were walking along a lane of shadows, music all around them, thudding or twisting like a corkscrew into inky blackness.

Rose said, 'It's okay, Sharif. You don't need to hold me I'm fine.'

'I'm not holding you.'

'Really, Sharif, please, I mean it, take your hands away.'

'Rose, it's not me. I'm not touching you.'

'Then who is? Ow! Bastard hit me.'

Mohammed felt something pound across his shoulders and almost stumbled to his knees. He shouted, 'Rose, are you, all right?'

He heard a scream of agony but could see nothing in the darkness. He yelled again, the effort making him wince from the intense pain in his back. And then a window opened, and a petulant male voice rang out. 'Who's making all that bloody noise? People are trying to sleep. Clear off or I'll call the police on you.'

In the light from the open window Mohammed could see Rose crumpled unmoving at his feet. Her tee shirt was stained black with blood. With a mounting sense of horror, he called out, 'Please, call the police and an ambulance. My friend has been attacked, she's bleeding badly.'

He bent down to Rose's torn body and desperately fought to keep her alive until the ambulance arrived. It was more than ten minutes before he saw the blue lights and by then he could no longer feel her pulse. Tears blurred his eyes.

'Don't die,' he said to her prone body. 'Don't you dare fricking die on me.'

[23]

Mohammed didn't know it at the time, he was too wired with adrenaline, but he had badly bruised and cracked ribs in his back caused by blunt-force trauma. Rose had been stabbed in the side by an eight-inch blade that luckily missed everything vital, but she had nearly died from loss of blood. Without his first aid she wouldn't have stood a chance, but as it was she needed multiple transfusions, dozens of stitches, and spent the night in intensive care.

Mohammed also didn't know if his confused state of mind was due to shock or the strong painkillers he had been given in A&E. When Maryam arrived and hugged him he had winced in agony. The details of his experiences that night still hadn't clarified in his mind, even after multiple iterations, to medical staff, the police, and now his wife. All he could say was that their mysterious assailants had arrived unheard and unseen and then vanished into the night, and the attack appeared motiveless.

Mohammed himself got several sideways glances from attending officers until his friends from the local police service arrived. A young officer had asked him if anyone had yelled 'Allahu Akbar' before the attack and insinuated that he and Rose might have been holding hands, opining that 'that sort of thing was an incitement to violence in certain quarters, especially what with him being dark-skinned and her being a blonde white woman'. The addition of the phrase, 'begging your pardon, sir' didn't make it sound any better. Mohammed bit back his scathing retort.

It proved a long and trying night before Maryam was finally allowed to take him home, and he was exhausted when he teetered into the living room. They were then confronted with the difficulty of finding somewhere he could sleep. Bed was out of the question, he couldn't think of putting any direct weight on his back and the thought of stretching out on his belly was no better.

Maryam finally fetched him a sleeping bag and he spent long hours waiting for the dawn packed in pillows on an old recliner Maryam's parents had given them when she had damaged her neck playing tennis more than a decade before.

He slept when the para-codeine painkillers held the agony at bay, and woke when its effects lessened, and torment speared up his spine. He kept his mobile handy because he had been promised a text when Rose was out of danger. Every time his eyes fluttered open he reached for his phone with a groan of pain, but there was no news, not even after the sun filtered through the curtains to announce the dawn.

After nine, Maryam came down from their bedroom and assisted him to the downstairs toilet. She offered to stay and help him perform his functions, but he shooed her away. He was not, he told her, a cripple. He could manage a shit on his own, thanks very much. Then he almost regretted sending her away. The whole performance of moving his bowels and cleaning himself afterwards was torment. Even washing his hands was an exquisite agony that robbed him of his breath.

Anger and impatience threatened to overwhelm him, he had never been so close to tears since reaching puberty. He wanted to understand what had happened to him, why someone had struck at him and nearly killed Rose. Rose! He stumbled to his phone. There was a message, he swiped open the screen.

'Maryam! Ow, shit! Maryam!'

His wife burst into the living room. 'Should you be making all that noise? That shouting can't be good for your back.'

'No, probably not, but she's okay. Rose is okay. She's comfortable they say. She, ow, damn it, she spent a comfortable night. She's out of intensive care and in a private room. That's, ow, great.'

'Sounds like she spent a better night than you. Maybe I should have left you there with her? I heard you groaning from upstairs. You sounded like a puppy locked in the kitchen. Boots, I didn't know whether to pour you a saucer of milk or get you a pint of whisky. I can't even hug you! I feel useless.'

Mohammed held out his arms, 'Take it gently, all right? But I need a hug. Yeah, a hug from you is the best medicine in the world, but no raunchy stuff this time, promise?'

Maryam laughed aloud, 'You should see the state of yourself, Romeo. Raunchy is not top of my list just now.'

She circled him with her arms and held him without squeezing. He bent to kiss her and immediately had to straighten again, his teeth gritted.

'You wait right there,' she said.

She stalked off to the kitchen and returned with the stool/step she used to get things off top shelves in the higher kitchen cabinets. She stood on it and her face was at the same level as his. She looped her arms around his neck and kissed him warmly on the lips. Almost as if their touch had pressed the button the doorbell rang. Maryam climbed off the step and cast her eyes over his body, which was plainly visible under his open dressing gown.

'I'll get it. Best do your robe up, Boots. I like you like that, but we don't want to frighten the neighbours.'

When she returned Mohammed had covered his nakedness and was sitting back in the recliner. Behind her was Dr Bakewell, their GP from the local medical centre. Bakewell was thin and grey, and she wore clothes that accentuated her greyness. She looked at Mohammed with a severe expression on her face.

'I hear you've been in the wars. Did you have to beat yourself up just to force me to make a house call? Ah, well, I guess if Mohammed won't come to the surgery, the surgery will have to come to Mohammed.' She grinned dourly, 'I've waited years to say that! Now, let's see what we can do for you.'

Half an hour later Maryam left at the same time as the doctor clutching a prescription for a month's worth of much stronger painkillers. Mohammed had been told to rest for the next five days and then get as much exercise as he could manage.

Bakewell said, 'The tablets will make you feel a bit strange for a while, but don't worry about it. The bruising will start to come out over the next few days. You're young and fit and you'll hate being stuck indoors but you need to take it easy or you'll take longer to heal. Catch up on some daytime TV. As a psychiatrist you'll probably be able to write the week off as important research. Whenever I've watched that rubbish I'm convinced the lunatics are out there and I'm safer locked indoors, preferably with a loaded gun. Come and see me next week, by then you should be up and about properly. Take two tablets as soon as Maryam gets back, and then two every four hours, and don't take any other paracetamol products at the same time. You've got a healthy liver, let's keep it that way.'

Bakewell's matter-of-fact brusqueness had been as effective a tonic as his wife's kiss. He had feared it might be much longer before he felt better, five days was okay. He could catch up on some reading. None of his patient appointments were critical. He rang his service and told his shared secretary what had happened. He asked her to reschedule his diary, moving everything back a full working week. She sounded concerned and told him his health must come first. He thanked her. She asked him to stay in touch, he said he would.

Job done he settled back in the recliner and gazed at the ceiling. He was idly wondering how long Maryam was going to be with his new tablets when the phone rang at his side.

'Sharif, ow, Mohammed.'

'Hello, Dr Mohammed. How are you feeling?'

The female voice was strange to him. It sounded cool, well tutored, and formal.

'Who is this?'

'A friend, you might say, a concerned friend. I would not have had this happen to you. You are in danger if you pursue your researches along the secret path. You must stay away from there. So, must Rose.'

'I'm sorry but I need to know your name. I don't take orders from mysterious callers.'

'Not orders, no, more like friendly and informed advice. Avoid the path, and the boy Jerome Talbot. He is in no danger, but you are if you interfere.'

'Look, what is this? Who are you?'

'Very well. My name is Florence Mayhew.'

'Don't be stupid. Florence Mayhew is dead. I saw her body. She killed herself.'

'So, I did. Must you hold that against me? Look out of your window Dr Mohammed. Say hello.'

When Maryam got home she found her husband sprawled on the floor, his hands reaching out as if trying to fend away something terrifying. She took his shoulders to help him up and he flailed wildly at her, his mouth open in a wide, distorted O. His eyes fluttered blindly as if he was finding it difficult to see her. And then she came into focus and his gaze settled on her face. And he wept.

[24]

Rose floated in and out of consciousness. She could remember very little after joining Mohammed to walk the secret path. Somewhere she had fallen into an empty void of pain, and if the state of her body was anything to judge by she must have fallen very hard. It was difficult to judge where the pain started and ended, it burned through her torso like acid.

She remembered being surprised when Flo' had popped into the room and sat with her for several minutes, chatting away animatedly the way she always did. She had apologised for not bringing flowers but explained that they had become difficult to get hold of. And, she said, Rose was on nil by mouth at the moment, so fruit was out of the question.

Flo' must have left when the nurse came in, because suddenly she was gone and replaced by a smiling, blue uniformed, dark-skinned woman who called Rose "darlin" and told her she was doing fine. The woman fussed around her, checking her drips, and making notes on the tablet she wore at her waist. The nurse reacted to the sudden spasm that passed through Rose's body.

'What is it, darlin'? You seen a ghost?'

Rose was shocked at the growling weakness of her own voice.

'Was there anyone else here when you came in, nurse?'

'No, my darlin'. Too soon for visitors, and anyway, it's too early in the mornin' for most good folk to be out of bed yet. You should be asleep too, you got a lot of mending to do and you won't get it done while you're awake.'

The door to the room opened and Rose heard a low voice mention something about tea being ready. The nurse replied but Rose couldn't make out what she said. The world was slipping away again. Rose heard a familiar voice say, 'See you soon'. The nurse answered, 'You can be sure of that, darlin'. See you very soon. Good to hear you sounding stronger.'

Rose sank into warm dark waters and floated away. She felt her free hand taken in a cool, dry grip, and then nothing at all. She awoke to daylight and an Eastern European sounding nurse who said very little beyond, 'Good morning. How are we feeling today?'

Rose answered, 'I feel like shit. How about you?'

The nurse nodded, checked a tablet at her waist, and then left the room.

Rose lost track of time, she dozed, but was jarred awake when a tall, white-coated man bustled into her room ahead of a group of younger people. He introduced himself as the consultant who had treated her the day before, gave his name, and then asked if it was okay if he examined her in front of his students.

'We understand if you'd prefer not, but you really are quite an interesting case. Do you mind?'

She shook her head. The consultant smiled encouragingly.

He then peeled down her bedclothes and lifted her cotton gown to expose her naked body from groin to breasts. Rose turned away from the intense scrutiny of the students, her face burning with humiliation. The consultant touched her dressings, spoke at length, and then gently covered her again.

'Thank-you Ms Platt,' he said. 'Everything seems to be looking very good.'

'I'll say,' said a younger male voice.

The consultant rounded on one of his students. 'What was that?'

'Nothing, sir.'

'I'll have a chat with you later, Kelly. Thank you again, Ms Platt. We'll leave you to enjoy your peace and quiet.'

She was alone once more. Alone with the whirring and beeping monitor at her side and nothing to do but lie quietly and think. Think about the dead Florence Mayhew talking with her during the night. About Flo's voice being heard and answered by the West Indian nurse. How could that be?

Her pain had largely subsided to an uncomfortable sensation somewhere between an infuriating itch and an acute stitch. And something was tugging at her insides every time she took a deep breath, so she worked hard at not doing so. She fought a tendency to yawn.

Nobody had told her what had happened to Sharif Mohammed, but then nobody had yet told her what had happened to *her*. One minute they were setting off towards the silver lights of the distant bypass and wondering at the gloom of the secret path, the next she was waking up in hospital and finding herself described as 'quite an interesting case'.

She felt heat flush through her at the memory of her intimate and unexpected exposure just minutes before. The consultant seemed a nice enough man, but she wouldn't mind getting her hands round the throat of that creep called Kelly when she was back in uniform. The door to her room opened again.

'Ms Platt? Ms Rose Platt? Please, forgive the intrusion. May I take just a few minutes of your time? Nice room you have here, so much nicer than a ward. They have mixed wards here, that wouldn't be pleasant for a young woman such as yourself. May I take a seat? My name's Klebb, Michal Klebb. A pleasure to meet you I'm sure.'

The man was hollowed out, his face gaunt. He wore a three-piece suit of a colour best described as 'dust' under which was a grey oxford shirt and a striped tie that might have indicated a good school, an old regiment, or a careful purchase from a charity shop.

His shoes were polished to a subtle shine. His hair was lank, steel coloured and parted in the middle, and his eyes gleamed under aggressively shaggy brows. They too were grey. He had that unfortunate kind of complexion that looked as if it would benefit from a thorough scrub with soap and hot water but was probably clean.

But then again, perhaps not. Rose could smell his breath, it was meaty and sour. He also had brought with him a pervasively musty body odour and a faint tang of urine. He perched uncomfortably on the orange fabric covered, wooden framed chair he had pulled away from its place by the wall and positioned beside her bed, careful not to tangle its legs in any of the lines trailing towards Rose's body. She fought for a moment to remember his name.

'Mr Klebb? What can I do for you?'

She wondered how he had got as far as her room. Her question unleashed another torrent of words, all delivered in an insinuating, nasal tang.

'For *me*? For *me*? Oh no. This visit isn't about *me*, the Lord forbid. Slap me across the belly with a wet kipper if I'm here for *me*! No, I'm here about you. You and Dr Sharif Mohammed, the poor man. He's suffered enough for a whole platoon, and he don't know why neither, no more than you do. The path chewed the pair of you up and spat you out like old tobacco, chewed you up good and proper didn't it. But what did you hear when it happened? Old Klebb bets you heard the drums, didn't you? Drums, was it? Some as hears drums and others hear voices. I bet you heard drums? You did, didn't you!'

This last wasn't a question.

Rose gritted her teeth with frustration. 'I'm sorry, Mr Klebb. I don't know who you are or what you want. I don't even know how you got into my room. You'll have to leave.'

She prayed one of the nurses would come in and show the man the door. She wished she had the strength to throw him out herself. She felt helpless.

When Klebb leaned forward and sighed deeply she almost gagged at the reek of his breath. He lifted a grimy finger and wagged it at her.

'Mustn't say leave, not until Old Klebb has had his say. Not leave. It's important you hear what he must tell you. He's like you, he's an old friend of *hers*. *She* looked after him. *She* was kind to him.'

His face creased up and he seemed on the point of tears.

He whined, 'She done it with a blade. Klebb knows. He saw her do it. And now look at what she's doing. She's out there getting the spirits all agitated and stirred up like hornets. I can't sleep for all the noise they're making. Even the animals are staying away. Why's she doing that? Klebb knows. Shall he tell you?'

'So, why is she doing it?'

'See, see what I said, she wants to know. Klebb's right again, right as a spirit level. Well, Rose Platt, let Klebb tell you. She's doing it because she has no choice. She must protect the path. The town cut it the way she cut her throat and that can't be allowed. She gave her blood to the stones and now she's ready to fight. Klebb's here to tell you. Get in her way and she'll let them cut you down, she will. Like grass to the sickle. And it won't be a nice bed in a nice room you'll be sleeping in then, no, it won't. It will be your coffin.'

[25]

Four days later Rose was sitting gingerly in an armchair and facing Mohammed on his recliner. Maryam had made tea and then left them to talk. She was desperate to find out what had happened to her husband and she believed letting the two of them thrash out everything they remembered from that evening might break through his amnesia.

Mohammed had been sleeping badly, and when he was awake he scribbled thoughts about his hazy recollections and mind jarring dreams into a notepad. He was filling the pages with a wild looping script that was barely recognisable as his handwriting. The lines were littered with question marks. There were precious few answers. And now here at last was Rose.

They heard Maryam close the front door on her way out. Even so they continued minutely examining each other in companiable silence. Rose was shocked at Mohammed's condition. She had learned how he had saved her life on that darkened street, but that it had been touch-and-go for several hours before her condition was stable enough for an optimistic prognosis.

Mohammed had been allowed home that same night, but now he looked by far the weaker invalid of the pair. He looked cowed and haunted. His silky hair and beard had lost its lustre. His dark brown eyes seemed dull despite bright sunlight pouring through the windows. It was a hot morning, but all the windows were shut, Rose wondered if she should ask if she could open at least the smaller lights to allow a breath of air into the humid room. Her friend shivered as if he was chilled.

Rose spoke first. 'Have you met a man called Klebb?'

Mohammed shook his head and blinked tiredly. 'No, I don't recognise the name. How are you, Rose? You look better than I feel, I must say.'

'I still hurt. I have to be careful when I reach for things.' She held her hand out in demonstration. 'See, if I stretch further than that, ow! You know?'

Mohammed smiled weakly, 'Then don't do it, doctor's orders.'

'How're you feeling?'

'Truth? I'm exhausted. I'm not sleeping and the pain in my back's no better. They said I should be up-and-about in five days. Well it's been more than five days, and I think the painkillers are wearing off.'

He moved restlessly and grunted in agony.

He said, 'Dad always told me a good man should be able to stand on his own two feet. God, knows what he would make of me now. He'd be

104

ashamed. I can't stand without Maryam's help. I can't even use the toilet or take a shower without her. It's pathetic. I mean, you were stabbed and here you are coming to see me! I should have come to get you, but I haven't been out of this house since the night I got back from the hospital.'

Rose leaned forward as far as she could. 'Sharif, I think the problem's more than just physical. It's about more than just pain and injury, sore though we are. Look, this man called Klebb came to see me in the hospital. I don't know how he got into my room or even how he knew which room I was in, but that isn't the point. He said he was a friend of Flo's. He's some kind of unpaid gardener. He lived in the shed back in the trees. He saw Flo kill herself, said he saw it through the kitchen window...'

Rose explained everything the gaunt man had told her about Mayhew stirring up the spirits and how they had been attacked. She spoke about the drums she now remembered hearing, and that Klebb had said Mohammed had likely heard voices. That was why she had been stabbed with a sword and he had been clubbed with a staff, they had attracted different kinds of spirit.

She said, 'Klebb explained that living people burn with different kinds of light, so they attract different levels of spirit activity, a bit like moths to flames. But now the spirits are aggressive, so they attacked when we drew near. Klebb says Flo' was partly responsible. She didn't intend for it to affect me, but I nearly died anyway.'

She looked towards the hallway and the front door beyond.

'When do you expect Maryam back?'

Mohammed shrugged, 'She left us alone to talk. Said she needed a haircut so she's off to the hairdressers. She goes by bus, so I doubt she'll be back much before lunchtime, why?'

Rose carefully lifted her bag. 'Is it okay if I get a glass from the kitchen?'

'Sure, of course. Help yourself.'

The blonde limped out of the room. When she returned she carried a tumbler half filled with a dark green liquid and a whiskey glass with two fingers of the amber spirit in it. She handed the tumbler to Mohammed.

'Drink this. It's better if you knock it down in one, trust me.'

'What is it?'

'It's kind of a tonic. Drink it.'

'What's the whisky for?'

'To take the taste away. Come on, get it down you. There's a good boy, in one.'

Mohammed drained the tumbler and shuddered as he swallowed the liquid. He grimaced, and his teeth and tongue were stained green.

'That was disgusting.'

'I know.' She quivered. 'Looking at you drink it brings it all back to me. Yeah, it's vile. Now this.'

She handed him the whisky. 'Sloosh it around your mouth like mouthwash before you swallow it, it helps get rid of the aftertaste. Trust me, it will be better that way. Don't sip it, neck it down.'

'What a waste of good whisky. Cheers.'

He did as he was bid and pulled a comedy face once he had swallowed.

He said, 'That bottle of *Glenmorangie* was a gift from my parents, I hope they never find out I used it as mouthwash.'

He belched. 'Excuse me.' He belched again. 'Pardon...' He lurched to his feet and dashed from the room. Seconds later Rose heard copious vomiting echoing from the downstairs toilet.

'Yeah,' she said. 'Took me like that too.'

The sounds continued for nearly a full minute and were followed by mournful groans. Then the toilet flushed after which she heard the door closing. She shut the living room door. Mohammed's body was being completely purged. She thought it better not to listen to the turbulence of everything he would suffer for the next minute or so.

At least he was undergoing it in the privacy of his own home. Rose had taken Klebb's tincture once she was off the monitors and unplugged from the drips in hospital. Everything was flushed noisily from her system in a patients' lavatory in a busy hospital corridor. When she had finally emerged, ashen faced, at the end of her ordeal, she had found two concerned nurses waiting for her.

She was almost kept in for another two days for observation as a suspected case of food poisoning, but instead they had allowed her to enjoy a long shower, being careful not to soak her stitches, and then a quiet afternoon in her room watching TV.

The toilet flushed again, and then once more, then there was a moment's silence. Through the living room door, she heard Mohammed shout, 'I'll be a minute, I'm just going to have a shower. Help yourself to a drink, read a magazine. I won't be long.'

She had found a recent magazine called *1843* and was leafing through it when he finally reappeared. He had changed his clothes and his hair and beard were still slightly damp. He was a little pale, looked chastened and trembled slightly, but otherwise looked stronger and had recovered some of his core vitality.

He sat next to Rose on the sofa. 'What on Earth was in that stuff?'

'I don't really know. Klebb told me it had been distilled from herbs and a select group of fungi. He described it as "The Queen's Flush". I thought it very apt.'

'Apt? I feel as if I've been hollowed out like a gourd. And everything that came out of me was black! I mean everything. What just happened?'

Rose put the magazine down. 'Before I answer that can I ask you a question? How's your back?'

'My, what?' He placed his hands against the base of his spine and arched backwards. 'It's still a little stiff, but it feels fine. It feels really much better.'

His face lit up. 'It feels a lot better.' He stood up and walked around the room.

'I don't understand.' He walked to the bay window and opened it.

'We need some air in here. It's stuffy.' He rolled up the sleeping bag he had lived in for five days. 'This is going in the wash.' He threw it back onto the recliner.

Rose smiled and patted the sofa by her side. 'Take a seat, this might take a minute to explain.'

[26]

'What do you mean, "melted"?'

'I mean melted, Sarge, you know? Like something that's melted. It's melted. Ice cream in the sun, candle wax in a flame, and our scene of crime tape up at the Close. Melted.'

'I know it's been a scorcher but surely it hasn't been that hot. Must be kids playing silly buggers.'

'Not likely. I can imagine kids burning a bit of it but it's all melted, all of it. Not a bit left around the yews, not any of it. Melted.'

'Any sign of fire up there?'

Constable Phil Coombe pulled his helmet from his sweat soaked head.

'More likely to find me catching fire under all this crap we have to wear these days. Hottest day of the fucking year and I'm wearing three layers. I'll have to wring the sweat out of me underpants when I get home. I fucking hate this time of year.'

Sergeant Fowler nodded sympathetically. Large wet patches at his armpits and down his spine amply demonstrated how the heat was draining the fluids from his body. He smacked his lips.

'I think a cold beer would be best once we're off duty, Phil. Fancy joining me? First round on me.'

'Best idea I've heard all day. But first I'd better get that tape back around those yew trees. That's still a murder scene even though it is a week later. You know I'm surprised CID didn't put a proper barrier around it. A bit of tape won't keep anyone away if they put their minds to it.'

'Nothing will, you know that. You be careful up there, lad. They haven't caught the killer yet. Don't go putting yourself in harm's way.'

'If he rips this stab vest off me to get at the soft bits he'll be doing me a favour. I'm cooking in here. By the way, if you hear a "bing" it means I'm done. Take me out and baste me with beer.'

Coombe tucked the roll of blue and white tape under his arm and sauntered to the exit. Fowler heard him shout 'bing' just as he reached the door and stepped out into the afternoon's white glare. He looked back over his shoulder and grinned.

'I'm looking forward to that pint.'

Fowler waved him away, 'Get on with it, lad.'

Coombe rode to the Cathedral Close on his bicycle, which was all uphill and caused another flood of hot sweat to saturate his clothing. He took off his helmet and peddled along with it under one arm, just one hand on the handlebars. He was almost blinded by stinging sweat washing into his eyes and he took his hand off his handlebars to wipe it away.

An elderly woman shouted out, 'Oi! You there! Coppers should know better than that. Riding about like a clever kid. What do you think youngsters will do if they see you? Eh? You should set a better example, you should.'

Coombe nodded, 'Sorry, missus. You're right.'

He set his helmet back on his head and took a firm grip of his handlebars with both hands.

When he reached the Close he dismounted and pushed his bike to the racks by the cathedral entrance. He chained its front wheel securely and took his roll of tape from the box above the rear wheel, replacing it with his helmet and locking the lid. Someone would steal it as a trophy if he hung it from the handlebars by its chinstrap, which was the logical thing to do.

He shook his head ruefully. 'Welcome to the high-tech world of the twenty-first century police service.'

As he always did when he came to the Close he entered the cathedral and walked down the nave towards the altar. The coolness of the large airy space chilled the sweat on his body, sending an unexpected shudder up his spine. He knelt before the altar and genuflected, bowing his head in a brief prayer.

He had once said to his wife, 'If you visit someone's house it's only proper to pay your respects. That's what's wrong with the world these days, there's no respect for anything or anyone. What's wrong with saying thank-you sometimes? Why not?'

She had hugged him, 'Thank-you, for you, Phil. Mad as a box of frogs but I wouldn't have you any other way.'

He thought himself a lucky man; lucky in having a good marriage to a woman he loved, lucky in having a job he enjoyed – most of the time – and lucky in having bought the house they lived in with money from an inheritance from an uncle he used to spend time with in London when he was a boy. His uncle had died in an accident, killed by a hit-and-run driver in a stolen vehicle who was being chased by the Met.

Phil knew it was wrong to feel lucky about something that happened as the result of another's misfortune, but Carole and he would never have been able to afford their house without his uncle's generosity. He assuaged his guilt by praying for uncle Alan's soul whenever he had the chance.

The sticky heat of the cathedral grounds struck him with redoubled force when he walked back outside. He was tempted to forget replacing the tape around the circle of yew trees until the following day, and instead take the easy option of freewheeling back to the station and accepting sergeant Fowler's promise of a cold beer. That he didn't was a measure of his self-respect rather than his devotion to duty.

The sexton, Charlie Croker, called out to him. Coombe was a regular and popular visitor to the Close and had proved useful in dealing with cases of criminal damage and petty theft from the cathedral and its grounds over the years. Croker liked to think they were friends.

'Any closer to catching the killer, Phil?'

'I shouldn't think so, Charlie. We're chasing our tails on this one, and frankly it's too hot to be running after anyone these days.'

'Blinding heat, horrible. I don't like it and it don't like me. My wife loves it, she's out in it all the time. I tell you, she's starting to look like a perma-tanned lizard. She's been going topless in the back garden; can you believe it? I'm waiting for complaints from the neighbours.'

'I'm sure she looks lovely. You're a lucky man, Charlie. Few women in their fifties would risk it, but your lady has kept her looks, and you know it.'

'Yes, she's all right. I just wish she wasn't sharing it with all and sundry.'

'You know the saying, "If you've got it...'

'...flaunt it. Yeah, I know.'

Croker went to his office and fetched out an ice-cold bottle of mineral water for the young police officer. He walked it around the west end of the cathedral just in time to see Coombe dragged headlong into the yew trees by an unseen assailant. Croker dropped the water and ran to his friend's aid.

He could hear choking shrieks coming from within the circle of trees and tore at the branches to get through them. When he reached the clearing containing the two ancient stones what met his gaze froze him in his tracks. Outside the trees the air was still and breathless as a corpse, and yet from nowhere the Sisters had become the focus of an icy tornado of wind. Coombe was pinned full length to the fallen sister, and even as Croker watched narrow gouges were sliced into his stab vest.

Without a thought for his own safety Croker threw himself forward and grabbed Coombe around the waist with both arms. He wrenched the man away from the stone, careless of the blood that spattered across both. Coombe tried to speak but all he could do was pant in shock. Around them the yew trees seemed to crouch lower and knit themselves more tightly together.

Croker gasped, 'Don't worry, mate, I'll get you out of this.'

While Croker wrestled with the needle-like branches of the conifers he felt stinging pain lash across his back, neck, and shoulders, He dropped to the ground and pushed Coombe ahead of him. The yew branches seemed to press down on him as if trying to hold him captive. Something pulled one of his shoes off and tugged at his ankle. He kicked out fiercely with the other foot, scrabbled at the ground, and then with a final grunt of effort he was free.

The two men rolled out into the silent heat of the Close. Coombe lay ominously still, his stab vest sticky with bright blood and stained yellow with dust from the parched ground. Croker fished his mobile phone from his trouser pocket and tapped nine, nine, nine.

It seemed an age before he heard a voice say, 'Which service do you require?'

He coughed out, 'Ambulance and police to the Cathedral Close. A police officer is badly injured, he needs help...' He reached up to place his free hand against the back of his neck then brought it round in front of his eyes. He looked at the wet redness dripping from his palm.

'Please, hurry. You've got two men injured here. Please, hurry, no time to...'

He passed out, his head and shoulders slumping across his friend's legs. Their blood pooled together on the scorched earth.

'They wanted to arrest Croker? You're kidding me.'

'No, I'm not, but it wasn't for long. At one point the Worthing CID guys were thinking of remanding him for questioning, but first they had to wait until he was patched up. Phil was almost cut to ribbons, poor sod was badly beaten up and he'd suffered a major loss of blood, but as soon as he was conscious he told everyone how Charlie had saved his life.

'I don't actually know if Croker was ever aware that he was a suspect. Sounds like the man acted like a cast iron hero. Phil's sure he'd be dead as mutton if it wasn't for Charlie stepping in. Says he owes the man a damn good drink.'

'A drink? And the rest. So, what are they saying happened up there?'

'Exactly the same as the place where you got stabbed and Sharif got clobbered. No evidence of anything untoward. No evidence of anything at all. There's blood of course, and plenty of it. And there's footprints and scuffmarks all over the place, but they all belong to the victims. Hines is calling it a forensic dead end. And you can bet she's not happy about losing her gopher to a hospital bed. I bet she's already got her feelers out for some other poor sod she can push around. I'd stay away a bit longer if I was you, Rose. You might look like the favourite.'

'Thanks for the warning, Sarge. I'm not due back until next week anyway, but I'll keep my head down in the meantime.'

Rose raised her pint and tipped it towards Fowler. He drained his and asked if she could face another, his round. She nodded, and he levered himself up from the table and headed towards the bar. She had been enjoying her quiet drink with the sergeant. He was good company away from the station.

She wondered if she should get some of Flo's tonic to the latest victims but decided to see how they were doing after a few days. Two of the town's police force off the beat in a week. It reminded her of the five officers who had volunteered to help police the Notting Hill Carnival, three of whom had ended up in hospital. She remembered Fowler's comments at the time, 'Carnival? Fucking carnage more like. They should shut the bastard thing down; and they would if it wasn't for where it is and the sorts who run it.'

Cutbacks in numbers left them with no reserves. Injury and sickness always meant the station was short-handed, which was great for overtime but lousy for stress levels. She had become so exhausted trying to help fill gaps left by those three being off work she nearly drove a marked car into a wall. The sergeant was sure to be trying to work out how to compensate for her and Coombe's absence. He returned with two pints and two packets of dry roasted nuts. He handed one of each to her.

He grinned, 'Nice to see you out of uniform, so to speak, Rose. I'd forgotten how well you scrub up. Cheers, anyway.'

They each took a long and companiable pull on their pints. Fowler opened his packet and took a handful of peanuts. He chewed ruminatively while he studied her.

'I know what I said about staying away, but you're looking so well, lass. Any chance you might be back in harness a bit earlier?'

Rose shook her head. 'I've already tried, but there's a problem with the insurance or something. They don't want to risk it, Health and Safety, you know the drill. Sutton told me to enjoy my time off and come back Monday week like the quack told me. She reckoned that by the time they make an appointment and assess me to come back earlier – and we get the results – I'll have been back a fortnight anyway. You know how long these things take, Sarge.'

'Yeah, like watching a year's worth of *EastEnders* Omnibus editions in one go. It takes forever, and you've gained sod all during the wait. Sutton's right. She usually is, I guess. It was just a thought, I should've known you'd already tried.'

He fisted some more nuts into his mouth and chewed slowly before swallowing.

'I eat peanuts because I'm having a drink, then I drink more because I'm eating peanuts. You'd think I'd learn, wouldn't you?'

'No Sarge, we never do, none of us do. I think we stop learning sometime while we're still kids. I think I read about it once.'

'I read enough just keeping up with the paperwork for the job. Haven't got time for anything else.' He finished his nuts and swallowed the last of his beer.

'I'm getting comfortable,' he said. 'That's dangerous. Next thing I'll be here 'til closing time. I'd better make tracks; the missus is doing Sunday lunch. You want me to wait while you finish that?'

Rose still had most of her drink in her glass. 'No, thanks, really. It's okay. Sarge, you get home. I'll be fine. Thanks for the company. I've got a book I'm enjoying and reading a few chapters with a slow pint is just what the doctor ordered. You take care and give my regards to your other half.'

'Reading? Bah! Bad for your eyes in this light. See you soon, Rose. Stay away from sharp places, they don't agree with you.'

'You've got a promise there. Cheers.'

She watched Fowler stride away with his customary measured step. She tried to imagine him running after a suspect, even as a younger man, but the picture eluded her. He turned and nodded at her when he reached the exit and then was gone. The few other patrons had watched their silent exchange with mild interest, and then returned to the important business of putting as much alcohol as possible between their sodden brains and the hard, real world.

Rose's stomach rumbled. Beer did that to her. She pondered the idea of ordering some food from the bar but decided to cook something quick when she got home instead. She fetched her book out of her bag and opened it at the bookmarked page. It had been described as a 'page-turner' in the blurb on the back cover, and she was finding it engaging enough. She liked the banter between the female leads, and idly wished she had a friend with whom she could swap snappy one liners.

She had barely reached the cliff-hanger at the end of the chapter when a distinctive stench assailed her nostrils. She gazed over the top of her novel at the gaunt and twitching face of Michal Klebb. He was still in his suit and tie and looked as if he had managed to avoid any trace of soap and water since she had last seen him. His body odour was just one of the layers of serious olfactory assault he could he charged with. He grinned, his teeth as mottled as his skin.

'Hello, Ms Platt, hello, Rose. You're looking a lot perkier than when I last saw you. Old Klebb knew the jollop would work. Better than anything from the chemist it is, and I got the secret receipt. I can make more.'

'Receipt? Don't you mean recipe?'

'Fangled and fashions, I knows what I'm saying. Recipe comes from the word receipt. The cooks kept the receipts for any dish they prepared and that's how they knew how to do it again.' He licked his lips and studied her glass. He swallowed, hard. 'Making the jollop gives a man a fearsome thirst, but it's worth it to tend to the sick, you see. I'd buy you a pint for conviviality's sake, but I left my money in my other trousers. Came out without a sou to me name. Embarrassing. I'd better go.'

She sighed, 'What can I get you?'

'Anything real ale would be champion. If it has the word ferret, bishop, or cock anywhere in its name then it's the very chap for me. And bless you. May you be safely in heaven before the Devil knows you're dead.'

'Not too soon I hope.'

'Noo, not before time. Let the horny red bastard wait until we're ready, that's what I say.'

At the bar Rose pointed at random to one the casks of ale lined up under the large framed mirror on the wall behind the counter. She also purchased a large bag of pork scratchings and ordered a hot sausage sandwich. She doubted Klebb had eaten anything substantial since Flo' had died.

The barman eyed Klebb quizzically then turned back to Rose.

'You want to add a bowl of fries to that? It's only an extra seventy-five pee. Your mate looks like he needs a meal more than he needs a bath, and he desperately needs a bath.'

She nodded and tilted her head towards her dinner guest.

'He's all right once you get used to the smell.'

'You get used to the smell?'

'I don't intend to find out. Thanks, Sam, and take for another pint when he finishes this one. He says he's thirsty.'

'Float him in a beer barrel and he'd drink himself out and he'd still be thirsty. I know the sort.'

Rose chuckled, 'I guess you're right.'

She fetched Klebb his beer and handed him the scratchings.

'Something to keep you going until your lunch gets here. I've ordered you a sausage sandwich and fries. I hope that's all right.'

His reaction to this information surprised her. The narrow man seemed to shrink in on himself. He hung his birdlike head between his skeletal shoulders and gazed into his glass. A heavy tear splashed into the dark ale. He raised his face to hers as if looking up from the bottom of a deep well, a picture of profound misery.

'I'm not a sponger, you know? Honestly, I'm not. I do have my own little pot of money. I'll pay you back for this, I will. You're being too kind, and Old Klebb has forgotten the face of kindness could be so sweet; and that it could be so lovely.'

With archaic dignity he reached out, took her hand, bent forward, and kissed it. His lips felt dry and warm, and they sent a shock of gooseflesh up Rose's arm.

He offered her a tight-lipped smile.

'The Lady will keep at her mischief until the bypass has been severed from the sacred path. She don't think of death the way you and I do. She sees it as moving from one place to another, for a bit of a change like. We living folk

115

are like batteries to her; she taps us for energy the way the barman taps a barrel. You be careful she don't drink you dry, Rose Platt. Old Klebb has respect for you; and you're too young to be dodging the devil just yet. You mark what I say, you want to enjoy plenty more Christmases before you meet the birthday boy in person. And old Klebb will help you.'

[28]

In the evidence locker at the back of the police pathology lab wisps of blue vapour escaped from an Iron Age cauldron while the jellified remains of a newborn child evaporated. Its energy was needed elsewhere.

Nearly two miles away in the Cathedral Close the stone Sisters moved. It was during the time when the veils between realms were at their thinnest, and dreams were easily scattered to nightmare. Toll bridges could be constructed between worlds. The price of passage? A life. Within the circle of yews, no living thing stirred; no insects, no birds, not even a worm. All was silence.

The Sisters moved, and the earth exhaled. A figure of mist and deception stepped out into the night. It was almost invisible. It drifted from the yews as an absence of light, a shadow deeper than darkness, and it slipped along the ancient line of the sacred path.

When it passed through the locked gate that separated the silence of the Close from the streets of the town the heavy padlock had shattered into fragments – as if it had been frozen in liquid nitrogen and smashed with a smith's hammer. Fragments of it tinkled away, glinting blood red in the streetlights.

The wraith flowed along the middle of the street that traced the path to the Queen's Mount. What had once been a broad line of chalk worn white over long centuries by the passage of worshippers' feet, was now a line of tarmac, parked cars, and pavements. Before the shadow the streets glowed in the sulphurous orange-yellow glare of lamps. Behind it streetlights dimmed.

This was the sacred path, it marked the passage from one world to the next. On the Mount had once stood tall defensive palisades surrounded by deep ditches Boreshame, the abode of warriors, monarchs and heroes, their names long since forgotten.

Captives had been forced to walk the chalk path from one hill to another. Their arms bound as they walked to the circle of Sisters. And there they would pay the price of embracing the fallen Sister, their blood flowing along the spirals and grooves cut into the Sister's stone. Their blood would pay the price for the bright sun and sweet rain that would reap a rich harvest. It would pay for ewes' bellies filled with healthy lambs and sows ripe with fat suckling pigs.

The blood token was accepted by Agrona, and she was a generous deity. But sometimes she was displeased, and she would turn her face from the people of Boreshame. Crops would fail, and the cattle's milk run dry. The land would become barren and the people faced starvation. Then the people's king or queen would be sent to personally entreat Agrona's mercy.

Not for them the short path. They would trace a spiral that ran around the circle of Sisters. They wore their best clothes and finest weapons, and in their hands, they carried a piece of silver as a gift for the goddess. During that long walk, the passage from the world of heroes to the realm of gods, priests and handmaidens taught them the sacred words of transition. Without these words they might be lost in the underworld and fail in their mission.

Their final destination was to lie on the fallen sister. There they accepted their fate, unbound and stoic. The last thing they would hear would be handmaidens thanking them and wishing them well on their journey. Priests would ask them to repeat the sacred words one last time, and then, with a blade of razor sharp obsidian, their throats were quickly slashed back to their spines.

Death was quick and noble. If the sun shone that day and the people's fortunes improved everyone knew the messenger had remembered the rote and succeeded in winning Agrona's favour. If the sky remained sullen and the future remained bleak another messenger would be selected, this time from amongst the priesthood. And then another. Until finally the sun shone.

Over long years the royal spiral path had been lost under the town that grew up around the cathedral, and all but two of the Sisters had gone, but the short path remained. It was still walked by those who understood what it meant, and by others who sensed something powerful along its arrow straight line.

The gardens of the houses along the path had always flourished and their inhabitants enjoyed good fortune. It was no accident that house prices along these roads were amongst the highest in the county, which put them amongst the highest in Europe. And then the bypass had been completed.

The shadow stalked down the path at the crest of the wave of darkness that streamed out in its wake. Insomniacs touched by the darkness felt their skin crawl with dread; dreamers stirred in their sleep. Wise cats slunk silently away to find safer haven elsewhere. Dogs quivered like beaten curs, crouching mutely in their baskets. A wave of night dwellers silently streamed away from the gathering shade as it approached the bright silver lights of the bypass.

Eammon White liked driving in the early hours of the morning when he all but had the roads to himself. He was listening to one of the *Harry Potter* novels. He had heard them all so often he could practically quote them from memory, but, although Stephen Fry's rounded, avuncular tones sometimes came close to inducing sleep, he loved to visit JK Rowling's world of witchcraft. He wished he too had received messages by owl inviting him to Hogwarts. It was worth risking Fry's mellow delivery to revisit the adventures of Harry and his friends.

It was another hot and humid night. White had been experiencing problems with his truck's air conditioning that had yet to be put right. It was cold enough, he had told his boss, to freeze the balls off a polar bear. Royal Marines had been running Arctic training exercises in his bunk at the back.

His hands, he said, were sliding around on the ice on his steering wheel, which is bloody dangerous because the only thing keeping over eighteen tons of articulated lorry on the road was the solid grip of his hands on the wheel. His boss had reminded him that there were plenty of other drivers who weren't so fussy, it was up to him. Eammon waited until he was out of earshot before making his response.

His truck was currently laden with a container full of Spanish toilet paper destined for a retail hub warehouse near Croydon. He had ensured the seals on the doors at the back were still intact before accepting the paperwork for the load, he didn't want to be the driver who delivered a container of 'illegals' to the Airport Estate. Toilet rolls were enough, and he didn't plan to freeze to death while delivering them.

Funnily enough, he mused, he preferred driving freezer containers. Nobody ever tried to smuggle themselves into one of those, and if they did they didn't cause any problems at the other end. Which still didn't help solve the problem of how he would cope with the combination of a steamy night and an over-enthusiastic air conditioning unit. He had finally compromised by keeping his air con on and his window partly open. He knew that doing so would prove fuel expensive, but if his tight-ass boss couldn't pay out to put the air con right, he could put out for the fuel instead.

The surface of the dual carriageway suddenly felt smoother under his wheels. Everything about the road looked bright as a new pin, as if it had just been taken out of its box. White realised he had reached the new stretch of bypass leading to Brighton and the M23. That was another way of saying he would be unloaded in another hour and a half and looking for somewhere to catch a few hours kip before moving on to his next load and then heading back towards despatch.

Not long now. Then he squinted through his windscreen. Something seemed wrong with the streetlights ahead. He wondered if there might be a power outage affecting everything. The area to the left of the road was pitch dark and it looked as if a solid wall of darkness had been stretched across his path. With a cold shock that was nothing to do with his air conditioning he thought he could just make out a slew of twisted wreckage on the northbound carriageway. He couldn't be sure, but he thought something might be burning on the other side of the crash barrier.

The air seemed thick and murky enough for an oil fire. He slowed to fifty and put his powerful headlights on full beam. The twin cones of light hit the darkness but seemed to be swallowed by it. *It must be smoke,* he thought. He stared hard trying to make out details of what was happening beyond the safety of his windscreen. Confusion and something else gripped at his heart, something he almost had time enough to recognise as fear. He slowed further, his foot hovering over his brake. And then the night poured through his open window and his final terrified scream was wrenched from his throat.

[29]

Jerome sat quietly on his bedroom floor. The only sounds in the room were his breathing and the fluttering patter of his drawings as he carefully riffled a thick stack of them through his fingers. When he got to the top he began again from the bottom. Before his glazed eyes the animated Lady performed her mystical gestures over and over again.

Lines of blue light spiralled from the pages and danced around the boy's head before streaming away into the night. His face was flushed and slick with sweat. It was a hot and humid night, but his sweat was not due to the heat. It was thick and glutinous, and it glowed with a green phosphorescence, a glow that also pooled deep in his wide blue eyes.

Jerome was dressed in just his underpants. His legs were crossed as if he was at school assembly and his thin ankles seemed on the point of snapping while he leaned into his work, such was the intensity of his concentration. His lips were compressed into a thin white line and he panted hard through clenched teeth. His breath was a metronomic beat to counterpoint the whirring sound of his flickering pages.

He didn't know it, but Jerome's pulsing breath perfectly matched the ancient drumbeat Rose had heard on the path. It was also one of the last sounds victims had heard when stretched out on the fallen stone Sister thousands of years before. That and the hiss of hot blood gushing freely from their slashed throats.

Jerome crouched further forward, and his thin shoulder-blades spread wide. They stretched the tender skin of his back, looking like the open carapace of a beetle. It would have been easy for a blind person to count the knobs of his spine by touch.

The magic had dissipated all trace of his youth. Instead of a six-year-old boy he appeared more like a gaunt old saddhu of a hundred years or more. The son who had sat on his mother's lap that morning and been told how much he was loved, and the boy who had eaten sausages with spaghetti hoops for his tea, had vanished away like steam.

Quietly, so quietly that a listener would have had to press their ears against his lips to hear him, Jerome began to chant. He was little more than a human machine, an enslaved marionette dedicated to the Lady's needs. Every drop of his vital energy had been drained away for her use. Even if exhaustion had wasted away his brain and body his nimble fingers would have continued their task until only his bones remained; and they would have continued their sacred dance until the job was done.

Just over two miles away and right across the blasphemous stretch of bypass the Lady and her dead followers were wreaking havoc. Vehicles struck the dense wall of her vengeance and were being flung to scraps and tatters. Drivers and passengers alike suffered the same fate. All the while the fresh tarmac of the road surface was being churned and split like a ploughed field.

In the heart of the destruction stood an inky form. She was no shadow but the absence of all light, a hungry vortex ready to suck the life force from any whom she touched. She grew stronger with every life she took, in her belly an insatiable appetite fed by death – and shaped by Jerome's enchanted stack of drawings.

Mike Talbot was snoring again. Stephanie lay restlessly on her back and listened to him with increasing irritation. He sounded like two rough stones being ground together in a tin bucket. Then, whenever he stopped, he seemed to stop breathing altogether. Sleep apnoea she thought hopefully. She'd read about it online. She didn't really care if he never drew breath again, just so long as the pig-like snorting noise ceased, and she could find peace and sleep. The relief was invariably short-lived. Within minutes his grinding growls and snorts would start once more, and Stephanie would have to fight back her overwhelming impulse to punch him.

But even if she had been alone she doubted she could have slept. She was so tired her body felt leaden and her joints ached, yet she couldn't get comfortable and her body was agitated. Her head was spinning, thoughts circling inside her skull like fat black flies.

She was worried about Jerome. He had been strangely eager to go to bed that evening. Normally he would drag his feet and cling to her, asking for just a few more minutes of TV, another story, another hug. That night he had kissed her, said goodnight, and padded off without a whimper. She wondered if he was sickening for something.

When she had crept into his room on her way to the bathroom before going to bed, she had found him sprawled across his mattress in a profound sleep. He looked flushed and was sweating profusely, his mop of hair plastered to his head, but, she told herself, of course he was sweating, it was a sultry night. *Or was it a fever?*

Four hours later and lying numbly awake and exhausted in her loveless marriage bed, Stephanie wondered whether she should rouse her husband and share her concerns. Then she chided herself for being a typically foolish mother with a small child and too much imagination. Jerome was fine, she told herself, he was just hot. She was sweating uncomfortably too, and Mike's sleeping body was soaked. His pores oozed the damp, ripe stink of beer and something else, something musty and unpleasantly organic.

That was when Talbot jerked in his sleep, belched an unpleasant laugh, then muttered something sly sounding yet incomprehensible. His hand reached down to his groin and he tugged at himself as if offering it to someone. He chuckled fatly. It was too much. Stephanie slid out of bed and went to the bedroom door to make her escape. Out on the landing she was faced with the prospect of another night downstairs on the sofa, which managed to be just a little too short to be comfortable, or visiting the medicine cabinet in the bathroom.

Too high for inquisitive little fingers to reach she kept her bottle of Nitrazepam at the back of the shelf. Two of those and she would be asleep in minutes no matter what Mike got up to. She hated the way she felt the next day, sluggish and headachy, but at least she would get some sleep.

Her route to the bathroom took her past Jerome's room, from which she heard an odd fluttering noise, low and continuous. It sounded like a curtain caught in a breeze, or perhaps the whispering blades of a fan. She shook her head. Jerome didn't have a fan, and the night was as airless as a tomb. The sound continued. Her curiosity piqued, Stephanie pushed open her son's door just enough to see what was going on.

What met her gaze wrenched a shocked bleat from her mouth. A skeletal figure sat on the floor by her son's bed. It was pale as bone and thin as a reed. It was humming and muttering to itself while it flicked nimbly through a neat pile of Jerome's drawings. She could just make out the way the finely scribbled renderings seemed to dance on the pages like an animated figure.

With trepidation she looked at Jerome's bed, convinced she would see him stretched out on the mattress unconscious – or worse. The bed was empty. With sick dread she turned her gaze back to the strange, crouched gargoyle. It was hard to reconcile its angular form with the little boy she had said goodnight to just hours before, but by concentrating on familiar and beloved things, the curve of his ears, the long delicacy of his clever fingers, his gawky oversized feet, she realised the truth. This nightmare creature *was* Jerome.

With a shriek of anguish, she rushed forward, her arms outstretched to take possession of her child. She would hold him and love him and make things better again. The nightmare would be gone, and Jerome would be back with her, his dear face his own once more.

Before her fingers could touch him, the boy snarled up at her. He leapt like a wild thing, his jaws open wide. He gripped her tight, and his bared teeth snapped shut in the flesh of her throat, then he wrenched his head away, tearing loose a big mouthful of his mother's meat and gristle. Even as blood spurted from her ruined neck and she frantically pressed her hands into the ragged wound to stem the flow Stephanie saw the wicked grin spread across what had once been her son's face. He chewed greedily.

[30]

Emergency services sped to the scene of what was being described as 'total carnage' by the news services. Those few who had managed to stop in time had instantly got on their mobile phones and the story was all over the social media. Confusing descriptions were pouring into local police stations. Reports included thick black smoke, explosions, terrorists dressed all in black, bombs, and gunfire. There was no talk of casualties, yet, but bodies had been spotted.

The first pale glimmers of morning were already threatening the eastern horizon, but no light could pierce the dense wall of darkness that stretched like a pall across the bypass between the town and the Queen's Mount. A police helicopter had been sent to the scene to get a better idea of what was happening. At first its crew had reported only a band of darkness and the odd orange billow of what they believed where oily plumes of fire. The pilot said he would go in to take a closer look, maybe land on the road and take a careful walk towards the 'accident'.

'Victor one five from despatch. Are you sure it's an accident?'

'Hello, despatch. No, I can't be sure of anything from up here, I need to see what's under that smoke. Strange looking smoke if that's what it is. Seriously, it looks almost solid. We're coming in to land n...'

The conversation ended in a short burst of harsh static. The team of despatch controllers looked at each other.

'What's happening out there?'

'Sounds like somebody's declared war on the bypass.

'That's crazy.'

'I'd be happy to hear an alternative theory.'

'I'll be happy to provide it as soon as I can think of one. Have we called the army yet?'

'Already on their way.'

Then the sun lanced out from behind the cathedral and shone down the secret path like a spear of light. Darkness scattered. It evaporated the wall of blackness and illuminated a scene of complete devastation. The men and women standing by their vehicles on the unaffected stretches of the dual carriageway were shocked to realise just how close they had come to death. Just a car's length away, no more than a few seconds later on the brake, and they would have become part of the destruction.

In the dawn light they could now see how the normal world of tarmac and cat's eyes – the accepted straight-line world between motorist and road surface – had been shattered beyond recognition. The front part of a helicopter had been smeared like wax into the earth. The burnt-out shells of cars and trucks were barely recognisable, and the final number of vehicles involved would be impossible to calculate other than by counting their wheels and axles.

It would take a lot of hours to write the final butcher's bill. Some bodies were discernible shapes amidst the wreckage, others were little more than scorched outlines, mere indications of a life ended where the body fell. The charcoal graffiti of death.

A small convoy of military vehicles rolled up to the site and stopped just outside the area the captain in charge described as the 'blast zone'.

He turned to his lieutenant. 'Murdoch,' he said. 'You were over in Afghanistan and saw time in Iraq during the worst of it. You ever seen anything like this?'

Murdoch examined the scene with his binoculars. He answered, his voice rich with a soft Highland burr.

'Sir, everything seems quiet enough just now. Shall I go take a bit of a gander on my own? I'd have a better idea what did all this once I've got wind of it in my nostrils.'

The captain sniffed the air. 'Seems pungent enough to me. What are you looking for?'

'Sniffing for is more like it. I'll ken it better once I smell it, sir. You know, I'll know once I smell it? The nose has a wonderful memory, sure enough.'

'Very good, lieutenant, very good. I'll come with you.'

'I'm no the right one for holding hands, sir.'

'Lord no. I want to learn from the master. Feel free to chat while we walk.'

The rest of the team were arrayed to form a perimeter around the affected area. Captain Trenchard and Lieutenant Murdoch moved gingerly forward until they were walking on disturbed raw earth. Trenchard looked around.

'What could do this, Tom?'

'Can I reserve judgement until I see a bit more, please, Maitland? First guess I would say earth moving equipment, localised earthquake, industrial grade ploughs, but none of this makes sense. It feels wrong.'

They moved forward, very aware of police vehicles joining their olive drab, light armoured ones.

126

Maitland Trenchard nodded, 'Boys and girls in blue look out of their depth again.'

Tom Murdoch shook his grizzled head, 'Them and me both. None of this shit makes any sense to me.'

He planted his booted feet on bare earth and carefully studied the immediate terrain. They were at the centre of a strip some twenty feet wide and thirty feet long. It bisected the road with the precision of a map-maker's rule. Where the damage began and ended was clear as if drawn by a giant ruler. The helicopter was intact, clean, and blue beyond the line, nothing but molten, cremated outlines inside it. Murdoch sucked his cheeks in, then puffed them out. He twirled around, looking at marks on the ground, melted vehicles, partly cremated bodies, and ashen outlines.

'Am I allowed to say that this mess is a pile of fucking shite?'

'Say it, old lad, but you need something to back it up.'

The lieutenant held out his arms like a showman to indicate everything around them.

'This. All of this. It looks like a badly staged film set. It's pure theatre. It would be laughable if it wasn't for the dead bodies in there. It makes no sense, no sense at all. It's our mini-Lockerbie and I don't like it.' He hissed, 'And another thing. The press is going to love all this, and the public are out there right now taking selfies with all this shit behind them on their fucking mobile phones. Those shots are going to be worth several pennies in the right grubby little hands, but we need to study them first. Can you get the lads onto it, sir? Let's start a little bit of a collection, shall we?'

The captain barked some orders into his radio. His men moved quickly, and shortly afterwards every smartphone and tablet in the area had been documented and confiscated.

Trenchard turned back to his friend who was now looking up at the sky.

Murdoch said, 'News copter up there. We need to clip its wings.'

'We can't go blowing up the bloody BBC, Tom!'

'We don't need to, *sir*.' Murdoch added a lot of inflection to the word 'sir'. He continued, 'Obviously I don't need to know about the *Sparkler*, never heard of it. But this would be a great time to use it if it existed, which I'm sure it doesn't.'

Trenchard studied his friend with quiet regard for no more than a second, then he changed the channel before barking more orders into his radio. A few minutes later the helicopter, which was cautiously hovering at the very edge of useful filming distance, wobbled, and dipped as if caught in an updraft, then it peeled away and vanished over Queen's Mount.

'How do you know about the *Sparkler*?'

'Me, sir? No, sir. Never heard of it. But, if I could build a cost-effective focused electromagnetic pulse projector that could scramble all the communication devices in a tight area without killing civilian personnel, or bringing down aircraft, I'm sure I would be on the Christmas list for several interested parties. Including the covert military anti-terrorist squad that you're not part of and neither am I, sir.'

'Murdoch.'

'Sir?'

'One day we must have that beer we keep threatening each other with. Now, back to the here and now. What are you seeing? Looks to me like a forest fire.'

Murdoch nodded again. 'Exactly, Maitland. But how do you have a forest fire that fits perfectly into an area the size of a bowling green where there is no freaking forest? That's question number one.'

'And number two?'

'Number one, no forest. Number two? Wrong nose. I can smell diesel, I can smell petrol, but that's all I can smell. I can't smell any explosive or accelerants. It's as if vehicles drove onto this bit of road and exploded without any reason.' Murdoch tapped his nose.

'I've used this fine instrument all over the globe and I've always managed to detect causes. IEDs, bombs, grenades, fertiliser bombs, you can see the list on *Google*, and even print instructions on how to build the bloody things if you want to, but the thing is they all got a specific stink, a distinctive odour. I'm not getting any of that here, in fact quite the opposite.'

'What do you mean?'

'What I'm smelling here is old. It's rotten. It isn't chemical it's organic, and I don't mean fertiliser. What I'm getting has been old for a long time, and I mean, a really long time. Whatever happened here stinks, and it stinks like an old corpse.'

31

Hours earlier Klebb had been trying to relax on the floor of his shed. He had been attempting, and failing, to catch up with his sleep in the nest he had made for himself from an old mattress and some bedding donated by Florence Mayhew. His mind insisted on replaying scenes from the last few days. He watched them as if he was in the audience at the opening of a mystery play. The curtains opened, and the lights sprang to life.

He saw Mayhew, the Lady, bring the knife to her own throat and then fall to the stone flags of her kitchen floor. He remembered the look of triumph on her face just before she made her final slashing cut. He had felt the power of her actions spread out like a living thing. It had thrilled through his body and whispered a message to him that he didn't quite understand.

It was later, and he was looking down at the body of a young woman in a hospital bed. He had expected to see moving darkness hovering in the eyes of Rose Platt when he had visited to bring her the gift of the Lady's tincture. The shadow in the eye was the sign of a wraith infection. When the ghost blade had entered her body, the spirit wielding it had also taken possession of Rose's living flesh. It would press its roots deep into her unless it was stopped. He knew that the Lady's remedy would dispel such an infection. It would purge her. He was glad to see it had worked when he met her in the pub, her eyes were clear once more. She would also have administered it to the one the Lady called the Moor. That was good. Rose Platt, yes, she was the one the Lady had sometimes called the Beauty, and sometimes the Witch.

And the girl had shown him pity and kindness. Unbidden she had given him the gifts of food and drink and shared the bounty of her smile. He found himself smiling back at the memory.

'Care for her, Michal,' the Lady's disembodied voice had told him the night after she died. 'Care for them both, The Witch and the Moor. Bring them my distillation you call the "tincture". I would not have them suffer for my act.'

And now Klebb could feel the vibrations of power becoming stronger, rippling like a silent storm through the trees and disturbing the creatures of the soil. He was alone in the garden that night. The natural folk had slunk away while they still could; the badgers, foxes, deer, and mice, had joined the rats in leaving the sinking ship. The branches of the trees were empty of birds. Klebb too felt compelled to go, but reluctantly admitted he had nowhere else to be.

Trying to silence his boiling thoughts he had been reading a book in his head. Klebb lived with nature, when the sun shone he had light, when it sank in the west he lived in darkness. A candle in Klebb's cluttered shed would have been enough to ignite a furnace, and he didn't believe in electricity. His was close to a stone-age existence. Except for his love of books.

Thanks to his astonishing memory, he had been able to devour whole books in Mayhew's library then he could dip back in and read them again at any time of his choosing without losing a single word.

That night he was attempting to distract himself by re-reading one of his favourite collections of short stories by the American author Rex Stout, *Homicide Trinity*. The fondly remembered words had scrolled across his vision like spoken script, and he was enjoying the inevitable conflict between the great detective, Nero Wolfe and Archie Goodwin, Wolfe's right, and left-hand man. And then the ruckus had erupted beyond the fragile wooden walls of his narrow, dusty, sleeping quarters.

Klebb never thought of the shed as his home. His home was much larger. It was out there in the woods, the Lady's garden, in fact anywhere he chose to walk on God's earth. The shed was just his bunkhouse, his billet for the night. His retreat.

He had slept there every night for decades, but even though he never accepted it as home, it was the only place he found the peace he needed to listen to his mentally archived books without disturbance. But now there was a 'ruckus' he must deal with. He sighed and climbed from his nest. *What now? It would be kids most likely. Most problems are down to kids.*

But, he had to admit, whatever it was it didn't sound like child mischief. It sounded like trouble. Klebb fetched a mattock from the corner of the shed, then hefted its weight in his hand. If the troublemakers didn't have guns *they* would have trouble with him. He knew the Lady would protect him if things got messy.

He put aside the empty scotch, wine and beer bottles that littered his nest, trying to make the least possible noise; but the bottles clattered together loudly in the silent night. The clashing glass rang out a warning, but that didn't stop the ruckus. It was obvious the kids out there were set to create mischief. It was a challenge. Klebb liked challenge. He clenched his mattock firmly in his right hand and stepped out into the open air.

The damp scent of freshly turned earth filled his nostrils, but what met his eyes stopped him in his tracks. The Lady was destroying her home. The plaster and lathe of stout walls that had survived six hundred years of war and council planning were spiralling towards the sky. Everything Mayhew had valued; her books, the tools of her craft, her books, her artworks, her books, her kitchen, and those magical, wonderful books, were spiralling out across the garden.

Klebb watched the precious pages flutter like snow from broken bindings and he fell to his knees in horror.

'Lady,' he cried. 'Lady, why are you doing this? What's happened? Your books, my Lady, my goddess! Your books!'

There came no answer. Instead he watched the flickering black shadow dance across all that now remained of her house, the stone floor. Klebb levered himself back to his feet with his mattock. He carried more than eighty years in his bones, but had never felt that old, not until now.

His spine twisted with fatigue, and for the first time since he had hitchhiked his way to England as a seventeen-year-old, he could smell the unwashed stench of his own body. The joints of his knees and hips ground painfully like spoons in a cup of sand. His neck ratcheted against the base of his skull. It was as if the years had suddenly pounded on his joints like hammers. They creaked.

Then the familiar commanding shape of Florence Mayhew stood regally, regarding him from the stone flags of her home. She was little more than a dark silhouette, but she was still everything Klebb had grown to worship and adore. A secret voice in his head thought of her as his wife, but he had never told her this. He had been afraid to. He heard her words, gentle yet compulsive.

'Michal, it's time. Are you ready?'

'My Lady, ready for what?'

She chuckled, low in her throat. 'I think you know.'

He coughed, a rasping wet sound.

'Please. Not yet.'

The first flagstone erupted from the ground and hit Klebb in the chest like a cannon shell and he was tossed into the air like a broken doll. The second nearly took his head from his shoulders while he was still in mid-air. The blow catapulted him towards the treeline yards behind him. He hit a redwood and crashed through its branches, where he was held for a moment, then dropped limply down. He was dead before his body hit the ground. The slices of flagstone drained Klebb's blood and energy, then slotted back together. They resurrected into the five lost Sisters, and for several minutes the massive Sarsen stones stood tall in Mayhew's garden.

All physical trace of the dead man had been subsumed into the stones. Even the wooden shaft of his mattock was gone. Mayhew's black shadow spun magic across the empty space where Klebb's body had been. With ancient enchantments Mayhew called his shade up from the earth, and his spirit was that of a teenager once more.

'Time for you to go home, my old friend,' she sighed, taking him into her arms.

She kissed him, and then he dissolved, and she was alone.

The resurrected Sarsen stones spun in a heavy, lazy circle above the destroyed garden for long moments, then darted like missiles to the Cathedral Close. Events were entering their final phase.

Even as they landed amidst the yew trees the sun rose. The stage was set for horror, but its clean light would hold back the final reckoning until the sun set once more.

32

Mohammed was largely back to his old self. He was still taking painkillers and could only sit in a right-angled chair for a few hours before he had to get up and walk around to relieve the pain, but he could sleep in his own bed, shower, and even talk about getting back to work. He had also been told to avoid too much heavy lifting, so Maryam had purchased a sturdy three-wheeled shopping trolley from one of the town's many charity shops, the idea being he could still help her bring the week's shopping in from the car. He had tried to refuse to use it in case the neighbours saw him.

'They're going to say you're married to Miss Daisy,' he said. 'I'm happy with you doing all the driving for a bit longer, sure I am, but do I really have to use the granny trolley? I can carry my share of the shopping without it.'

'Sure you can, Boots. But I like having you back on your own two feet and I'm not going to let you put yourself back on your back just because you're too vain to be seen pushing a cart. Be brave now, my big man. I won't let the nasty people make fun of you, I promise. If anyone asks I'll tell them, you hurt your back when we broke the bed making love for the fourth time in one night. That work for you?'

He grinned, 'I bet you would too, you crazy woman. Tell you what, tell them you can't say anything because the cause of my injury is still part of an ongoing police investigation. Let their imaginations run riot.'

'Oooh, I like that. That will really get the tongues wagging. But you use that cart, or I promise you there *will* be an ongoing investigation, and you will not like it. You will not like it at all.'

'Like what?'

'Like a proctologist *investigating* the best way to pull it out of your sweet little backside, which is where it'll end up if you don't use it. You hear me?'

Mohammed loved her vocabulary and everything else about her.

They had laughed together and retired to bed. Life was returning to normal.

And then the next morning it seemed as if Hell had come to town.

It started with the breakfast news which was running a special edition about the terrible events on the bypass. Reports were still incomplete, but brief footage of the blackened wreckage on the stretch of road by the Queen's Mount was repeated on a regular basis. There was also a sequence showing a man on a bridge over the dual carriageway. He was reporting the gridlock and increasingly chaotic tailbacks the road closure had caused.

Police were battling to cope with traffic that had quickly got out of control. No one was able to use the road past the old Iron Age fort, and it looked as if it would be a long while before the road reopened. As a desperate measure the crash barrier down the centre of the road either side of the scene had been breached and motorists were being sent back the way they had come. It was a slow process and would be many hours, if not a day, before the roads were cleared.

The authorities were remaining tight-lipped about causes, which gave free rein for 'experts' to put forward their theories. The situation had been worsened by reported violent clashes between 'cultists' dressed as Druids and the military and police personnel at the scene. Arrests had been made and weapons confiscated.

The local news added little to the story, except a piece from a noted historian who lived in the town close by the cathedral. Something odd had happened to the yew trees around the ancient Sister Stones, said the historian who was filmed standing in front of the trees, and who, Maryam observed, would be better suited to breakfast broadcasts if she wore a bra under her copious yet flimsy top.

'The yew trees,' explained the historian, 'have always acted as a protective barrier around the stones; but previously one has always been able to press through the trees to visit the historic site. I can still remember dancing around the stones as a child.'

She demonstrated, and proved surprisingly light on her feet. While she was waving her arms around and rocking back and forth, her large bosom offered a substantial counterweight to the rest of her body.

Maryam chuckled, 'She'll have somebody's eye out if she's not careful.'

Once her body had resumed a state of repose the woman had continued by explaining that she had attempted to visit with the stones that very morning and found the trees to be an impassable barrier.

'I know I come in the larger economy size,' she concluded. 'But it's almost as if the yews are conspiring to keep me out. They seem somehow knitted closer together. It's a mystery; they were fine just a few days ago. Maybe it has something to do with all this weather we've been having?'

In closing, the slender and petite young interviewer admitted that she too had tried to push her way through the trees and had found them impenetrable. Then the station cut to a weathergirl.

Mohammed's skull itched with questions. Something told him the situation on the bypass and the mystery of the yew trees were somehow connected. He would have happily driven to the Cathedral Close to see the circle of trees for himself. He also wanted to look down the secret path to see if, as he suspected, the incident had occurred where the secret path met the bypass.

It was almost lunchtime and he was trying to work out how he could get into the town through the nightmare traffic conditions – and whether Maryam would let him try – when his phone rang. The screen told him it was Rose. He thumbed 'accept'.

'Rose, hi, what can I do for you?'

'Sharif, thanks for taking my call. How are you?'

'Me? Fine. I have to be a bit careful how I move but otherwise I'm fine. How about you?'

'That's why I'm calling. I'm not officially back at work until next week, doctor's orders, but something's come up and the Chief wants me to take a look at it. It would be great if you could be there too.'

'What's up? Are you talking about that nightmare on the bypass? Are some children involved?'

'Oh, no. But you're right about it being a nightmare. A team of army specialists are working with Sandy Hines at the scene, but no one can make any sense out of it yet. None. No, no kids involved that we know about, they can't actually work out how many people *are* involved yet, but no it isn't that.'

'So then, what can I do for you?'

'Sharif, it's about Jerome Talbot.'

'Is he, all right? Rose, has something happened to the boy?'

'Sharif, please. I'd rather tell you face-to-face. It's just something else to add to an already weird day. Can you meet me at the station?'

Mohammed chewed this over, then said, 'Look, I'm not really in a fit state to drive. The pains in my back are much better but it might be a bad idea to put my body under that kind of strain just yet. Also, I can't work out how to get into town without hitting all that traffic. According to the news it's practically a no-go area. I don't see how I can do it. I'm sorry.'

Rose agreed, then said. 'Can I call you back in five minutes?'

'I'm not going anywhere.'

He was in middle of explaining the conversation to Maryam, who was wondering very vocally what the police expected from a man who was recovering from severe injury, 'And only just back on his feet, for God's sake.' When his phone rang again.

'Hi, Sharif. It's Rose. We may have an answer. Can you get to the playing field just down the road from your house?'

'Well, yes. I'll need time to shower and get dressed, you know, but I can be there in about forty minutes. Why?'

Maryam watched him while he listened to Rose, her face creased with concern and curiosity. He nodded at something he had been told.

'Okay, right. I'll be there. Tell the man I'm fragile, so no funny stunts, okay?'

He listened again, then said, 'Right, bye, see you then.'

Maryam eyed him angrily. She said, 'So, *what*? They sending a motorbike over to get you? You're not fit to go on the back of a bike, it will twist your spine like a pretzel. I won't allow it. Ring her back and say no! Do it right now, do you hear me?'

He took a deep breath. 'No, love. I've got to go. Something's happened and they need me there. And no, they're not sending a bike, they're sending a chopper. I'm meeting it at the rec in less than an hour. Let's see what the neighbours make of that!'

33

'The ancient Roman empire took a laissez-faire attitude to most religions. It preferred to assimilate its freshly conquered people's beliefs on the principle that people were much easier to control if they retained their gods. When Rome became Christian it kept some of the major pagan rituals, including the yuletide mid-winter solstice festival of the sun's rebirth, which later became known as the Christ Mass, or Christmas.

'The spring festival of fertility in the form of the worship of the Germanic goddess Eostre or Ostara, who took the form of a hare, is still with us to this day. Hence the bunnies and eggs we use to celebrate Easter, which have nothing to do with the death of Christ, although I suppose it can be claimed to have a marginal connection to all that rolling away of the stone and his resurrection.'

Local historian Professor Pamela Clarkson was still in need of a bra, but she was thoroughly enjoying her fifteen minutes of television fame. The journalist from *Channel 4* had asked her about the history of Queen's Mount because it was the largest and best-known landmark near the tragic 'disturbance' on the bypass.

Clarkson had taken the bit and run with it, and the young woman who had asked the question was receiving withering glances from her colleagues. Clarkson heaved a great sigh, which set major sections of her anatomy on the move like tectonic plates during an earthquake.

'Such, however,' she continued, 'was not the case with the Druids. The Romans suppressed them wherever they found them. There were reports of Druidical blood sacrifice and even cannibalism, which the Romans frowned on despite their own barbarism in the arena. Something about the Druids frightened or disgusted the Romans, and the last of the poor chaps were finally exterminated on the island of Ynys Môn, which you know as present-day Anglesey. They went down fighting to the last man.

'What I'm saying is that the Queen's Mount is a remnant of Prydain, old Britain. It's an Iron Age Celtic fortress. Most likely it would have fallen soon after the second Roman invasion of 43AD. All Druids were Celts but not all Celts were Druids. Some Celts got along fine with the invaders, even taking Roman names and titles. However, all the evidence indicates that the Mount was likely a Druid stronghold, perhaps home to the wise ones, also known as men of the oak, and Celtic priests. The fact that it has survived almost untouched to the present era is a measure of how much it was, and still is, respected by people in the area.'

Like every other local, Clarkson had kept her mouth firmly shut regarding the secret path. Like many others she had campaigned to stop the bypass slashing through the path, and like them she believed there must be a connection between the creation and completion of the bypass and recent tragic events.

Clarkson could openly say nothing about such matters for fear of a backlash from her social group and her academic peers. She also had a strong suspicion that retribution might come from a source other than human. Many historians and archaeologists hold a deep respect for the supernatural elements of Britain's ancient landscape. Albion's spirits run deep in her veins, and some of those veins are close to the surface. Something odd was going on, something more than events on the bypass. Clarkson had been in the daily habit of feeding a small family of hedgehogs in her back garden, but just recently the soup of cat food, snails, and slugs she prepared had been left untouched. She had also not seen any trace of urban foxes for a while, and birds had not only stopped singing they had vanished from the sky. Even pigeons, which she considered to be little more than dirty tree rats, had disappeared.

Tucked in her bag Clarkson had her tickets ready for a train to London later that afternoon. She had contacted an old friend and got herself invited for a little holiday to Carshalton, a village she found almost bearable on the very outskirts of the great city. Until the spirits in her home town calmed down, *anywhere* else might prove a lot safer.

The mystery of the yews might not interest the national media – and only be worth a passing item on the local news desk – but it played on Clarkson's mind. Something had turned the circle of trees into an impenetrable fence of tightly woven and hostile fir branches. Her hands and arms still bore witness to how much damage the vicious needles could do. The delicate skin was criss-crossed with thin red lines that itched and stung like insect bites.

She was so distracted by her own thoughts that she missed a question asked by a middle-aged journalist who had tapped her on the arm to attract her attention. He repeated his question slowly and loudly, as if she was a little deaf or feeble minded.

'As a local, Ms Clarkson, what do you think happened on the bypass? Might it be a geological or a meteorological event, or has something perhaps disturbed an ancient ley line leading to the Mount?'

Clarkson tilted her head to one side, her jowls folding into her shoulder. The man's question had come disturbingly close to her own thoughts. The other journalists chuckled as if the man had said something witty, but his face remained deadly serious. He raised his eyebrows, waiting for her answer.

She said, 'I'm sorry, Mr...?'

'Williams, Marcus Williams. *The Strangeness Papers*. Perhaps you've heard of us? We like to keep an open mind.'

She had heard of it. The journal veered from subject to subject, from UFO sightings to hauntings to possessions, and included articles on witchcraft, spiritualism, and mythology. She had found it entertaining, informative, and batty as a church-tower in equal measure. She took stock of Williams with hooded eyes.

'What do you mean by "ley line" Mr Williams?'

'Marcus, please. And I think you know, Ms Clarkson. A ley line is an ancient secret path, a sacred line of spiritual energy. Britain has a network of them leading from noble sites of power such as Stonehenge, Avebury, even Canterbury. The list is long. People of sensitivity can feel the energy leaking from a ley line. I would say there has been a great disturbance of spiritual energy around the Queen's Mount, so much so that it is giving me quite a headache even now.'

Clarkson heard one of the other journalists whisper 'Feel the force, Luke' and saw knowing smiles on some of the younger faces. Time and experience had yet to give any of them much in the way of personality. She thought of them as pretty, pouting, unweaned puppies. In her mind's eye she saw the milk still dripping from their soft faces.

In Williams' face was the weariness of a man who had seen too much. She thought it might be good to break bread with him. She certainly wasn't going to let him be mocked by callow youth. She stood up and gave her audience a little bow.

'Thank you, everybody. I think we're done. I think we've covered everything, and these nice people want their library back.'

Her impromptu studio by the science fiction and fantasy shelves of the local library had been a last-minute inspiration. They had been there an hour while cables and cameras were set up, and then there had followed another half-hour of questions and answers. That was long enough. She doubted they would use more than five minutes of her presentation in any case. Clarkson picked her way through the journalists with surprising daintiness and vigour. The man from *The Strangeness Papers* had drifted away from the pack

'Marcus,' she murmured when she caught up with him. 'Would you like some lunch?'

Williams looked surprised and then smiled.

'I should be very pleased.'

'Then let's get away from these schoolkids and find somewhere a bit quieter. Follow me, I know the perfect place. We shall be able to talk in peace.'

She took his elbow and steered him out into the carpark. The sun was high in the sky and the day promised to be hot once more. Clarkson led the journalist up the hill towards the cathedral. She spoke in a confidential tone.

'I have a few hours before I catch my train to London. I am reluctant to spend another night here in town.'

She explained about the lack of birds and wild animals, and about the secret path which she strongly believed to be a ley line, just as Williams suspected.

The journalist nodded while he listened and followed Clarkson down into the cathedral's undercroft and its *Crypt Café*. Within minutes they were both spooning mouthfuls of delicious lamb and lentil soup into their mouths.

'Well then, Marcus, what do you think?'

'Think, my dear lady? I believe I think the same as you. This town will become a killing field until it gets its secret path back, and I'm afraid there's nothing we can do to stop it.'

[34]

Rose watched the familiar tall figure climb carefully out of the marked police car and stride up the drive of the Talbot's house towards her. Her relief was so intense she almost wept, and she ran to greet him.

'Sharif, thank God you're here. I'm so sorry to drag you out in the middle of all this mess, but I couldn't think of anyone else. It's wonderful to see you. You're looking fine. How do you feel?'

'As if most of my marbles have been shaken loose. People *choose* to climb into those boneshakers? I tell you I had to put my eyeballs back twice and we were only up there for a few minutes. Still, from up there we could see the state of the roads around here. There's no way I would have got here by car. Not a chance. But I'm here now, special delivery from a helicopter straight to you. So, then. What's up? What's wrong with Jerome?'

Rose screwed up her face. 'Not good. It looks like he tried to murder his mother. She's in a bad way, Sharif. She lost a lot of blood.'

'My God. What did he do?'

'All the evidence says he used his teeth. It appears Jerome tore a chunk out of her neck the size of his fist and then he ate it. Do you know how difficult it would be for a little kid to do something like that? I can't imagine it, you know? I can't get my head around it. It seems impossible. Then, yeah, the father slept through everything. Deep sleeper, probably a booze coma. When he finally got up this morning he found the mother curled up on Jerome's bedroom floor in a pool of blood, and the boy asleep in bed with blood spatter all over his face and body. He's not handling it very well.'

'Jerome? I'm not surprised.'

'No, the father. You remember, Mike Talbot. Jerome's in a daze. He's drawing a total blank about the whole thing. He can't remember anything from the time he went to bed last night to the time we arrived this morning.

'He's upset because we won't let him wash or brush his teeth, not until you see him. Forensics have taken swabs and samples from between his teeth. They took photographs of the scene, the boy's face, everything.'

She looked over her shoulder at the open front door as if expecting something to pounce from its shadows.

'Stephanie's gone. She's been taken to St Joseph's A&E. She was in a critical condition, but I don't know how she's doing now. Sharif, tell me, what kind of nightmare turns a nice little kid into *Hannibal Lecter*?'

'How badly shocked is he?'

'We were hoping you'd tell us. Shall we go in?'

The atmosphere in the house was dense and gloomy after the heat and light of the street. Mohammed felt intense pressure building behind his temples. His eyes ached. He pressed his fingers to the bridge of his nose.

Rose glanced up at him. 'You feeling it too? This house is giving me a migraine. Feels like something's taken a grip on my head and started squeezing it to see how long it takes before it goes pop. I've never felt anything like it before, have you?'

'Yeah, I have. On the way here when the helicopter flew over the cathedral. I thought it was just down to the flight but now I'm not so sure. Felt just like this, but I think this is worse.'

Rose climbed the stairs and Mohammed followed. The sensation of mounting pressure increased with every step. Rose groaned.

'I think we can agree that this is not a great way to spend a Monday. Let's tell them we're still off sick and get out of here. Why don't we? I'm finding it tough to breathe.'

Mohammed tried to rally a smile but neither of them was convinced by it. He ducked his head down into his shoulders and sucked in a deep and unrefreshing breath, then forced himself through the door leading into Jerome's bedroom, Rose at his shoulder.

A small, spare figure sat on the bed. A uniformed police officer filled a wooden chair in the window bay next to a bright blue and yellow chest of drawers. He looked bored and evidently felt none of the distress experienced by the new arrivals. Mohammed nodded to him and the officer climbed to his feet.

'Perfect timing. I'm breaking my neck for a piss and I haven't had a smoke all morning. Is it okay to leave you two to it while I take a quick break?'

He didn't wait for an answer before he hustled out onto the landing.

He called back over his shoulder. 'Boy's not saying much, and when he does he's not saying much.'

Mohammed couldn't take his eyes from the reed-like creature on the bed. Jerome looked almost like one the wax anatomical figures Mohammed had seen years before at *La Specola*, a macabre section of the Museum of Zoology and Natural History in Florence. Except none of those intricate figures had clots and smears of dried blood around their mouths and down their chests. Even Jerome's hair was spiked with blood, his nostrils were caked with it.

The boy gazed up at him as if awakening from a reverie. Amazingly, he smiled with genuine warmth. His eyes came into focus. He was a small-boned, very young boy who was naked apart from a pair of slightly too large underpants which sported a colourful image of Spiderman swinging through New York.

Jerome sighed, the cage of his delicate ribs rising and falling under their thin layer of taut pale skin.

'My mouth tastes funny.' He said, in a small voice.

Mohammed pulled up the chair the policeman had been using and settled down near the bed, his eyes gentle on the serious little face.

'Hello, Jerome,' he smiled. 'Do you remember me?'

The boy nodded. 'Dr Mohammed.'

'That's good. Yes. Nice to see you again, Jerome. How do you feel?'

'Feel?'

'Yes.'

Jerome chewed over the question. 'Dirty,' he said.

'Why do you feel dirty?'

The boy picked a flake of clotted blood from his narrow chest and held it up.

'I'm covered in this stuff. It feels dirty. It smells.'

'Where did it come from?'

'I don't know. I would like to wash, please. And brush my teeth. Please.'

'Can you remember where it came from? Try, Jerome.'

Under its gory mask the boy's face changed. He grinned, exposing blood stained teeth. Mohammed tried hard not to recoil from the sight of shreds of dark maroon flesh still jammed between them.

'Don't pester the child, my Moor, my dear. He cannot know, he was not here. Even for you it's plain to see, the one who did the deed was me.'

The voice was mocking and educated. It chilled the room, even though the words held little menace. Mohammed leaned forward slightly.

'Tell me, why do you talk in rhyme?'

'I don't, my Moor, not all the time.' The face changed. 'Enough of that. Yes, you are right. The mystery has served its purpose, we must put childish things away. Another time, another day. Oh dear, it does become something of a habit, doesn't it? Please, let the child wash. And he needs food.'

Jerome then appraised Rose, who was standing in the bedroom doorway.

'So do you, my sweet witch. The black bile is gone but you must feed the body to redeem the soul. And now to surrender this sweet shell to its owner

144

once more. Should I see you again? If we should meet again you will know me first by my perfume. English witch and Moorish knave, not quite *Chanel*, much more the grave.'

In front of their eyes Jerome seemed to transform into a desiccated corpse. His belly bloated into a blood streaked grey ball and his jaw swung wide open. Then his stomach squeezed itself flat and air whistled from his open mouth, it smelled rank and rotten. The bedroom reeked of the charnel house and Mohammed gagged at the stench.

'Fuck me, what's that stink? What died in here? Smells like dead fish.'

The policeman stood behind Rose in the doorway, his hand over his nose and mouth. He bustled into the room and flung the windows wide open. As soon as he did so there came the sound of gentle laughter which seemed to float for a moment in the air and then was gone. Jerome blinked his eyes. He looked around him in confusion and began to weep.

He reached a hand towards Mohammed. 'Where's my mummy?' he said.

35

They stood by the ruined gate that separated the path in the town from the Cathedral Close. Neither took much notice of the gate's condition, they were more interested in what lay beyond it.

'There's your ley line, Marcus. See it? That's the secret path.'

'Why, yes, Pamela, I can see it quite clearly. Once you point it out it becomes very evident. And what a beauty. You say it starts at some sarsen stones? A henge? How exciting!'

'The Sisters. Archaeology tells us of a henge, you know, a circle of six standing stones with an altar stone in the centre. Before that there were wooden posts, two circles of them, one within the other. All that's left now is what I showed you in the museum.'

After lunch Clarkson had taken Williams for a tour of the corridor just off the *Crypt Café*, in which was a half-hearted attempt at a cathedral museum. Pieces of delicately carved architrave shared space with Roman sarcophagi and the ubiquitous clay pipes of a previous age. Gnarled leather straps, ancient boots, old bottles, and pots cluttered the glass display cabinets, each marked with a cardboard label that had been hand printed in now faded ink.

On the walls were images of the cathedral, including old watercolours and etchings, and a long, framed, sixteenth-century map of the town; which had important locations, including the cathedral, drawn larger so a visitor could find them easily. There were also black and white photographs of the building and its grounds, some dating back to the reign of Queen Victoria. Among these were shots of the Sisters in their circle of trees, a few of which included suspiciously scantily-clad young girls dancing suggestively in a circle around them.

Williams had purchased some postcards of the Sisters and one of the circle of yews. He studied this now while he examined the trees in the flesh.

He said, 'I suppose the trees have grown somewhat since this was taken?'

'Not really, Marcus. They were already mature by then. The English yew, or *taxaceae*, grows like a bastard when it's immature, but that soon tails off. These should be roughly the same size now as they were then. The fruits are edible but taste like snot, the seeds, however, are not, they will kill you. Some people say you can make tea out of the yew's bark, bad idea. Treat the whole tree like a big bucket of poison and you won't go far wrong.'

Clarkson held out her arms. Williams could see the raised red welts on her hands and forearms.

She continued, 'Buggering trees bit me when I tried to get in there this morning. Look what they did. Mildly infected I guess. I've put some anti-histamine on there, but they itch like the devil.'

Williams tutted in sympathy, 'I got poison ivy like that once. Drove me mad. I'm afraid anti-histamine cream is the only remedy. Now, if I may, I'd like to work out where this photograph was taken.'

'That's easy, I can show you. I used to do a history walk and talk around the Close, I know it by heart. Come over here.'

She took his elbow and steered him towards the shadow of the cathedral walls. When they turned the sun was almost directly behind them and shone on the circle of yews like a giant white lamp. She bade Williams to study his postcard, he did so with a grunt of satisfaction.

'Spot on, thank-you, Pamela.'

After a few moments he lifted the card up before his eyes then lowered it. He did this several times then turned to Clarkson.

'You might want to try this. I'd like to know what you think.'

She took his postcard and followed suit. She quickly realised what had caught Williams' attention. Gravestones and features of the Cathedral Close that had been visible at the edges of the yews in the photograph were now obscured by the circle of trees.

She turned to her companion, 'The circle has got wider.'

He nodded, 'Considerably so, by my estimation. Perhaps up to ten feet or so. Please forgive me, Pamela, my head won't work with the new metric money of metres and centimetres, I am an old feet and inches man. But by my reckoning that circle of yews is ten feet wider, give or take a blade of grass.'

They both moved to the densely packed group of yews. Clarkson tilted her head to one side and squinted at them with frustration building on her broad features. There was no sign of any way in.

She mused, 'How can it become both denser and wider? That's perversely counterintuitive. Surely it should have thinned out, not become thicker?'

Williams didn't answer. He got to his knees and then lay flat on his belly. He held his glasses to his eyes and wriggled sideways towards the base of the yews.

Clarkson protested, 'What are you doing, Marcus? You'll get filthy down there.'

147

His answer was slightly muffled. 'I've done much more than get a little dusty in the interests of my enquiries before now, my dear Pamela. At least I should be able to see the ivy covering the stones from...'

He had forced his head forward under the trees and inched further in. Then suddenly his feet jerked, and he seemed to be caught in a tug of war with himself. He moved forward without using his feet or hands, Clarkson heard his cry of surprise. She made her mind up. She had made a new friend that day, she was not going to lose him to a bunch of bloody trees.

With considerable effort Clarkson bent down, grabbed the journalist's ankles, and heaved. He groaned but didn't come free. She tugged again, and only managed to pull the man's socks down around his ankles. She whimpered with frustration then a fresh shadow fell across Williams' struggling back and a pair of strong hands reached out and gripped the trapped man's legs.

'Let's pull together, shall we?' grunted Charlie Croker. 'Now, heave!'

They wrenched at the trapped man, once, twice. Clarkson had forgotten to breathe and choked out a ragged breath. Croker cursed through gritted teeth.

'Let go of him, you bitch! He's done you no harm.' Clarkson realised that he wasn't talking to her when he continued, 'Okay then, Pam. Let's do this!'

They both put all their considerable weight into the battle and just as Clarkson began to fear they were wasting their time Williams burst from the yews like a cork from a bottle. The three fell backwards in a tangled heap. Williams' head and shoulders were scratched and bloody but otherwise intact. He had lost his glasses during the fray and his face looked less defined as a result.

He put his hands up to his face as if to push his glasses back into place and his fingers found only flesh. He looked over his shoulder at the yews. Croker followed his gaze and then touched his arm.

'Are you all right, mate?'

'I... my glasses. I've lost my glasses, they must have come off in there. I've got to...'

He moved back towards the trees, which seemed to quiver with anticipation in the windless air. Croker strengthened his grip.

'Let her have them, mate. We only just got you out this time, she won't let go so easy if she gets her hands on you again.'

Williams sat heavily in the dust. Clarkson pushed herself up into a sitting position. Her blouse had lost some of its buttons and fallen open to expose a large expanse of her plump left breast. She tugged feebly at it, trying to recover some degree of dignity. Her hair was dishevelled, and her long skirt had risen to her knees. Her nylon knee-highs were badly laddered.

Croker climbed to his feet and offered her first one hand, and then both of them. He almost had to lift her forcibly upright. She was trembling with shock after the effort of freeing Williams, her lower lip was quivering uncontrollably. She searched Croker's face as if she didn't know him.

Williams rolled onto his knees and with an effort pushed himself upright. His eyes darted from Clarkson to Croker and back. Then he looked sideways at the viciously waiting evergreens. A ripple stirred the branches with evident intent. He turned back to Croker.

'I think I owe you my life, sir. I don't know how to thank you enough. I don't know what happened there, but I'm grateful you came along and that's a fact.'

Croker attempted a grin, 'Names Charlie, Charlie Croker, and that bitch in there had a go at me too, and not long ago. Look.'

He opened his shirt and showed them the surgical dressings on his neck and shoulders. 'Fifteen stitches. Cut me like a knife. Mate of mine is still in St Joseph's thanks to the evil bitch in that bastard circle of trees. I tried to burn them down, but they won't catch. I tried to cut them down, but they won't cut. I tell you, I wish I had a hand grenade I'd blow the bastards back to Hell where they belong, I swear I would.'

Williams stuck out his hand, 'Marcus, Marcus Williams. Glad to make your acquaintance, Charlie, and right glad at that.'

Croker took the hand and shook it firmly, then pointed his thumb at the yews.

'So, what were you doing to get yourself stuck in that Devil's trap? I don't find many grown men wearing a decent suit scratching around in the dirt like a schoolboy. Were you looking for something?'

Williams nodded, and seemed a little embarrassed. 'Sort of, I was trying to get a look *at* something; the famous stones. Pamela told me about the stones, the Sisters, and I wanted to see them. I'd barely got deep enough in to where I could see them when all hell broke loose, it was like the branches of the trees had come to life and grabbed me. I was being dragged in and there was nothing I could do... Thanks again for pulling me out, I don't know what would have happened, really.'

Clarkson looked at him intently. 'Marcus, you say you got a look at them? But I told you, there's nothing much to see. Just the two ivy covered Sisters, one standing and the other flat on the ground. You saw that?'

149

He shook his head, 'No, that's the thing. That's not what I saw, that's not it at all. I saw the ring. I saw the henge intact, all the stones standing except the altar on the ground. I saw them clear as I see you now. All of them.'

Croker's mouth became a grim line. 'Yeah,' he growled, 'and it didn't want to let you out to share that bit of news. The bitch would have killed you to keep that secret. Killed you and swallowed you whole. But thanks be to God, all she got was your glasses. And I hope she chokes on them!'

36

Mike Talbot went to work that morning, after explaining that he was in the middle of a major project and that there would be serious ructions if he didn't show up. He told Rose he was already late as it was, and he had just been waiting for someone to, 'Come look after the boy, you know?' Rose was thoroughly disgusted. His wife was critical in hospital and his son was probably the person who had put her there, but all Talbot could think about was his job.

His breath stank of stale alcohol even after using mouthwash, and she was certain he would fail a breathalyser test. And yet he had climbed into his car, left his family in a state of crisis, and buggered off to work.

And yet, the creep had still found time to check her out as if she was a car he badly wanted to test drive. She kept her peace, but mentally she labelled him as a prime example of grade 'A' wanker with bells on. She thought he would look better on a butcher's hook than in shoe leather. She had almost willed him to try for a bum squeeze when he passed her on the way out; he would have ended up with much more than the offending hand in a sling if he had.

Jerome was washed and dressed and talking with Mohammed in the kitchen while he ate some breakfast cereal and drank some milk. It looked as if the run of blistering Mediterranean weather was going to last a few more days, and the boy had chosen to wear an *Iron Man* tee shirt and cerulean blue shorts.

He had tucked his bare feet into matching blue ankle socks, and then a pair of canary yellow sandals with Velcro straps. When he walked little lights built into the heels automatically flashed. Mohammed asked if they were his favourites. Jerome shrugged. He wasn't bothered about them, he explained, he couldn't even see them; but they made his mummy laugh, and mummy said a good laugh and a big hug was the best medicine.

He had chosen his wardrobe for the day as if it was his customary routine, much as he had chosen his breakfast. Even though Mohammed had told him it was lunchtime Jerome had insisted on having his cereal rather than an omelette or beans on toast.

'Breakfast,' he explained, 'is when you break your fast. That's why it's called breakfast. I haven't had anything to eat since yesterday, so I must break my fast and that means cereal. Mummy told me.'

Rose heard the exchange from the hallway and smiled. How could such a smart kid have such a prat for a father? When it came time to leave, Jerome had been very excited when Rose told him he would be riding to the hospital in a police car. But he was visibly disappointed when an unmarked, dark blue BMW pulled up outside the house. He soon perked up when he climbed into the back with Mohammed and saw the car's dashboard.

A large Automatic Number Plate Recognition screen stood proud next to a brightly coloured digital panel with flashing buttons for the sirens and lights. The car was filled with the murmur of radio chatter. Jerome's eyes gleamed when he heard the uniformed driver mention his name and he looked brightly at Mohammed, a happy smile on his face. Even so he still hugged his blue bunny comforter to his narrow chest. Mohammed pointed at it.

'So, Jerome, what's bunny called?'

Jerome lifted the toy to his eyes as if wondering where it had come from.

'Rabbit,' he answered. 'It's a rabbit. A blue rabbit. They aren't blue you know, not the real ones. Daddy said they are if they get cold enough, but he was just being silly. Mummy says he can be a right idiot sometimes, "a class idiot", she says, but not when he can hear her. He shouts at her, he does, but mummy says it's just the beer talking.'

Jerome's feet were lifted from the floor when he sat back in the seat and his legs swayed loosely from side-to-side with the motion of the vehicle. He sat quietly and idly stroked the ears of his rabbit while he watched the graphic displays on the ANPR screen. *A little boy on an outing* thought Mohammed.

Rose looked over her shoulder at him with a serious expression on her face.

'Jerome, can you remember anything about last night. Anything about your mummy and you?'

The boy's face looked vacant for a moment, he chewed one of the rabbit's ears while he thought about the question and Mohammed noticed how the ear was already slightly mangled. The chewing must be a stressor symptom. Rose's enquiry had stressed Jerome out. Why?

Through a mouthful of ear Jerome replied, 'I kissed her goodnight and went to bed. I was tired and hot. I fell asleep and had dreams. When I woke up I was all sticky and dirty, and a policeman was in my room. He was a nice policeman. He put cotton buds in my mouth, but he wouldn't let me brush my teeth. He used a prodder and a thing like mummy's tweezers he called four-steps to pull stuff from my teeth. Mummy had gone out. I heard daddy being loud. Sometimes he's loud and rude. He uses ugly words we mustn't say.'

Mohammed smiled at Jerome's interpretation on the word 'forceps' but said nothing to interrupt the boy's flow of consciousness.

Rose asked, 'What did you dream about?'

'The Lady.'

'What was she doing?'

Jerome moved his arms around. 'She was doing that and making blue light from her fingers. It was pretty. I felt happy when I saw it.'

Mohammed said, 'Why did you feel happy?'

'It was like sparklers on bonfire night, whoosh, whoosh, whoosh. And the Lady was happy, so she made me feel happy. Whoosh, whoosh...'

He hesitated. 'Her dog wasn't happy though. It was a big dog and it growled because of the lights. It wanted to protect the lights. It wanted to bite anyone who tried to stop the lights, bite them hard. It bit her. It bit her...'

'Bit who, Jerome?'

The boy put the rabbit's ear back in his mouth and began to chew again. He said nothing more and kept his head bowed most of the way to the hospital. He wouldn't respond to Rose's questions about the dog. She glanced meaningfully at Mohammed. He shook his head and fought a tremendous urge to hug the child next to him. He could feel the deep well of confusion filling the boy's heart, and his own heart had become choked with empathic pain.

A sudden inspiration grabbed him. He said, 'What was the Lady's dog called?'

The boy mumbled around his rabbit's ear.

Mohammed tried again, 'I'm sorry, Jerome. I didn't hear that. What was the dog called? Did it have a name?'

The boy pulled the ear from his mouth and looked up into Mohammed's face.

'It was called Jerome, like me. It was called Jerome and it bit her and made her bleed. She was so surprised she fell down. Okay? She fell like a cushion, plop, on the floor. And she made a noise like a squirrel when a fox catches it. The Lady did something that made her go all quiet and she touched her on the neck where the dog had bitten her. The dog was all dirty too, like me.'

'What did the Lady do to your... what did she do to the woman's neck? I don't understand.'

'She put magic in there. She filled the hole with magic. It didn't get better, but she stopped bleeding. Mummy stopped bleeding. Mummy?'

Jerome put his hand to his mouth in horror.

'It was mummy! The dog bit mummy and made her bleed!' He began to weep. 'Bad dog, bad dog, bad, bad dog! Bit mummy and made her bleed, bad, bad dog. The Lady tried to make it better. Where's mummy? Where is she? Where is she?'

Mohammed held him while all the pent-up shock exploded from his small, narrow frame in a high-pitched wail that sounded as if it had surged up from his bright yellow shoes.

The driver said, 'Should we take the lad home? Look at him, poor little bloke. He's in no fit state to visit a hospital. There are sick people in there, it isn't right.'

Mohammed took Jerome's balled fists into his own and held them.

He said, 'Jerome, we're going to see mummy now, but you have to be calm or they won't let you in. You must be good, you must be good now. Do you understand? It's all right, it's all right.'

Just as the car pulled into the hospital carpark Jerome used his fists to wipe the tears from his eyes and nodded. He blew his nose and gazed out at the blue and grey walls of St Joseph's. His eyes were those of a soldier, fresh from the field of battle.

37

Rose and Mohammed left the police driver in the Hospital Trust's Friends Café after promising to be back in less than an hour. Then Mohammed took one of Jerome's hands and the three made their way down the busy corridors. Stephanie Talbot was in the High Dependency Unit, or HDU. This gave her a degree of privacy she wouldn't get in an open ward.

When they reached the lobby at the entrance to the HDU the trio were stopped by a middle-aged nurse in a dark blue uniform who introduced herself as Adiba and asked who they were there to see. Jerome said, 'Mummy' which earned him a smile.

'And what is mummy's name, young man?'

Jerome frowned at this. Rose answered, 'Stephanie Talbot. She was brought in this morning.'

Adiba consulted a computer screen. 'Ah, yes. Partially healed neck trauma. She's doing very well but she has been sedated. I think her dressings are being changed at present. Would you wait here while I see if she's ready for you?'

She smiled brightly at Jerome, 'A lady likes to look her best for her men.'

Jerome shook his head, 'I'm her son, not her boyfriend. Daddy's her boyfriend but he's at work so I'm here. I'm wearing my flashy shoes to make her laugh, look!' He walked in a circle. 'See? Mummy thinks they're very funny, so I wore them.'

He marched around again, holding his arms out like a tightrope walker.

Adiba clapped, 'How delightful, and how very thoughtful. Your mummy's very lucky to have such a thoughtful boy. Now, I'll just be a minute.'

She vanished into the silent ward. The HDU is not so well staffed as an Intensive Care Unit, but it offers a higher degree of nursing than a standard open ward. Rose heard a stifled groan during the moment the doors were open, and then all became silent once more.

Jerome looked up at both of them. 'I need a wee-wee, please. I need it quite badly.' He hopped on the spot. 'I really have to go, please. Now.'

Mohammed scanned the signs overhead and spotted an arrow with the ubiquitous cut-out man and woman.

'Okay, Jerome. This way.'

The boy was skipping urgently by the time they reached the toilets, and Mohammed heard him sigh with relief through the cubicle door. The sound of urine splashing into the bowl continued for what seemed a long time. Jerome must have been nursing a full bladder for quite a while. He came out after flushing the toilet and sombrely marched to the lowest placed sink against the wall to wash his hands, which he did with a thoroughness that surprised Mohammed who was used to children giving their hands a cursory rinse.

Mohammed lifted Jerome up to the hand dryer while he rubbed his palms together with intense concentration. His hand was warm when Mohammed took it in his own once more.

When they returned to the lobby of the HDU a white coated man was talking with Rose and Adiba. All three gazed directly at Jerome as he and Mohammed made their approach. The man tilted his head inquisitively and touched his index finger to his lips thoughtfully. He said something to Rose who nodded. The man folded his arms tightly across his chest and drew his chin down and back against his protuberant Adam's apple. Mohammed had never seen such defensive posturing in a grown man before. He was acting like a five-year-old who had just been told Christmas was cancelled.

When Mohammed and Jerome reached the small group, the man spun on his heel and marched back through the double doors of the HDU without saying a word. He cast a solemn glance over his shoulder before the doors closed behind him, his lips twisted as if he had caught a strong whiff of something very unpleasant.

Adiba looked flustered. All trace of her smile had gone to be replaced by an expression of confused concern. She looked as if she was out of her depth and her feet couldn't touch the bottom.

'That was Mr Hyde,' she said. 'He's Mrs Talbot's Consultant.' She glanced at Rose who returned a blank stare. Adiba continued, 'Mr Hyde isn't sure it's a good idea to let Jerome see his mother just yet. Mrs Talbot has some, ah, issues, she needs to resolve, and she's been sedated. Mr Hyde believes visitors might be a distraction Mrs Talbot doesn't need at present. It might be a little too much for her, you see?'

Mohammed raised a hand, 'Surely a visit from her son will be acceptable? He's a quiet lad and won't make a fuss. He just wants to see his mother. He only needs to see she's all right. We'll just be a minute, that's all. Just a minute, will that hurt?'

Adiba shrugged and squirmed uncomfortably, looking behind her at the closed doors.

'Mr Hyde said he thought it was a bad idea. That's what he said.'

Rose frowned, 'He also said there was nothing he could do about it if we took Jerome in there anyway, isn't that right?'

'Well, yes. We can't ban family from the HDU, only make recommendations and requests. Mr Hyde strongly *requests* that you do not trouble Mrs Talbot today.'

Mohammed thought back to the petulant sulkiness of the Consultant's face. He looked down at the earnest and intelligent expression on Jerome's. He crouched down until they were eye to eye, never releasing the boy's hand from his own.

'Jerome,' he said. 'The doctor says that visitors might upset your mummy. He says it might be best to come back another day. What do you want to do?'

Jerome gazed at the double doors. 'Is mummy in there?'

'Yes, yes she is.'

'Will you come with me?'

'Yes, of course I will.'

The boy looked around. Mohammed followed his scanning eyes.

'What are you looking for, Jerome?'

'I'm looking for the Lady's dog that hurt mummy.'

'Is it here?'

Jerome pursed his lips then shook his head.

'I think it knows it was bad and it ran away. It's gone now. Can we see mummy, please?'

'Just for a minute, okay?'

The boy nodded, solemn as a priest. Something in Mohammed's chest tugged loose and he felt himself on the verge of tears.

'Right you are then, Jerome. Let's go see her.'

He rose back to his full height and addressed Adiba.

'Where is Mrs Talbot in the Unit, please, nurse? We are going to see her.'

'Mr Hyde said...'

Mohammed raised his hand palm out and nodded.

'Yes, we heard you. Please, relax. We will accompany Jerome. I am Jerome's friend and a paediatric psychiatrist; Miss Platt is an undercover police officer. She too is Jerome's friend. I can assure you and Mr Hyde that Mrs Talbot is safe from attack, and Jerome will only be in there long enough to see his mother and see that she's all right. So, please, where is Mrs Talbot in the Unit? Or do we have to disturb every patient in the room until we find her?'

'She's in bed five, the third one on the left-hand side.'

Mohammed thanked her and led the way into the subdued light of the ward. Jerome tightened his grip on the tall man's hand. Mohammed heard him counting under his breath as they walked between the beds. They reached the third on the left and stood at its foot. A woman lay prone under carefully folded sheets. Her blonde hair made a tousled halo around her pale face. Her eyes were open but unfocused until she saw Mohammed. They widened in alarm. She brought herself up on one elbow and looked down the bed to where Jerome stood gazing at her. Her hand reached up and touched her neck, she shook her head with fear in her eyes.

A high voice hissed into Mohammed's ear. 'I said no to this. What are you doing in here? Get out before I call the porters, and have you dragged out. Get out I say.'

Jerome broke away from Mohammed and walked to his mother's side. Hyde made as if to stop him but was held back by Rose. The Consultant made a frustrated whining sound. Mohammed watched in fascination as the boy leaned over and kissed his mother on the lips.

'I love you, mummy,' he said in a small, clear voice. 'The doctor says we can't stay so I've brought rabbit to look after you. He loves you too. I'll leave him here on your pillow. Look he's right here. I'll ask Dr Mohammed to bring me back when you feel better. Rabbit promises to keep the dog away, he'll keep you safe.'

He kissed her again, a tender and gentle touching of lips that she returned. And then he turned away and walked back towards Mohammed. Behind him his mother reached out a tentative hand. Her voice sounded croaky and oddly metallic.

'And I love you too, Jerome. I love you so much.'

The boy ran back and hugged her, she winced and emitted a little groan of pain.

'Sorry, mummy, sorry. I didn't mean to hurt you. Look I'm wearing my flashy shoes for you, see?'

Stephanie smiled weakly and stroked his cheek. Then she fell back against her pillows exhausted. Hyde raged inside. He wanted to shout but didn't want to disturb his other patients. The shallow keening sound he made reminded Mohammed of an old-fashioned steam kettle just coming to the boil.

'Enough, enough! I must insist you leave. Enough! You are tiring Mrs Talbot and frightening her. Get out!'

Stephanie said, 'My son will never frighten me, Mr Hyde. Don't talk such rot. Now, please, people are trying to sleep here and you're waking them up.'

Jerome stepped away from the bed, waved, and then returned to Mohammed's side, taking his hand once more.

'Can we go to your house, please?' he asked.

'You took the words right out of my mouth,' Mohammed replied, with a catch in his voice. 'Come on then.'

38

Pamela Clarkson and Marcus Williams found first class seats next to each other. Their train would deliver them to Norwood Junction in just over an hour, and from there they would transfer to a train for London Victoria. They had time to relax and catch up with the day's events. As the town dwindled into the distance behind them they both began to breathe more easily. A sense of normality settled over them.

They had left Charlie Croker in the Close. Williams had given him one of his business cards and told him that if he was ever in London he should give him a call and he would be Williams' guest for 'A bloody good dinner; my treat'. And he should not worry about expensive hotels. Chez Williams had a spare bedroom that was at his disposal whenever he needed it.

He had made the same offer to Clarkson and she had accepted without hesitation, accepted for that very same day.

'You and I,' she grinned, 'have started a conversation that I'm unwilling to put down just yet, if Mrs Williams has no objections?'

'Divorced these twelve years,' he told her. 'And well rid of the old hag. You know she never believed in the supernatural, called me a superstitious hack. Imagine that!'

'Ha, well, invite the woman here and ask her to fetch your glasses. Then see what she says. What time is your train back to London?'

'I've got a first class all day return, so whenever I like.'

'Brilliant, I'm in first class too, but mine is at twelve minutes past three. We've got just over an hour, come on.'

They had reached the platform with five minutes to spare after stopping off at Clarkson's house to grab her luggage and allow her to change her torn blouse and laddered knee highs. The archaeologist had made a quick phone call to her friend to let her know that she had made other arrangements so wouldn't be coming to stay. She couldn't mistake the faint note of relief in her friend's voice, something she mentally tucked away for future discussion. If the woman didn't want her there why did she keep saying yes?

After she performed her final checks around the house and locked her front door Clarkson wondered if she would ever see her home again. She looked up and down the quiet, familiar street and set her mouth into a grim line. She placed a resolute hand on Williams' arm.

'Let's go catch that train, shall we?'

Their sense of urgency began to ebb while the steady clatter of the train put miles between them and the town. British railway carriages are neither built for quiet nor comfort. They are basic conveyances for people who have no other option but to use them. Even first class was an example of minimum consideration for the customer, the only difference between it and the main part of the carriage being the doors and the plastic 'first class' covers on the head rests. But at least Clarkson and Williams had seats, no matter how uncomfortable, while the rest of the passengers suffered the misery of being tightly packed together in standing room only. This was largely due to the hordes of chattering, uniformed schoolchildren who had boarded after three thirty like an invasion of energetic puppies.

Williams sighed. 'Have you ever noticed that they never make the seats quite wide enough for normal people?'

'Yes, every time I climb into one of these miserable cattle carts.'

'So, then. What compelled you to suffer the slings and arrows of outrageous Southern Rail, and in rush hour too, instead of staying at home in your charming cottage?'

Clarkson dimpled, 'The thought of staying in your good company for a little while longer, my dear Marcus.'

He smiled back, 'The pleasure is all mine, my dear Pamela. But I believe you are being a little disingenuous with me, are you not? You had purchased your ticket before ever you met me. Am I right?'

Clarkson poked him in the shoulder, something she did when she was very pleased with someone. A rare event.

'There it is, the journalistic brain. The keen insight that made Mr Charles Dickens such a particular reporter of the human condition. See what is truly there and not what you expect to see. And yes, you are right.'

He nodded at her to continue, she looked at him blankly.

'Come out with it,' he said at last. 'So, why did you buy the ticket?'

'Oh, yes,' she almost purred like a satisfied cat. A sudden burst of noise interrupted her when the door to first class slid open and a dishevelled woman stepped inside.

'This is first class!' barked Clarkson. 'Have you got a ticket?'

'Oh, oh, sorry,' said the woman, and pressed back into the crush of the main carriage where the crowd swallowed her.

'Where was I?' said Clarkson. 'Oh, yes. History, my dear Marcus. History is why I bought my ticket. History and mystery. It is just, as you may say, just up your editorial alley.'

And she told her companion about a series of unusual finds around the Queen's Mount and what the latest events had told her.

'To begin with a Roman road was discovered while the by-pass was being built and we, the local historical society, were invited to dig it before it disappeared forever under the dual carriageway. So much of Britain is built on top of the relics of ancient times, much of it lost to us, Marcus, lost and gone.'

She breathed deeply, an impressive act that Williams appreciated with a connoisseur's eye. He had always told his friends that he liked his women the way he liked his dinner plate, plenty of meat on the bone.

Clarkson leaned towards him conspiratorially, pressing her bosom against his arm. He could feel her heat burning his flesh and experienced a thrill of excitement that had been missing from his life for more than a decade. He found it difficult to breathe, let alone concentrate on what she said next.

'The thing is,' she told him. 'The road ended suddenly in the middle of a field. Curb stones had been laid for a few yards after the metalling stopped, but that was it. It looked as if the workers had just put down their tools and walked away, except there were no tools. And that never happened. Roman roads always ran from one place to another, they never just stopped like that in the middle of nowhere, never.'

She leaned back, leaving Williams feeling a little bereft. Then she pressed forward again, to his great satisfaction. He began to realise how very attractive she was, almost kittenish.

'And there's more,' she breathed, warming to her subject. 'We found a charnel pit on the Mount. A mass grave. Hundreds of people, men, women, and children. Artefacts dated the find to around the time of the Roman invasion. It looked as if someone had murdered an entire settlement and dumped the bodies in a pit. Now, we know the Romans torched Boreshame – or Bosham as it became later, a lost Rotten Borough like Old Sarum – they burned it to the ground about then. So, are the road, the bodies and the burning connected? One would have to say yes, very likely. They were certainly contemporary. Romans would do such things if the locals gave them a good enough reason. We called it the "Mount Massacre", a bit cheesy, I know but it hit the local headlines.'

She pressed closer to him. 'And then we have the real mystery. This will fascinate a mind like yours, Marcus. The Legate in Chichester at the time was a chap called Vespasian, he would go on to give the whole of Dorset a good kicking and later became Emperor of Rome. We're talking about an important player on the fields of Mars. This was not some reed-backed, wet boy who got where he was thanks to his powerful father, no, Vespasian was the real deal. He had control of the Second Augustan Legion camped at Noviomagus Reginorum, sorry, Chichester, which was only about twelve miles from the Mount.

'Vespasian kept records, Romans were very like the Nazis in that respect, and we have access to some of them even today. These records tell us that something happened on the Mount back then. Something like two hundred men just vanished one night while they were camped there. The same thing happened to five hundred men a little later. We have no precise details of what happened, or how, but whatever it was Vespasian put the Mount out of bounds to his men and they marked it as a "cursed place".

'Your wife may have labelled you as superstitious, Marcus, but you would understand such a label as well as any Roman soldier. A cursed place that must be burned to ash because a gateway had opened to something terrible on the Mount and it had taken hundreds of seasoned men and swallowed them whole.'

She shivered at the thought. 'We're talking about men who had conquered the entire known world at the time, hard men at the height of their powers. And something on the Mount terrified them. It scared them away and they stayed away. What was it? What could do that to the pride of Rome? We don't know, but something is waking up in the town, and in the Cathedral Close. Something is playing with the landscape and turning trees into weapons. Something tore the bypass to shreds on the precise line where it crossed the secret path. People are being torn to pieces and the police are baffled. And who can blame them?'

She leaned back and gazed out of the window at the passing landscape.

'That's why I bought my ticket, Marcus. Because I believe that whatever it was that once terrified some of the hardest bastards who ever lived, has woken up once more after nearly two thousand years. It has a purpose and it will destroy anyone and anything that gets in its way. Let's watch the news tomorrow and see how much of the town's been left intact. I told them not to build that stupid bypass, but did they listen?'

Williams took her hand. 'They will tomorrow.'

She smiled bleakly, 'If there's anyone left to hear, Marcus. That's why I bought my ticket. I don't want to die just yet, I have too much living to do.'

Williams kissed her cheek, she turned and kissed his mouth.'

The other side of the glass of the first class partition a schoolboy nudged his friend and nodded towards the middle-aged couple embracing.

His friend pulled a face, 'Ewww, gross! And they're old! Is that even legal in a public place?'

[39]

The traffic congestion had eased enough for the police driver to choose to drop Rose at the station and then chauffeur Mohammed and Jerome back to the tall man's house. There was no need to resort to a helicopter, much to Mohammed's relief. Even so he was distracted. Rose had seemed to enter a fugue state during the drive as if she was listening to music no-one else could hear. Jerome had tried to engage her in conversation, but she had answered his comments with nothing more than monosyllabic grunts and vague noises.

Thoughts wove and flickered behind her startlingly blue eyes. If she was wool-gathering, Mohammed thought, she would soon have enough wool to knit blankets for every household in the UK. Her lips moved soundlessly while she gazed fixedly out of the car window.

Mohammed would have asked her what was on her mind, but he was very aware of Jerome and everything the boy had been through just recently. It would be wrong to add to his concerns by indicating that one of the few adults he had come to trust was acting strangely.

When the car swung into the police station grounds Rose climbed quickly out, muttered her goodbyes, and was gone without a backward glance. While the car edged back out into the stream of traffic Mohammed watched her. She didn't enter the station but headed away from it with a determined stride. Jerome took his big hand in his smaller, more delicate fist.

'I like her,' he said. 'But she's acting funny, like a puppet person.'

Mohammed smiled quizzically. 'I like her too. But, what's a puppet person?'

Jerome became animated. 'Nanny took to me to the theatre and there were puppet people and animals. And the people and the animals were on strings, except for the ones with people inside them making them work.' His eyes shone. 'It was magical, really amazing, better than telly. Nanny told me that people called puppeteers were making everything move. They seemed real, but they weren't, they were being controlled. Nanny said, "They couldn't move a thing if people didn't pull their string." It was like magic. There were flying fairies and dragons and a caterpillar bigger than me.'

Rose had moved out of sight. Mohammed wondered where she was going.

He said, 'And you think somebody is pulling Rose's string?'

Jerome frowned. 'No, silly. She doesn't have real strings. But she looks like she's being controlled or something. Don't you think?'

165

'I don't know. I do know what you mean, Jerome, but maybe there's somewhere she needs to be, something on her mind, you know?'

Jerome nodded. 'I know. Nanny calls it "Having a bee in your bonnet". She said I had so many bees in my bonnet that it flew off, which is why I don't have a bonnet anymore. It's a type of hat, you know.'

Mohammed smiled, 'I like the sound of your Nanny.'

'She looks nice too, like mummy but a bit fatter.'

Mohammed heard a muffled sound and looked up to see the police officer at the wheel. His shoulders were quivering with supressed laughter. Mohammed grinned at the man's eyes reflected in the rear-view mirror. The police officer winked gleefully.

Rose was not a puppet person that afternoon. But she had a bee in her bonnet, and it was a large noisy buzzing bee that wouldn't let her rest. She had to go back to Florence Mayhew's cottage to see if she could find *something* there that might explain what was going on. She knew where her old friend hid her spare key and she could spend the rest of the afternoon rummaging around to see what might turn up. Flo' had never been a bad person, Rose reasoned, but something wicked had come to West Sussex and Flo' was involved. How?

Rose quickly traversed the town centre and crossed the bridge over the canal. Within minutes the sounds of traffic had ebbed away behind her and she was walking along the lush, tree-lined road that led to Mayhew's cottage. It was a familiar route and brought the same surge of excitement she had always felt when she approached the beautiful house and garden.

Whatever happened during her visits with the older woman she always came away feeling as if a greater world had touched her, almost as if she had breathed the air of Narnia, or Oz. Mayhew lived at a different angle to reality than most people, she made life more fun. The world was a much poorer place without her in it. At that thought the sunlight seemed suddenly darkened.

Rose slowed her pace as she approached the gate. There was a strong smell of dust and damp earth on the air, almost as if someone had been digging a deep trench. She wondered if it was wafting up from the ruin of the bypass, but the scent seemed earthier with no trace of burned fuel and melted tyres. She gave a mental shrug and opened the gate.

The winding path towards the cottage was the same as it ever was, right up to the time one rounded the corner to experience the reveal of the building's fine Tudor lines. What met her eyes brought a stunned gasp to her lips.

Mayhew's beautiful home had gone, and the site where it had stood for some five hundred years was a scene of utter devastation. Not one brick remained on top of another and an arc of water gushed up from the torn and twisted mains pipes.

Sparks of electricity flickered in the spray, which told her the supply was obviously still live, and now she was closer Rose could also detect a strong smell of gas. She quickly got herself well away from what had once been a picture postcard slice of Ye Olde England. She put distance between herself and it, before an errant spark could cause the gas to erupt. How there wasn't already a sheet of flame pouring from the ground escaped her. She positioned herself the other side of the road and rang the station to get someone onto the gas people. She made her call and started to replace her phone in her back pocket.

That was when the world went white and she was thrown several feet back into the line of trees and tangled shrubbery. She was stunned, and her ears rang oddly. Rose could almost imagine a line of small singing birds circling her head, as if she was a cartoon character who had been hit with a rock. When she struggled to her feet she found her clothes caught on long thorns. Her hands and legs had also been badly scratched.

When she regained her trembling feet and tried to walk she slipped and sprawled headlong deeper into the thorn bushes from which she fought to extricate herself again. She battled a strong urge to weep with frustration and anger. It took her several minutes to get back to the road, and during that slog the tender areas on her back began to twinge in earnest.

The gas had caught, just as she feared it might. The cottage's front garden was now a twisted mess and a column of flame erupted towards the flat blue sky. Rose had never been blown up before and wasn't sure of the protocol for reporting it. She was saved the trouble when she fished her phone out and studied it for long seconds. The cracked screen told her the phone was useless.

Should she walk into town for help? Or should she stay where she was and keep the public away from the fire? That decision was taken out of her hands when she saw two marked squad cars hurtling towards her with lights and sirens given full play.

Sergeant Fowler was the first by her side and he insisted she be given a lift back to her place as soon as she had completed her report.

'You've been in the wars, Rose. On top of everything else you've been through I'm surprised you're still on your feet. If you were a cat you'd have precious few lives left. Go home, it's either there or back to the hospital. Your choice.'

She went home where she showered at length before tending to her wounds. Rose was surprised. They seemed to be healing very quickly and her bruises were slighter than they should be. Her clothes were ruined, and she should have been a mass of welts and contusions. However, her skin was smooth and almost unblemished. *Had she been very lucky?* And then she thought about Flo's tincture, *or was something else at work in her body?*

She climbed into fresh clothes, something lightweight that reflected the sticky heat of the early evening. There was nothing of the police officer in the beautiful woman she saw reflected in her full-length mirror. And then she decided to go out for a good meal somewhere local. It had been a crazy day, so she believed she deserved a bit of a treat. Who knows it might be one of the last meals of her short life, so she might as well savour it.

She knew the battle for the sacred path wasn't over, but she had to do what she could to stop more carnage from happening. And she had decided to hold a vigil every night, lay in wait to confront and plead with the Lady, whom she believed to be Florence Mayhew. If she was right, she would win much more with her feminine charm than she ever would with a gun.

40

Councillor Larry Shay believed himself to be an astute man. He knew he had recently become very unpopular, and he knew why. He had Chaired the working committee that had agreed the new bypass placement between the old Iron Age fort and the town. Folk wisdom and popular opinion had been strongly against him, but the alternative had meant putting the road in a long loop around the other side of the ancient Mount, and that would have added miles and millions of pounds to the cost. Millions the Council didn't have. But the locals weren't happy.

'What would you have?' he had argued. 'Happy tree huggers or hospital beds and bobbies on the beat? We can't have both. And anyway, this is the twenty-first century not the fifteenth. We must be pragmatic about this, can't you see? What do you think's going to happen? Will a bunch of witches come flying down on broomsticks and kill us all in our beds? The fuss will soon die down, don't you worry. So, please, give me a show of hands. Who says aye to the proposed route? Thank-you, the ayes have it.'

Even so it had been a narrow victory and he had had to veto the idea of a recount, despite the clamour from some of his team. The Clarkson woman from the local historical society had since become something of a pest after the plans for the new bypass had been posted, as had the Mayhew creature. Shay had promised an independent review, which, unsurprisingly, had since outlined the clear 'economic and logistical' benefits of the bypass.

It was noted that the track of an ancient public footpath would be lost under the dual carriageway, and the review had insisted that the plans include either a bridge or an underpass. The people's right to ramble must never be usurped by town planners.

The bridge had been built after a competition to find a design that would best reflect its location in the heart of an area of outstanding historical and natural beauty, a description that would appear to ignore the four lanes of fresh tarmac that the bridge was destined to straddle.

The judges had discarded as impractical designs that called for wooden supports or looked like the lost palisades of the old fort. They finally plumped for an almost art deco design, one that used pierced steel to depict the ring of the Sisters and the old fort as they might have appeared when new, the rays of the sun blazing across them.

Shay had walked down the secret path to the bypass when a local TV 'celebrity' he didn't recognise opened the bridge and had declared it 'an instant classic and a fine addition to the architecture of the old town'.

He had pretended to ignore the sullen glances and growled threats he received from the locals and was glad for the strong police presence on that day. He had never been back, neither to the secret path or the bypass, although he had gazed across to the gate when he visited the cathedral on a Sunday for the morning service.

'What do they want?' He had asked his wife over their breakfast toast and coffee. 'What do they want? Ancient myths and magicians or modern midwives?'

That had been his theme during his interviews about the bridge and the bypass on local radio and the TV news channel. It had also been picked up by the press, and the headline 'MYTHS OR MIDWIVES' had been blazoned across Thursday's editions.

Shay did not equate the secret path with events on the bypass over the previous Sunday night and Monday morning. He preferred to toe the party line and regard what happened as an unfortunate multiple vehicle collision caused by freak localised weather conditions. The fact that the surface of the road had been ploughed up was a side-effect that would be explained by logic, not magic.

He looked out of his office window. The sun was still shining, and it was casting a warm orange glow across the town. He could just see the canal and it rippled like liquid gold.

You want magic? He thought. *Well, there it is. In the light of the late summer sun across the beautiful place I call home.*

He stood and walked to his window and gazed out at the view. He could see the park to his left, and the hill rising to the Cathedral Close on his right. To the south was the sea, he knew that, and to the east the Downs, which rolled in chalk swells across miles of land. Sway breathed deeply, almost as if he could take a sip from the exquisite brew of light and colour that met his eyes.

The roads still looked jammed, though. He looked at his watch. Coming up for seven o'clock. Time to call it a night. Sway was a first man in, last man out, kind of boss. He believed in setting examples for his team. He had no idea how much they resented him for it. He fetched his jacket from the back of his door and shrugged it on before turning off his table lamp.

He had begun walking to work because the roads had been so bad all week. He would enjoy his walk home, building up an appetite for dinner. He wondered what Brenda would delight him with that evening. No microwaved 'recipe bing' from the good Mrs Shay, no sir. Everything she prepared was fresh and delicious, and tonight was a Friday. She would be sure to delight him with a weekend special.

He chuckled at the memory of a teenage nephew who had spent time with them earlier that summer. He had gone into the kitchen to grab himself an afternoon snack and had come out again looking baffled.

'You've got no food in the house,' he exclaimed. 'Just a load of ingredients!'

Shay brought himself back to the here and now with a wrench. The lift doors were just closing as he approached. He quickened his step.

'Sorry, excuse me! I say!' He yelled. 'Please, just a second. Hold up there. Room for a little one inside?'

After a brief pause the doors opened again to a darkened interior. The lights from the corridor seemed unable to illuminate the space. Inside he could just barely discern a single shadowy figure. It was a woman.

'Are the lights out again?' he asked 'They really should do something about this. It's the second time this year.'

He received no reply. The doors started to close again. He hastened to step inside, and they shut behind him. The only light in the lift was the faint line of red emergency lighting around the edges of the ceiling. It took his eyes a moment to adjust to the gloom. The woman seemed to be standing with her back to him. He found her silence unsettling, which made him garrulous.

'I say, are you, all right? I'm Larry Shay, you know? Councillor Larry Shay? You must be one of the cleaners I suppose, this late in the day? Most of the other workers will have gone home I expect, it is nearly seven. You people do wonderful work keeping the place so clean after we spend the day messing it up. So, then, what time will you finish? Hmm?'

She turned to face him. At first, he thought she must be one of those dark-skinned women he sometimes saw on the telly. An Ethiopian or Somalian. She was certainly slim enough. He continued his stream of questions.

'Ah, nice to meet you. Have I seen you before? I thought I might recognise such a distinctive face.'

And then his brain finally accepted what his eyes were seeing. He stepped away from the shadowy figure and pressed himself back against the lift's wall. The woman's face had no features. She was a woman-shaped shadow in the gloom.

'I don't... who are you? *What* are you? Please, don't hurt me.'

Shay also realised that the lift had come to a stop.

'What's happening? What do you want from me? What do you want?'

And then the shape of the woman melted away before his eyes like ice in a furnace. She flowed downwards and puddled on the floor like black water. At first, he looked down with a sense of relief. Perhaps he had been overworking and his mind was playing tricks on him. He had always known he had an overactive imagination.

He spoke aloud. 'Seeing ghosts in the lift, Shay? You're working too hard, time you booked a holiday old lad. Brenda needs the break too.'

Something stroked his ankle and he looked down. With a growing sense of panic, he realised that the surface of the puddle was rising up his legs. He forgot to breathe while he watched the black liquid climb the walls of the lift, all the while immersing his body. He began to thrash helplessly about, frantically crying for help, and then screaming while hammering on the lift walls. The swelling sounds of his panic echoed up the lift shaft and around the empty Civic Offices. The sounds stopped when the liquid finally filled his mouth and nostrils and he began to drown. Death took several minutes. Agonising minutes.

41

Phil Coombe was feeling worse despite his doctor's assertions that his wounds were healing well. Rose had been in to see him and had brought along a strange green drink that she made him promise to swallow as soon as she had left him alone. He couldn't get past the smell of the stuff and had dumped it down the toilet without tasting it.

Charlie Croker has also been in to see him. Phil thought Charlie was looking much better. He too had been given a green drink by Rose and he had done as he was told and downed the stuff in one, followed by a large shot of whisky.

'I don't know what was in that stuff, Phil, but it gave me a dose of the trots something terrible. I've never felt so bad, I mean it turned me inside out. And I was throwing up this horrible black muck too. I didn't know which end to put over the pot. I got myself in a right mess. I think I lost a stone in weight in less than two hours. It wore off quickly enough, but I had to spend over half an hour in the shower trying to make myself feel clean again, you know what I mean? Would you like a mint? Sorry about my breath, I'm still trying to get rid of that taste. Never drunk anything like it.'

And Croker had shuddered at the memory. Coombes was glad he had passed up on that one, and he wondered what Rose had been playing at. It wasn't like her to play tricks on people like that. She was a nice girl, in fact if he was honest about it, he had fancied her ever since he first met her at the station. His own wife, Carole, was a pet, but Rose was top notch. He knew she was well out of his league, but she never acted like it. She always smiled when she met him, and she sympathised with him when Hines treated him like her own personal minion. She had spent her time there, under Hines calloused thumb. She knew what it felt like.

So why would she want to make him ill like that? Was it meant to be funny?

And there it was again, the building surge of irrational anger that had him clenching his teeth and balling his fists into tight knots, his mind a boiling mass of furious resentment. He felt like a pressure cooker about to explode.

Police medical insurance had paid for his private room at St Joseph's for the last few days, same as it had for Rose, but ever since he had arrived he had suffered the constant to-ing and fro-ing of nurses, doctors, and visitors. He couldn't settle, and he was sure Rose hadn't had to put up with this much disturbance. Things had seemed quiet enough in her room when he had visited her, very peaceful in fact. What was it about him that brought every bugger in the building to his door every five minutes?

There sounded another knock at his door and a white-coated, middle-aged, solidly built woman walked in. She looked him over as if she was judging him for a dog show. He tried to keep his irritation out of his voice.

'Can I help you, miss?'

She shook her head, 'I doubt it. You're Coombes, yes? You're the stab victim. I'm Alice Stubbs, pathology. Doctors say you're not responding to treatment very well, so I'm just going to check a few things to see if there's residual infection in any of your samples. We'll take some blood but first we need to get a nice stool sample. Have you used a bed pan recently?'

He thought about it. 'No.'

'Would you be willing to try for me?'

'I don't know if I can.'

'Well, let's have a crack at it, shall we?'

The word 'we' ignited blind fury in Coombes' normally placid heart.

'All right,' he hissed. 'If *we're* going to try, you go first. Show me how it's done.'

And he climbed menacingly from his bed.

The sounds of the pathologist's screams brought her colleagues running. It took two of them to pull Coombes away from the cowering woman and a third to drag the bedpan from his hands before he could wield it like a club. All trace of the mild police officer was gone, replaced by a snarling demon in human form. He kept hissing like a snake and repeating, 'Shall we try it, shall we? Shall we try it? You go fucking first, lady, you go first! Shall we try it...?'

Coombes didn't calm down until he had been sedated with an injection administered by a junior doctor. Stubbs had been led away weeping and explaining that all she wanted was a stool sample. No-one had ever reacted like that before, she said. Was the man mad? Crazy people didn't belong in a hospital, they wanted locking up. She would be talking to her union rep before the day was out, you see if she didn't.

In his bed the sedated Coombes writhed and muttered. Dark foam flecked his lips and nostrils. Bright blood flooded from his mouth when he bit his tongue, but in every other respect he was grey. A sheen of oily sweat gleamed on his skin and his eyes glowed as thin white crescents, opened barely a crack.

174

Within his skull flowed dark images of violence, macabre scenes of the very worst things one human can do to another. And all the while the presence that had taken root in him during the attack by the Sisters dug deeper into his tissues. It crouched in his bones and waited, biding its time until it had its next opportunity to lash out and hurt and maim. The Lady had released it from its ancient grave and given it this flesh to use, and its time would come. It would come soon.

Even though he was unconscious Coombes' bitter smile sent a chill of fear up the spines of the two porters who had been asked to keep an eye on him while decisions were made about what to do with him. He was, after all, an injured police officer and had to be treated with respect. The obvious solution was to restrain the man, either physically or chemically. The porters would have been a lot happier if Coombes had been strapped down.

One of them looked at the door. 'Fancy a cuppa? I'll fetch it. Two sugars ain't it? White? I'll only be a minute.'

He stood up, the other did the same.

'Hold up, you don't think you're leaving me alone with this nutter, do you? Leave it out. I'm coming with you.'

'Yeah? Well I need a piss. I was going to do that first then grab the teas.'

'Well, so do I. Look, let's leave him alone for five minutes. He's out for the count, he's not going anywhere. We go, we shut the door on him, then we come back, okay? Nobody knows and everybody's happy.'

'I don't know.'

All right, look, how about this? I go for a slash and grab the teas. You wait here until I come back and then it's your turn. Sound good to you?'

'Fuck that, let's go. Better be quick.'

By the time the men returned Coombes was gone. The dishevelled, bloodstained bed was empty. In the vain hope that the policeman was hiding somewhere they searched under his bed, one of them even opened the bedside cabinet to look inside. Then they raised the alarm.

Coombes had staggered out of St Joseph's like a puppet with broken strings, but no-one had tried to stop him. He was bloodstained and drooling an odd black fluid, plus he was barefoot and wearing a hospital gown under a raincoat he had lifted from the porters' mess. Even so, hospital staff had seen stranger sights during their working day, and patients had enough to worry about with their own ills.

St Joseph's was over a mile from the town. The raggedy man walked the pavements past pedestrians who presumed he was drunk or drugged, and he doggedly wove his way around the Friday rush-hour motorists who just wanted to get home as quickly as their achingly slow, stop-start progress could get them there.

The gridlock caused by the incident on the bypass had eased somewhat since the nightmare of the previous Monday morning, but there were still long tailbacks and delays on every major route around the town. The haunted grey shade presented by Coombes wasted body flitted unnoticed through the crammed streets until he reached the secret road and climbed towards the cathedral.

'You all right, dear?'

The elderly woman asked her question with a note of genuine concern in her voice. Her eyesight wasn't too good, but she could see that the man walking jerkily towards her was in some distress.

She repeated, 'Are you, all right? Do you need a hand or something? Can I get you anything?'

She was one of life's lonely angels. Always ready to lend a helping hand, even to a stranger. Coombes bent and examined her softly lined face. He grinned and showed her the blood on his teeth. His answer was slurred because he had bitten his tongue.

'Fuck off before I reach down and pull your arse out through your mouth and eat it, you stupid old piece of shit.'

The woman gasped in horror and scurried away in tears. Coombes chuckled nastily and continued his stalking stumble towards the Close and the stone circle, his final destination.

As he approached the ring of yew trees they opened to him and made a gateway for his passage. He stepped through and saw the resurrected henge. He entered and lay down on the sacrificial stone. At last he could rest. The trees closed behind him. Within the hour his wife had become a widow and the thirsty stone had taken her husband's body into itself. The final stain of his spilled blood evaporated and was gone.

[42]

For four nights the Lady rested, and each night a keen wind blew across her memory. While she waited for her energy to build ready for her final act she cast her prodigious mind back, back to a time when she had been worshipped. Back to a time when she was known as Agrona. It was long ago, almost two millennia. In her mind's eye she revisited an ancient place, a grassed and wooded place under a winter sky of banded lead. It was 44AD and a small group of cloaked men rode small horses towards her. She sighed and settled down to watch.

The bypass was not the first time men had planned a road to cross the sacred path. The Romans had attempted to build a road to connect the city of Londinium in the east to the major military settlement they named Noviomagus Reginorum – or New Fields of the Regnenses after the local tribes who lived in the area – and known today as Chichester. The road's most logical route would take it close by the ancient fort of Boreshame.

The builders planned to skirt the earthen ramparts of the fort on its eastern side, while also avoiding the west flank of the hill facing it, on which stood a ring of standing stones. They would take their road straight through the middle, threading the shallow valley between them.

Forts and earthworks were things the Romans understood very well. Anything to do with warfare or defence was as meat and drink to them. However, rings and columns of standing stones meant little or nothing to them, although they had seen enough of them to know them well. There were plenty of them in the empire, but they were an enigma Romans chose to ignore.

They had found them in Gaul and the frozen north, and in the lands around the Mediterranean, including Egypt and Anatolia. The island Prydain, which the Roman's called Britannia, seemed littered with them. Their engineers could appreciate how much craft had been expended in shaping, moving, and positioning such heavy rocks, but who put them there and why was a mystery. Some said they were clocks, others believed they were calendars. The Romans considered them irrelevant. Stones were a mystery they had little time to puzzle in their drive to conquer and unite the known world under the Pax Romana – and bring whole countries under the shadow of the imperial eagle.

All of this ran through the minds of the engineers while they approached the cut between the fort and the hill and saw on one side the ring of white stones gleam in the chill winter sun and on the other the strong palisades facing it. They had ridden forward from the main party to map the terrain and plan the new road's optimum route. Much like modern builders they needed to get maximum return for their time and effort; however, unlike most modern builders they also built to last. The foundations of Roman roads were chosen carefully and laid well. The heavy curbs first and then the layers of metalling between. The technique had been proven over centuries. Once the roads were built the army could move along them faster than across any natural terrain. They could move quickly to attack or defend. Roads carried the life-blood of empire and the engineers who built them had status.

It is a common myth that Roman's only ever built their roads – known then as 'Via' or 'Cammini' – in straight lines. Straight lines were the shortest distance between two points, but the engineers would also always follow the path through the landscape that offered the least resistance. They knew it was usually faster to go around a hill than over it or through it, and it was less expensive to find a ford across a river than build a bridge. These engineers were skilled military men who quickly gauged the lie of the land and knew how to turn it to their best advantage.

And then they reached Boreshame.

Their names are lost to history, but the Lady watched in memory as the engineers, four of them centurions, reached the pathway between the fort and the stones, where they were met by a party formed of the fort's priests and a band of seasoned warriors. The priests spoke the ancient British language of Prydain as well as the local dialect. The Romans had at least one translator in their party. The priests and British warriors were on foot, so the Romans dismounted to parley on an equitable level. So far, so routine.

They met on the broad chalk path that ran from the circle of stones to the fort's great wooden gate, a path wide enough for four men to march along it in line abreast. The priests were cultured men, bearded and swathed in robes and intricate jewellery. Serpents and spirals featured heavily on their belts and torques. The warriors were armoured in wooden plate and iron, all bound together by leather. They carried long spears and their unbarbered hair was plaited to keep it out of their eyes when in battle. All the Britons were elaborately tattooed in blue and green woad, their skin densely covered with images of fierce, totemic animals.

The Romans wore lightweight iron armour and trousers under their heavy cloaks. The weather was too cold for the familiar skirt. They each had a gladius or short stabbing sword sheathed and belted to their waists. The air tasted of ice, but their reception by the indigenous people was warm. There was no hint of threat. Not yet.

The British politely introduced themselves, as was their nature, and asked the Romans the purpose for their visit. When they were told about the planned road they respectfully explained to the Romans that, for religious reasons, they could not allow them to bring their road across the sacred path on which they stood. It would be best to take it around the far, western side of the fort's earthworks. They would even lend them tribesmen to help with any extra work.

Through his translator the chief engineer brusquely explained why that wasn't possible, and that for expediency the road would have to come through the valley between the fort and the hill.

'It will come through here,' he growled. 'Here where we stand. And nowhere else.' He would brook no argument.

'No,' protested the head priest. 'Cross this path and you will anger the goddess Agrona. You must not do that. The people of Boreshame will not allow it. There will be bloodshed. It would be best to go around.'

Romans do not respond well to threats. The chief engineer was a blunt man, a soldier, and a centurion. In his mind the Britons were a conquered people and these protests angered him. He lashed out with a hard-practiced fist and knocked the head priest to the ground.

'The soldiers of Rome marched to this place through rivers of blood,' he barked. 'We've seen whole countries brought to their knees. One little fort in a backwater place like Britannia will be wiped away like so much shit from a woman's arse. This Roman road is coming right through here, and if your goddess tries to do anything about it she'll soon find out what it's like to be fucked witless by Roman men before we kill her with Roman iron and hand you her fucking head on a Roman spike!'

The insult was more than the warriors of Boreshame could stand. They rushed at the engineering party, quickly overpowering, and killing them all. The Lady felt the hot thrill of the remembered massacre deep in her belly. The action was fast and brutal, but it had been witnessed by three soldiers standing guard unnoticed several hundred yards away. They fled, running the few miles back to the work site, where they told the senior optio, the dead lead centurion's second in command, what they had seen.

180

He conferred with his peers and agreed that the situation was too grave for the work party and four centuries of untried troops to deal with. Thirty-two men against a fort, even if backed by over one hundred workers with road building tools, would most likely be slaughtered like sheep.

He sent messengers on fast horses to Noviomagus Reginorum, which hosted the winter fort for the Second Augustan Legion under the Legate Vespasian. The sun set on the Reginorum Downs and the optios settled their men in defensive positions, down amongst the dense treeline away from the road. They banned fires for cooking or heating, asking their belligerent troops whether they really wanted a hot meal in their bellies if it was to be followed by cold Britannic iron if the Fort's warriors saw the light.

The senior optio told them, 'The bastards already know we're here. Let's stay down, safe, and out of sight for just one night. We'll be warm and eating a hot meal soon enough once the Legion gets here. So, stop your grousing and get down out of sight.'

Grumbling, his men complied and settled down for an uncomfortable night. By sundown the next day the world of Boreshame would be changed forever

The sun had barely washed the faintest hint of pearlescent light into the eastern sky when the sound of a host of marching boots clattered and echoed from the southwest. There was nothing stealthy about the approach of the legion. Centurions bellowed, and the men stamped along in columns consisting of three cohorts of five hundred apiece. The centurions rode alongside them on small but sturdy horses.

The pilus prior, the senior centurion, was named Titus Petrus. He rode at the head of the column, all the while scanning the terrain with a keen and wary eye. The Britons had previously proved themselves to be clever guerrilla fighters and he didn't want to give them the chance to ambush his men or cut them down with arrows. The natives were brave and resourceful people and they were willing to die to defend their country. If they attacked, he would try to make sure they got their wish.

The first cohort consisted of unseasoned troops, which was the Roman way. Petrus didn't want to waste experienced men by throwing them at enemy lines from the front. Seasoned fighters could do more damage to an enemy by attacking once the Britons had exhausted themselves fighting well trained but greener troops.

The senior optio from the work party galloped his horse through the disputed cut between fort and hill, bent low over the creature's neck to make himself less of a target. He expected arrows to thud into the ground around him, but his passage was peaceful, and he reached the head of the column unscathed. Petrus greeted him with a salute, hand raised. He wasted no time on niceties.

'Optio, well met. So, then, to business. I'm told Romans died here. Is it true?'

'Yes, sir. Witness reports say that the Britons slaughtered them over there on that path. They didn't stand a chance.'

'How many did the bastards kill?'

'Five, sir. Four centurions and a road's man, all of them engineers. Experienced and valuable men.'

'The bastards will pay for that. What set them off?'

'We don't know. The guards were too far away to hear anything. One minute they were parlaying like civilised men and the next the Britons fell on them. I'm told my centurion punched a priest.'

'Antonius? He always was hot-headed. You've got to be careful around these people, they flare up like tinder. So would I if I had to survive in this shithole at the end of the world. What in Hades does Augustus Claudius want with it?'

'Who knows what the Emperor wants? So, is the Legate coming?'

'No, he's too busy politicking to worry about a single British fort. He's got his eyes turned to the west with plans to expand the empire and earn himself a Triumph in Rome. This is conquered territory, centurions' work. Don't get me wrong, he's brave enough. If there had been an army here he would have been the first in the field. So then, what have we got? What are we up against?'

Petrus learned what the optio knew, which wasn't much. Boreshame was more like a heavily defended settlement than a military fort. The friendly locals, the Regini of the larger Atrebates clan, said the tribe had always been there, but they didn't mix with their neighbours. Some said they might be part of the Belgae clan, but they never acknowledged it.

'They trade with the locals, and that's about it. Otherwise they keep themselves to themselves. The priests are Druids, they know that.'

'How do they know?'

'Rumours of sacrifice, human sacrifice. Up there.'

The optio pointed up the hill towards the stones. Petrus sniffed loudly and rubbed the back of his hand along his muscled jaw.

'Ignorant barbarian shits. Right, how many of them?' he asked.

The optio shook his head. 'We can't be sure. Locals estimate somewhere between five hundred and a thousand, could be more. Men, women, and children. These are families, they live and work here. This is their land. We've never needed to know their fighting strength, why should we? We didn't think we would be fighting them. We thought this whole area paid allegiance to King Togidubnus and he's got Roman coins in his pouch. But no, turns out these people plough their own furrow. How could we have known?'

'You couldn't, and no matter. They've killed Romans. That means if they're ploughing their own furrow it heads straight to Tartarus. They die today. All of them. Hello, what's this?'

Petrus pointed over the optio's shoulder. A group of men had exited the great gate and descended the path to where the attack had taken place. They faced the column and waited.

The optio said, 'Calm as you like. Looks like they want to talk.'

Petrus called for the translator and a century of men to join him.

He grinned at the optio, 'Let's see what the green faced bastards have to say, shall we?'

The optio grinned back. 'Then what?'

'Then? 'Then we burn the place to the ground with them in it. Come on.'

Petrus dismounted and the optio followed suit. The centurion led his party to the Britons, the optio at one shoulder and his translator at the other. Behind them marched eighty armoured men, gladii and shields at the ready. To their rear the column's sagittarii, or archers, moved forward and nocked arrows onto their bow strings ready to loose a deadly volley if the Britons made a wrong move.

The blue and green tattooed warriors carried spears as before, and as before one of the bearded priests stepped forward to be the spokesman. His voice was gentle and formal.

'Greetings, Romans. Welcome to Boreshame. May I ask, why are you here in such great numbers?'

Petrus answered tersely. 'Sweetly said. Do you always welcome strangers like that before you murder them? Is that your practice?'

'We do not murder strangers here. Why would you say such a thing?'

'You killed five Romans here yesterday, here on this very spot. See, there is the blood. Was that not murder?'

The priest looked at the blood spatter in the dust and smiled.

'No, my friend, not murder. That was self-defence. The men attacked us. They knocked me to the ground and blasphemed against our goddess. They said things I would not repeat for fear my tongue would be ripped from my mouth, and rightly so. My men defended me and themselves. We had no choice. We would not have war with Rome over five cruel and violent men who spoke foully of our goddess. We understand that you feel anger for your loss, but it was not murder. You have no call to be here, or to threaten us with your army.'

Petrus stepped closer to the priest, close enough that when he spoke his spittle glistened in the man's long beard.

He pointed up towards the heavy palisades of the fort. 'Army? Do you think Rome sends an *army* to deal with a wasps' nest like that pile of shit? Don't flatter yourselves.'

He prodded a hard finger into the man's chest. 'We're here as urban cohorts and we're committed to keep the peace and to protect innocent people from violent little gangs of murderous scum like you. You are charged with committing a crime, the crime of murder, and you will be arrested and tried fairly in the Legate's court. Then you will be found guilty and executed.'

He turned to his men, 'Take them. Take them in chains.'

From the walls of the fort the warriors of Boreshame saw their priests and leaders being manhandled by rough, armoured soldiers and they made their last and ultimately fatal mistake. The great gates were flung open and hundreds of men and women streamed out to attack the legion of Rome. They were skilled and brave fighters, but they stood no chance against the battle-hardened discipline of the column.

The first to die were the Britons and priests in the hands of Petrus' men. Mercy is always the first victim of war, and as soon as the warriors of the fort broke cover the captives were cut down without another word. Freed of their prisoners Petrus and his group ran full pelt back to the column under the cover of a hail of arrows, pursued by screaming British warriors. Prydain valued the fighting arm of a woman as much as it did the prowess of a man, and the ululation of female voices was just as loud as the cries of the men.

The column had smoothly raised its defensive shield wall, which opened just long enough to allow Petrus' group to rejoin the ranks, and then closed once more. Like the spines of an iron porcupine the shield wall bristled with pila, spears more than six feet long. The Britons' armour provided little defence against the jabbing spear points, and while they furiously tried to find a way through the impassable shield wall they were skewered and died.

Then, impossibly, the armoured column began to move. Despite being harried on all sides by the diminished ranks of desperate warriors, the soldiers marched forwards and climbed the path to the open gate, their feet stamping in unison like a terrifying automaton. The Britons couldn't believe how quickly they had been blindsided by their attackers, or how fast they were being slaughtered.

Rage replaced caution. Men threw themselves bodily onto the shields trying to breech the column, and fell away pierced by the Roman's gladii, the short stabbing swords that had proved lethally effective in close combat for centuries. Not one Roman soldier had sustained so much as a scratch, and yet the fighters of Boreshame lay dying in their wake in their hundreds. Ruthless efficiency met berserk Iron Age courage and the screaming Britons were cut down like grass under the scythe.

As soon as they had breached the gate Petrus sent a cohort of troops and his sagittarii to take the walls. The British fighters were now on the outside of their own fort fighting to get back in. The walls fell within minutes and soon arrows pelted down upon the surviving Britons' heads.

The cohort of experienced Romans had been ordered to hold the gate. They maintained their shield wall and invited the furious warriors to attack, then killed with machine-like precision. Meanwhile the third cohort was dispatched into the settlement. Their job was to kill the aged and butcher the children. Any men they met were cut down without mercy.

Less than two hours after the legion had arrived at the settlement the fight was finished. Of the entire ancient settlement only young and comely women had been preserved. Roman military wisdom allowed that after a fight a soldier deserves to take his pleasures, even if he must stand in line to take his turn with a struggling naked female held spread-eagled over a barrel.

Not everyone wanted their share of such spoils, but a good percentage of fifteen hundred men, plus the optio's centuries and his rough, road building labourers, took advantage of just thirty-seven women and girls. The luckier victims were soon unconscious, others had been beaten into passive silence. Once the rapists had finished with them the women's throats were unceremoniously slit, and their semen smeared bodies thrown into a great charnel pit, along with their families and friends. Some of the men used the pit as a latrine before the labourers backfilled it and stamped the soil flat with their shovels and boots.

Petrus gazed at the sun, now low in the south. It was midday. He called the optio to his side.

'I don't think you'll be having any more trouble here, do you? I've got to get the legion back to Noviomagus Reginorum or Vespasian will have my arse. You might as well camp in this fort and get your team back to building the road in the morning. Do you need any extra men?'

'I don't think so. We know where you are if we need you.'

Petrus saluted the optio, 'You did well today. Consider yourself the centurion in charge here. I'll get the documentation dealt with as soon as I'm back. Saves leaving one of my men here and you're capable enough. Congratulations.'

The optio stood on the wall and watched the legion march away. He thought he saw Petrus salute him, and he saluted back. Then he went to sort out his new command.

Along the path shadows clotted and moved with silent intent.

[44]

The day had been cold enough, but the setting of the sun promised to bring the Scythian breath of Hades itself to the road builders' camp in Boreshame. The avenue between the dense trees funnelled and accelerated the lightest breeze into an icy blast, and the fort's high position made it prone to chill winds that whispered and groaned around the palisades like vengeful ghosts. The men stood around their fires and like soldiers everywhere and in every age, they grumbled.

None of these men had taken part in the great massacre, but they had been enthusiastic participants in the rape and murder of the women. However, they had also seen what was in the burial pit, including the pathetic remains of children. Little bodies, even babies, had been ruthlessly skewered, and spitted on swords and pikes, then discarded like so many cuts of cheap meat. Warriors were one thing, but children? Some of those men were parents, the images of death haunted them.

They could have set up camp in the roundhouses of the settlement, indoors out of the weather, but they complained that the thatched roundhouses stank of stale cooking grease and soot. They didn't admit that they were also filled with the voices of dead children.

Their imaginations ran riot in the gathering gloom. They refused to sleep in the homes of the victims, but instead clustered out in the open, making themselves as comfortable as possible around blazing fires. Wrapped in their cloaks they sat, lay, or stood in loose circles and gazed into the flames, seeing broken figures twisting there.

The recently promoted centurion had set some of his soldiers to guard the gate, which he had ordered shut and barred against any hungry wild animals that might roam the forests of the Regini. He expected no trouble from the other local tribes, but then his centurion had expected none from Boreshame and he was dead. Better to be safe than sorry.

The new centurion was unsuited to his post. At heart he was a gentle soul. He had not taken part in the killings or the rape and was sickened by what he had seen. His workmen and soldiers were very aware of his lenient nature and would have taken advantage of it, if the optios hadn't enforced discipline with a firmer hand. He was on the wall, his heavy cloak wrapped tightly around his frozen body. He hopped on the spot trying to warm himself. One of the guards looked at him.

'We're wasting our time up here, sir. Fucking bears have more sense than to be out in a night like this. It's colder than my woman's backside, and that's cold enough to freeze the balls off Priapus himself. Why don't we call it a night and go join the others down by the fires? They've got hot food down there, and we haven't eaten hot food for two days. What do you say, sir?'

The other guards and the sagittarii on the wall mumbled agreement. The centurion sympathised with them, but after the day's bloody work he had no appetite for food and preferred to stay away from the other men.

'All right,' he said. 'Go and get yourselves some dinner but keep your ears open. I'll stay here on watch. If you hear me yell you drop your plates and come running as if all the bastard tribes of Germania were at the door. Understood?'

Within five minutes he was alone on the palisades. He watched his men heading for what little warmth they could glean from the fires and a bowl of hot food. The workers might have had little stomach for the Britons' roundhouses and beds, but they were a lot less reticent about taking the settlement's cache of food. Cauldrons of hot stew bubbled away above the fires, slung under three-legged, cast iron cooking tripods. He could smell the food from his position by the gate, he could hear the murmur of chatter and the clatter of spoons on plates, he could even hear somebody snoring, but he felt no trace of any heat.

He turned his back on the fires and gazed out into the darkness. He could see nothing. He had been momentarily blinded by the light of the flames and even squinting hard he could make out nothing in the moonless night. He cursed his stupidity. At that moment, he thought, the enemy could be approaching on a thousand elephants and he wouldn't be able to see them. If they took their boots off and walked quietly enough a hundred thousand men could be creeping towards him right at that moment and he wouldn't know.

Oldest stupid act known to any soldier; he told himself. Never turn your back on the darkness to look into the light, it takes valuable moments for your eyes to readjust to the gloom. He chastised himself with angry, gutter words that would have shocked and surprised his men if they had been close enough to hear him.

The path swam back into his vision as a faint silver stripe vanishing into the distance. He gazed at it because it was the only discernible feature in the blank, inky landscape. That stupid path was the cause of everything that had happened over the last two days. People had died because of that path. He was standing alone on a British wall because of that path. He felt a hot coil of anger knotting in his gut, the only hot thing in his whole body. He was tempted to open the gate and get every single one of his men to piss on the cursed thing, to spurn it with bodily waste. It already had drunk enough blood.

That was when he saw it and narrowed his eyes. A fizzing shock of wonder traced an icy finger up his spine. *What was happening out there?* The distant line of the path was vanishing from view. It was as if it was being erased by the night. He leaned forward and cupped his hands around his eyes to shield his vision from the slightest background glow from the fires. *What is that?*

He was tempted to call to his men and get some fresh eyes on whatever was happening but held his tongue until he had a better idea about what he was seeing. *Might it just be mist?* It was silent as mist and flowed like midnight water. He took a breath to call out, but fear snagged the words in his throat.

An arrowhead of shadow was swallowing the landscape. The path closer to the gate shone with a strange mineral phosphorescence but was swept out of sight where that 'V' shape had passed. Nothing moved in the shadow, and it made no sound. It was as if the path was silently passing from this world to another, more secret place. The centurion looked up, and he saw a flickering blue glow around the circle of stones on the hill. The stones glittered whitely like pale bone. To his startled gaze it changed and became a crown perched on an invisible brow. And then it was blocked from his view by an ebon figure that hovered before him.

He heard a single word that rang in his mind with the violence of a hammer blow and sent him stumbling backwards until he lay full length on the palisade's viewing platform.

'Witness!'

Like a cloak of night, the figure flowed over the wall into the fort, and then down, heading inexorably towards the fires and over one hundred and thirty men warming themselves around the flickering yellow flames.

The screaming began.

When the blackness touched a man he was devoured, torn apart like bread in a starving man's hands and consumed. The centurion watched as the eerie figure strode through the camp, trailing behind it a spreading wake of destruction. He saw men take up arms and burning torches to beat away the nightmare vision. He saw sagittarii fire arrow after arrow into the advancing wave of midnight death. And he watched them die. He watched them all die, watched them rendered into gobbets of torn flesh and hot sprays of blood. He watched until the last man fell, and the camp fires were extinguished. All became silent and still once more.

He was helpless. Lying on the wall like a terrified child he felt powerless to move or defend himself. And then the night before his eyes became darker than sin, and the clashing voice spoke to him once more.

'You are witness to the power of Agrona. I have taken the first steps in my revenge. Rome has killed my people. They sleep now, safe in my bosom. I shall take ten Romans for every man woman and child they killed here in Boreshame. I will take every Roman soul who crosses me; and I will slaughter their children and rend their wives until I have drowned your wicked empire in its own blood.

'But hold, I shall stay my hand if you and your tribe vow to preserve my sacred path. Cross the path and you cross me; and then you dare not sleep for I will come looking for you in your worst nightmares.'

He felt ice-cold breath upon his face. It was the breath of the tomb opening.

'Hear me, Roman. You must remember everything I have said and everything you have seen. This must be the last thing you ever see. I must prepare you to be my special messenger. Look at me. LOOK AT ME!'

The next day a patrol from Noviomagus Reginorum found the centurion alone in the settlement. The gate had been shattered and he was crumpled in a heap in plain sight just inside the wall. He was almost incoherent with terror, but he finally managed to stammer out that he must be taken to the Legate. He had a warning for Vespasian, the gods themselves had sent a message to him. Vespasian must beware. Rome itself might be destroyed.

The optio in charge of the patrol had known the centurion before the Roman fleet had landed on Britannia's shores. He knew him to be a calm, intelligent man, not easily disturbed. He barely recognised the human wreck quivering and weeping at his feet. He was shocked by the man's traumatised state, that, and the fact that his eyes had been brutally clawed from their sockets.

Back at the Second Augustan Legion's camp Vespasian looked down without pity at the only survivor from Boreshame. He believed such harm could only come to cowards. Brave men would overcome adversity or die in the attempt.

'Where are your men?' he barked. 'What happened to them?'

And then he listened with mounting horror to the tale the shivering, broken creature had to tell. He breathed, 'How did you survive?'

'To be witness. To tell you what she did. I wish I *had* died. That terrible night was the last thing I shall ever see. I must live as a blind man, unable to see anything else but that terrible nightmare until my dying day.'

In response Vespasian sent five hundred troops to the fort and they burned it to the ground. Then they set camp on the path and waited for the night. Not one of them was ever seen again by living eyes. No trace of them was found by scouts sent out the next day when the cohort failed to return.

The Legate was a pragmatist; he wanted no truck with vengeful gods and had no more men to waste. The west was calling. The Mount and the hill were marked on maps as cursed ground. The road was abandoned, and from that time on no Roman would walk there in the night; not once in more than four hundred years of occupation. At least none who talked about it afterwards. Boreshame was listed as a haunted, forbidden place, and there were more fruitful towns to conquer.

45

Present day. The sun slipped behind the Mount like a bloated orange disc bathed in blood. The ancient bones of the fort remembered the long-ago days when it had been home to bloodshed and fire. Magic leaked from its clay and seeped in a blue haze along the truncated line of the secret path. Those with eyes to see could have watched the magic flow down as far as the bypass and stop. It waited, ready for the command it knew must come.

After four days of fruitless forensic examination Tom Murdoch saw the movement from the corner of his eye. He was a soldier, he had a soldier's instincts. He called out to Maitland Trenchard.

'Captain, something's happening here. Get everyone off the road, get them away from the site. Make them move, sir. Make them move NOW!'

Trenchard didn't hesitate. He raised his arm and bellowed, 'Pull out! Clear the area, you men follow me. Look sharp now.'

Murdoch goaded the men to urgent action with frantic gestures. He yelled 'Come on, come on, drop everything! Move! Move!' and waved his arms as if he was herding geese. Most of the men had been with the lieutenant overseas, they knew when to listen. They sprinted away from the burned cars and trucks.

Just as the last of the sun's light vanished in the west the small group of specialist troops clustered around their armoured vehicles or crouched behind them, panting after their unexpected exertion. They felt safe, out of the scorched zone and well away from the perceived threat.

Murdoch stood by Trenchard's shoulder. They both gazed back towards the silhouetted masses of scorched vehicles. Nothing happened.

Trenchard made a sucking sound. 'What did you see, Tom?'

Behind them the sound of whispered conversation broke out. There came a low chuckle as if someone had said something witty. Murdoch pointed.

'See over there, sir. Where the blast radius touches the side of the road?'

Trenchard followed the line of his finger. He saw shadow and little else.

'What am I looking at? What spooked you?'

Another low murmur from the men and another chuckle. Murdoch stood more upright, pushed back his shoulders, and straightened his back.

'Can you no see that blue mist there?'

Trenchard nodded, 'So, are we scared of a bit of evening mist now, Tom? What's this all about?'

Murdoch drew a breath, 'Evening mist on a warm evening after a long, hot, and dry day? I don't think so. And when have you ever seen an "evening mist" that glowed blue like that? I never have, but *something* over there is doing precisely that. And why did it float to the edge of the burned road and stop? Why did it do that? That's not an evening mist, sir. Something fucking odd is happening over there, and something fucking odd wrecked those cars and killed several people here early last Monday. For my druthers, whatever happens next, I'd far rather be a witness than a victim, if you have no objections. Better part of valour, d'you agree?'

One of the men piped up. 'I believe mercury vapour creates a bit of a blue glow, sir. Might that be it?'

Murdoch replied, testily, 'Aye, lad, so it does. If you put it in a bottle and pass an electric current through it you'll get a lovely blue light, right handsome lamp too. But two things here; first, would you want to be breathing mercury vapour because I sure wouldn't? And second, how are you passing an electric current through open air? Answer me that. No cigar for that one, Lance Corporal Spelling, no cigar for that. Wait, what's happening now? Will you look at that?'

A curtain of darkness rolled across the dual carriageway like dense black smoke. It swallowed the blue mist and all trace of the tangled wreckage still scattered across the melted tarmac. It settled and boiled in place like a wall of pure malice.

Spelling spoke in a hushed whisper. 'What do you think's happening in there, sir? Have you ever seen anything like that before?'

'What do *I* think's happening? *I* think the devil's having himself a barbeque and he's looking for a gobby lance corporal to kebab and throw on the coals. Why don't you go take a look if you're so curious?'

Spelling stepped forward, heading towards the mysterious darkness. Murdoch grabbed him with a yell.

'You hold it right there you bampot! I'll give ye credit for balls, ye madman, but I'll no give you credit for any sense. I know your missus and she'd kick my arse if I let you loose in there, and she'd be absolutely right to do so.'

He raised his voice. 'All right, lads. I think we're looking at whatever shat fire and brimstone all over this road last Monday, and I think you'll agree it is not smoke from a bonfire. We don't know what it is – but we do know what it does. If it looks like it's heading towards us we get back and we get help, understood?'

Another voice asked, 'Sir, what if it moves towards the town?'

Trenchard fielded that one, 'We call in support, Mills. I agree with the lieutenant. We don't want to tangle with that, thing – but we can't stand idly by while the general public takes a beating. If it becomes a threat to the town, we call in an air strike. How does that sit with you, Murdoch?'

'I won't argue with you, sir. But first, have we got any grenades in the vehicles?

Mills replied, 'We've got a box of L109A1s, sir. High explosive frag grenades. They come in useful for shifting heavy objects and breaking up rubble. Effective range about ten metres, sir.'

Murdoch grunted his satisfaction. 'Swiss-made big bangs, excellent. Right then, who has the best arm? Come on! Don't be shy.'

'I guess I do, sir,' said Spelling.

'Right you are, bright boy! Get two grenades and chuck them into that shit. Let's see what happens.'

'Are you sure my missus won't mind, sir? I wouldn't want to get you in trouble.'

'No worries, son. You just volunteered in front of witnesses. Saddle up, now.'

Murdoch was one of those men who would never ask someone to do something he wouldn't do himself. He grabbed two of the heavy grenades and joined Spelling on his mission. The evening was warm and silent. The wall of darkness seemed to suck the life out the air itself. They both experienced a morbid sense of dread as they got nearer.

Spelling muttered, 'This shit is fair giving me the willies, sir. I'm all goosebumps.'

Murdoch spat onto the road. 'If a brave man like you wasn't with me I'd be off down that road like a screaming girl, so I would. Chin up, lad. Set me an example of British manhood I can be proud of.'

The Scotsman's guts were churning. He was a devout protestant, a believer in TULIP reformation and a Presbyterian of the Scottish kirk. He was not afraid to meet his maker. It was something he had come close to doing more than once. Death didn't trouble him. But he had never learned to overcome his fear of pain and suffering.

He had seen enough to know that there was no dignity in a man writhing in pain with half his face missing or a limb blown to minced meat and splinters of bone. He had seen the look of surprise and shock in the eyes of a man eviscerated by a shitty little IED, his vitals flung into the sand and dust. He had heard the desperate cries for help, the groans of agony. He knew here was no nobility in turning a soldier from a living man into a bloody smear on a butcher's bill. Murdoch's mouth was dry, and he fought to stop his hands from shaking. He needed to urinate, but he always did at times like this. He would hold his water. Spelling came to a halt.

'This is far enough, I think, sir. Mills said the blast radius is about ten metres, so we don't want to get too close. We've got three second fuses once we release the safety clip. I say we pull the pins, throw the grenades, and then run like shit back towards the guys. How does that sound to you, sir?'

'I love this plan. Okay, let's do it. On three... One – two – *three*.'

Four grenades hurtled into the black miasma to the sound of two men running away as if their lives depended upon it. Murdoch counted as he ran. When he reached three he leaned forward to make himself less of a target. Target from what? He didn't know, but he hoped it wouldn't blow his arse off or scythe his legs from his body. And then it happened.

The four grenades exploded simultaneously so that their reports made one great concussion. And there was something else, a furious screaming sound as if a host of voices had been raised in anger. Murdoch thought he recognised some of the words as Gaelic – the very tongue of heaven; but whatever the language none of it sounded polite. It was more like the banter outside a Glasgow pub at closing time. The two men sprinted, urged on by their fellows. When they reached the vehicles, they turned around to look at the damage they had wrought.

Nothing had changed. The sable curtain remained across the road, undamaged, unmoved.

46

Blue light had also seeped from within the circle of yew trees in the Cathedral Close, lancing out, needle sharp into the night to illuminate the graves around it. It brightened until it appeared almost white, and then, with a soundless concussion, poured upwards creating a solid column of light, reaching towards the stars. Within the henge the Lady stood on the sacrificial stone and allowed twenty centuries of death and more to soak into her spirit body and empower her. She coalesced and took shape.

At first, she appeared as a beautiful young woman with raven hair. A proud woman wearing a midnight dress and sable cloak that swept down from her fine shoulders. And then the transformation continued. The woman's fine features vanished, melting away into ebon shadow.

At last the beauty was gone and in her place stood the silhouette of the war goddess Agrona, the grim and vengeful deity who had once threatened to bring an end to mighty Rome itself.

She heard the grenades and the shrieking fury of her followers. They had been disturbed by detonations that shook the corporeal aspects of their shades. She sent calming enchantments along the path to still their pain. Silent once more they awaited her approach. It was time. She had absorbed all the power she needed.

Before the sun rose once more every vestige of that hated bypass must be destroyed, as would anyone who tried to stop her. She had been woken from the sleep of millennia when the people of the town broke the ancient promise. To her they were Romans. They would pay for their treachery with their blood.

She took on her mantle of power and sent out a greeting to the spirits of Boreshame. She felt their adulation and their fear. She was the dread goddess once more, the warhead who had once taken the blood of their enemies, their priests, and their leaders. She had taken their Roman murderers and scattered their shredded remains to the four winds, making them vanish as if they had never been. Agrona awoke once more to glory.

When she first awoke to this new time she had reached into the soul of a dying witch and hastened her death. She had entered the witch's spirit and devoured her mind. She had also reached into the boy who had once touched the gates of death and she had invited him to join her. The boy had been called away by another God, escaping her influence for a time, but he had performed the magic well for her when it mattered.

Michal Klebb had disembowelled the sacrificial baby he had stolen from travellers. Following her orders, he had abducted the newborn and vanished into the trees before its parents discovered it was missing. He had slashed its throat on the fallen Sister before he ripped the still beating heart from its opened body. Years before he had assisted the witch when she used a child's burnt remains to assemble the flesh token, a kind of battery in a clay pot from which the powerful could draw energy, but this time he watched while the fallen Sister drank the new-born's flesh, blood, and bone. The intestines remained behind because he had mistakenly placed them on the ivy instead of on the bare rock. His act had woken the guardian spirits of the henge.

It was they who had punished the man who had pleasured himself and splashed his seed onto the stone, using the Sister like a common whore. His act was unforgivable. Such behaviour was the domain of Ceridwen, the fertility goddess, or Damara, the spirit of Beltane, not fit for the temple dedicated to a goddess of war.

Agrona's abode was a temple to victory, to battle, and to death – it was not a cupped hand eager to accept the offering of a man's wasted seed. The revenge had been sharp and sweet, and his energy had been drained straight from his soul. And she had also drunk from the man who had allowed the crossing of the path. He thought of himself as a councillor, a noble of his tribe. But he had no nobility at the end. He died in terror and had screamed like a child. How fitting.

Michal Klebb and Phil Coombe had also helped fuel her resurrection. Their blood burned bright in her spirit, their sacrifices made all the sweeter by their helpless devotion.

Enough musing. It was time, time she walked her path once more. Time to accept sacrifice and taste the souls of brave men. Exulting in her reborn strength she screeched into the night like an eagle and howled like a wolf. People who had not heard a squeak from any wild animals for days pricked up their ears at the sound and felt the cell deep terror of the prey stalked by the insatiable predator. It was time.

The circle of trees opened for her and she stepped out from the henge in all her proud, dark, glory. A swathe of gloomy witch shadow swept away behind her, a broad and billowing V shape, an arrowhead for which she was the lethal blade. She strutted down her path like a queen born to rule, and she heard long lost voices praising her.

'Agrona, tha sinn gad adhradh bidh sinn a 'toirt aoidheachd dhut màthair de mheadhan-oidhche, piuthar bàis.'

Agrona, we worship you, midnight mother, sister of death.

And she answered, 'Coinnichidh mi thu ann an Annwn agus molaidh mi thu mar bhràithrean.'

I shall meet you in Annwn and praise you as brothers.

She breathed deeply, and her mouth filled with living air. A rich thrill passed through her and she almost moaned with pleasure. Where her feet floated over the ground it cracked as if crushed by a great weight, but she walked several inches above her path as if the soil was too mundane a thing to receive her touch. Her cloak of darkness streamed away either side of her as she proceeded across the Close.

A golden figure stepped out of the bosky shadows and approached the regal silhouette. It was Rose Platt. She was wearing a light, white, short-sleeved linen shirt dress that came to mid-thigh, and medium heeled tan shoes. Her hair fell around her shoulders in waves. All trace of the police officer was gone and in her place, stood an ethereal, beautiful woman.

She spoke, 'Flo', it's me, Rose. I know you're part of this spirit. Some of your personality must still survive in there, a light in the darkness. Talk to me Flo'. Let me know you've not gone completely, that this nightmare creature hasn't devoured you. If you can, please, stop this. Help me.'

The pitchy, featureless face turned to her. Words melted into her mind like hot wax and she felt her body tremble with fear. She took a step backwards.

Agrona hissed, 'So then, witch. You approach me without courtesy and I let you live because of the love of the woman who woke me to this fresh time. Kneel before me, pay obeisance, or I will forget the love she bore you and strike you down where you stand. DOWN!'

Rose staggered and fell to her knees, her head bowed low in supplication. The dark Lady sighed and bent towards her.

'So very fine, such a biddable soul. You walk in beauty, Rose Platt, you always have. I would protect you from what will happen next. Sleep. Sleep until the face of the sun warms your lovely cheek once more. My warriors shall guard you, my arms cradle you. No harm shall come to you. Sleep.'

Rose crumpled sideways in a boneless trance, her eyes shut and her breathing soft. The midnight spirit hovered over her for a long moment as if drinking deep from her scent. It quivered with remembered desire and the part of the goddess that had once been Florence Mayhew ached to touch the young woman's downy cheek just one last time.

The goddess chuckled at the thought. *Such mortal things we put aside. Let us take a walk along our path once more and leave her to her sweet dreams. We must now cast nightmares for those who have earned them.*

Agrona drew herself to her full height then began her journey into the town. She hesitated at the shattered gate where once had stood two wooden pillars that marked the transition from the human world to the sacred place of the henge, a place of sacrifice and worship.

She turned and regarded the cathedral itself, tilting her head to one side as if curious about the massy dark building. She saw through the skin of stone and brick to the light at the heart of the altar, the light that shone out in welcome to everyone who opened their heart to accept it.

'Men sacrificed themselves to me and I was powerful. You sacrificed yourself for the sake of men and look at how powerful you have become. Was that ambition that nailed you to the tree, or mercy? A goddess may not worship another God, no matter how humbly he lived and died, but I ask you not to interfere in my deeds this night.'

She bowed slightly, 'I will not touch your true worshippers, but I must take back that which has been stolen from me. It is my right to do so here in my own land. Stay there in your place of worship and keep your hands away from me. I shall not fight you if you turn your cheek as you promised you would. I cannot turn mine away but must bare my blade to the enemy of my grace. I cry "enough now, it is time". I bid you well, Nazarene. Watch if you must. I shall stay my wrath from your flock.'

She turned to the hill that led down the straight street to the blackened ruin of the dual carriageway. She chuckled to herself once more.

'Anyway,' she whispered. 'Where is the glory in punishing *sheep*?'

And she glided down into the town.

47

Promises made by gods are binding. Not a single true Christian died in the town that night, nor did the children who slept under His protective hand. But others were taken by darkness while they slept in their beds or sat watching the TV or were playing on their tablets. Some died while working or making love. During that short, hot summer night the town became a Necropolis of lost souls.

Agrona experienced every single death as if it was her own. The agony of loss coursed through her as each mortal light flickered out and was gone. She was the goddess of war, not murder. She had not sought this task, had not wanted to be awakened from her sweet repose in blessed Annwn. But now she had no choice, trust had been broken and she must become an engine for revenge to take back that which was hers.

'Are you all right, dear? You do look awfully thin; would you like to come home with me for some supper? I've got soup.'

The woman who had met Coombes on his way to the henge was still wandering the streets looking for a chance to perform a good deed before retiring to her bed. She thought of herself as a vessel of the Lord. Her neighbours thought she was a sweet but eccentric old darling and kept a fond eye out for her. She couldn't return the favour. Despite the bottle bottom lenses in her glasses she was almost blind from a combination of cataracts and glaucoma. The tall dark woman standing before her was little more than a rake thin blur.

'You would offer me food?'

The words dropped into the old woman's mind like stones into a well. She nodded and smiled.

'Yes, dear. I live near here, not much of a walk. I can heat you up some nice soup and the bread is nearly fresh. I can toast it. That would be nice. I can make us some tea, but I don't think tea goes with soup, do you?'

'You would break bread with me?'

'I don't think we should break it, dear. Just toast it with a nice bit of butter. And some soup. It's beef and tomato.'

Agrona reached out and placed her long-fingered hands onto the woman's shoulders.

'I have many names, but I am known best as Agrona.'

'Nice to meet you, dear. I'm Linda, Linda Dalmartin. I live at number 23, just along there. I've got a spare bedroom if you need somewhere to put your head for the night. I've got chucky eggs for breakfast if you stay, and a nice bit of toast for dippy soldiers.'

Agrona chuckled, a deep, throaty sound. 'I like soldiers,' she said.

'Nice girls love a sailor,' smiled Linda Dalmartin. 'I know I've loved, and lost, a few of them in my time. So, are you hungry?'

'I have something I must do first, Linda. Number 23 you say?'

'Just up there, with the black stone cat on the doorstep. He's called Merlin.'

Agrona leaned forward to study the woman's eyes and sighed. Soon this kind heart would be condemned to total darkness. She would not allow it.

'Go home and sleep, Linda. In the morning I will join you for chucky eggs and soldiers, if I may. I would like to see you again, to toast bread with you in number 23. But sleep now, dear heart, sleep. I shall see you in the morning.'

'Very good, dear. I'll see you then, I hope.'

'Yes,' said Agrona enigmatically. 'Yes, you shall.'

The goddess continued her stalking progress towards the bypass and the old biddy tottered home without feeling a thing. As she let herself into her house she patted Merlin on its stone head.

'Good-night old cat,' she said. 'I think we've made a nice friend today. See you in the morning, Merlin.'

And she sought her bed.

Murdoch scanned the town and beckoned Trenchard to his side. He pointed.

'You see what I see, captain?'

'The lights are going out. Power cut do you think?'

'I've never seen a power cut that rolls down the hill like that. I don't know what I'm looking at. I've never... Okay, look, I don't want to embarrass anyone here, but I really need to do something, something I always do when I'm neck deep in the shit and there's no fucking ladder. Is that okay with you, Maitland?'

'What do you want to do?'

'I'm going to ask for help from the one man who might know what's going on here. This crap is right off the page, I'm telling you. We need help.'

'Who you going to call?'

'Well, it ain't *Ghostbusters*.'

203

Murdoch fell to his knees and closed his eyes. And, in true protestant fashion, he clasped his hands in prayer. Trenchard looked around at the rest of his men. Two of them bowed their heads. Trenchard did the same.

'Our heavenly Father. You sent us your Son to deliver us from sin and eternal torment. Please, deliver us from evil now, we who worship you. Something terrible has touched this town and we must fight it. People have died here, innocent people. Reach out to these, your poor humble servants. Guide our hands, I beg you. Help these poor sinners to help others, I beseech you. Yours is the Kingdom, the power, and the Glory, for ever and ever, amen.'

When he began intoning the Lord's Prayer half the group joined in including Trenchard. Standing by their armoured vehicles just a few hundred yards from a devastated stretch of road and a mysterious curtain of drifting black fog, the men bent their heads and offered up the prayer they had learned at school.

All the while the eerie wave of darkness flowed through the town towards them. They would not run from it, but neither did they know how to confront it. Hand grenades had done nothing to dent it. It might be a thing of spirit, but it was obviously capable of affecting the corporeal world. It had killed and smashed and beaten the trappings of the modern world into a tangled ruin, and it stood unscathed in the face of its weaponry.

And that was when Murdoch got to his feet.

'Sir,' he said with a formal lilt to his voice. 'Sir, how fast do you think you can get the *Sparkler* here?'

Trenchard looked dazed and threw a glance towards the star-studded sky.

'What is it, Tom? Have you seen some press around here?'

'No, sir, not that. I've just seen something like a beacon pointing to the answer. Don't try to understand it, sir, but we need the *Sparkler* here. And we need it in a hurry.' Had his Lord answered their prayers?

'I'll give them a shout.'

He was on the radio for less than five minutes; all the while Murdoch and the men watched the tide of darkness drawing nearer and nearer.

Trenchard put his radio down, 'They say they'll be with us in fifteen minutes, tops. Can't do it faster than that. Sorry.'

'Right, then we'll just have to pray that's soon enough.'

And that was when the leading point of the darkness merged with the black curtain of mist. And it began to boil.

48

Mohammed was dreaming he was in a small boat and a shark was slamming into it, trying to get at him. He reached out to grab an oar and fend it off and the shark clutched at his wrist with its teeth and shook him. He cried out...

And woke up. Jerome stood at the side of the bed in his underpants, a thin, pale wraith-like shape in the night. He was still wrenching at Mohammed's arm and intoning, '...wake up, oh, please, wake up, please...'

'It's all right, Jerome. I'm awake. It's okay. What's wrong?'

Maryam stirred and muttered in her sleep. She distinctly said, 'It's on top of the wardrobe.' Then she issued a slight snore before her breathing became deeper once more. She had always been a sound sleeper and had once notoriously nodded off during a film sequence in a lecture. Ironically, she had been the one giving the presentation, and had to be woken up by one of her colleagues. Her talk was on the subject of sleep apnoea, and when she stood up, stretched like a lean cat, and covered her mouth when she yawned mightily before saying 'Where was I' she earned a laugh and a round of applause from the delegates.

The boy was agitated, his body bouncing up and down and his back curling backwards and forwards. He was evidently in an excited state.

'We have to go-o, we must go-o! We have to leave, right away, now!'

Mohammed thought Jerome might be sleepwalking, and then wondered whether he might be under the influence of an outside force.

'Jerome, its Dr Mohammed. Are you, all right?'

'No, Doctor we must go! We have to go now.'

Maryam sat up groggily, 'What the fu...? Sharif, what time is it?'

The boy's head was whipping from side to side. 'There's no time. We must go, we must leave here! We must go. Now!'

Mohammed made a decision, 'Jerome, get dressed. You too Maryam. The roads should be clear at this time of the morning. Be ready in five minutes. Go.'

Less than ten minutes later they were in the car with the engine ticking over.

'Okay, your call, Jerome. Where are we going?'

The boy was in the back, his face in shadow. His voice was tense. He was also excited that he was not in a kid's car seat.

'We must get away and high. Away from the town and high. Up is safer.'

Mohammed backed the car onto the silent road, and then nosed it towards the town. Jerome shrieked in terror and made to claw his door open. Maryam grabbed him before he could get away and Mohammed hit the doors lock button. Jerome whimpered at the snapping sound of the catches clicking into place. He pulled his knees up to his chin and wrapped his arms around them, making himself as small as possible. He had difficulty breathing.

Then Mohammed turned left onto a wider road, accelerated, and then turned left again at a roundabout onto a dual carriageway before smoothly hitting seventy away from town. Behind him the boy calmed down.

'Sorry, Jerome. I didn't mean to scare you. I had to come this way to get onto the A road. It's the fastest way to get away from town. What frightened you?'

The road climbed the South Downs. Either side of it fields and hedgerows stretched away across billowing chalk hills. One of the most iconic landscapes of England and all of it lost in the shadows of a moonless night. All that existed for Mohammed was the digital dashboard of his Mazda 6 and the bright cone of his headlamps lancing out onto the clean tarmac before him.

He glanced up at his rearview mirror. He had driven this route at night before and was used to seeing the lights of the town behind him, glittering orange in the distance. That night there was nothing. Not a streetlight not a house. Even the blue uplighters illuminating the cathedral had been doused.

'Sharif, careful! Watch the road. Are you half asleep, man?'

Mohammed dragged his eyes away from the stygian blackness behind them and quickly steered the car back onto the inside lane. He had veered dangerously close to the central crash barrier.

Maryam said, 'Do you want me to drive?'

'Look behind us.'

'What?' She turned around, so did Jerome. The rearview window was a featureless black. 'What am I looking for? There's nothing back there.'

'Precisely. There's nothing. Nothing. Where's the town? Where's everything? There are no lights back there, not even streetlights. Jerome, please, tell me. What do you know about this?'

The boy shook his head, then Maryam said, 'What time is it?'

Mohammed glanced at the clock on the dashboard.

'Just gone quarter past one, why?'

'Look, wasn't there something on the news about the council turning off the streetlights at night to reduce light pollution? I think they were turning them off after one. I'm sure I'm right, let me check. Just a minute.'

She switched on her smartphone and went to her search engine.

'Yes, here we are.' She swiped the screen a few times, 'And there it is! Dah, dah, dah, dah, hmm, oh.'

She switched off her phone. Mohammed cast an inquisitive glance at her. 'Well?'

'It starts at the end of September, when the nights are long enough for it to make a difference. It hasn't started yet.' She looked back towards the town.

'Hey, maybe it's a power cut. That could be it.'

Mohammed looked in his mirror at the silent child on the back seat.

'Do you think it was a power cut, Jerome?'

The boy shook his head. No.

'What do you think it was?'

He shook his head again. He didn't know.

'Has it something to do with the Lady?'

Jerome stared mutely down at his hands, knotted together on his lap. Mohammed flicked his gaze towards the road then up to the mirror again. The boy was looking at him now. His eyes shone silver in the shadows.

'It is the Lady, isn't it, Jerome?'

He nodded. Yes.

Maryam murmured, 'What's going on over there?' She pointed to a place where a popular café and large National Trust carpark proved a year-round draw for bikers, hikers, and sightseers. Lights glittered around it like fireflies, moving and congregating then breaking apart. Mohammed shrugged, 'Let's go find out, shall we?'

Seconds later he slowed and turned into the carpark. The place was a crush of vehicles and several people were walking between them with torches. Then he saw people with children, some obviously younger than Jerome. A bearded man with thinning hair approached the car and waved for him to stop. Mohammed lowered his window.

'Welcome,' said the man. 'Welcome, follow me. I'll show you where to park. Careful now, there are little ones running around. You know what they're like, they get excited and don't look where they're going. Keep your eyes open.'

Once they were parked Mohammed climbed out of his car and shook hands with the man who introduced himself as Lawrence.

'Which one of you got the call?' he asked. 'It was my wife Helen who woke me up and bundled me into the van. Moved like a squirrel with its tail on fire and she's not normally one to rush, if you know what I mean.' He cupped his swelling belly, 'She's like me, built for comfort, not for speed.' He chuckled ruefully. 'So, then. Who got the call?'

Mohammed had to think for a second, then answered, 'The boy. He's called

Jerome. He woke us up and made us drive away from the town.' He gestured into the night. 'What's happening down there, Laurence? What's happened to the lights? Do you know? My names Sharif, by the way.'

'Good name, we're practically brothers, yeah? Sharif? *Lawrence of Arabia*?' He chuckled, 'Have to be a big camel to carry a tall man like you. What's happening? Good question. Helen's been talking to some of the others and she's heard as many theories as she's heard answers. I guess this is one of those times when everybody knows everything, but nobody knows anything really. You know what I mean?'

'I thought that was just religion and politics?'

'Yeah, those and a man trying to work out what really goes on in a woman's head. Helen thinks it's something to do with the old religion.' He whispered, 'She's a pagan, talks to the sun and the trees, that sort of thing.'

Maryam had climbed out of the car and joined the two men. She shook hands with Lawrence who smiled. And then, before Mohammed could make introductions, a concussion of golden light threw the town into silhouette. The cathedral blazed, every part of its architecture picked out in the finest detail. The light burned like a halo, soft and warm.

A large woman bustled up to the little group. 'See, Lawrence,' she crowed. 'See, I told you! It's happening, it's the time and we're here to see it! It's the end of days, the bridge has opened between the worlds and the gods are here. They've arrived! And see, there? They blaze in all their glory!'

Mohammed looked back towards the brilliantly illuminated town and wondered what was happening. Maryam threaded her arm through his, and then he felt Jerome's small hand squeeze his other palm.

[49]

The town and its suburbs lay under a blanket of darkness. It was not fog or a mist but an absence of light. It moved and flowed like a living thing and wherever it touched life it brought death. But not everyone felt its fatal caress. The miasma flowed around St Joseph's Hospital without entering its corridors. Stephanie Talbot slept peacefully, dreaming of her son. She dreamed he was once more the happy, playful boy she remembered from years before.

Charlie Croker and his wife slept the sleep of the just. Phil Coombs' wife had an easy night. She didn't yet know she was a widow. She had prayed for her husband's speedy recovery before climbing under the single sheet that was all that covered her modesty. It was too hot for nightclothes, but she was too shy to lie naked on her bed, even when she was alone.

Surprisingly few of the townsfolk were taken by Agrona's curse, and most of those who died would not be missed. Not even by those closest to them. From a population of nearly five thousand the final tally of the dead would number in their tens of dozens. Mike Talbot would have been an obvious candidate, but he had not come home that night. He had not been home since Monday. He drank heavily after work and then spent the night with his girlfriend, a generous, well-proportioned woman who didn't demand the impossibly high standards expected of him at home.

Raychelle was an enthusiastic lover who knew how to arouse him even when he had enjoyed a pot or two too many. He thought of his wife as a tight-arsed streak of piss by comparison. Nothing there for a man to get his teeth into. He didn't even worry about his son, telling himself the boy was safe in police care. Parental duty dissolved as soon as he planted his sweaty hands on Raychelle's nakedly ample buttocks and she pressed him firmly between her thighs.

'Come to momma!' she moaned. And he did - eventually

Back on the bypass Trenchard moved his men behind their vehicles and watched the black wall across the road change its shape. Every instinct told him to get the troop out of there, and fast, but Murdoch said nothing. Everyone knew who was really in charge, they knew how important the battle-hardened Lieutenant Murdoch's advice would be for a team under fire. He was a lucky charm in battle, and a cool head in a crisis.

And yet the Scotsman did nothing. He merely scanned the sky and urged, 'Come on, will you? Come on,' as if waiting for the cavalry to arrive. He kept looking at his watch.

Spelling was the first to see what was happening.

He yelled, 'Shit! I don't know what that crap is but here it comes. What do we do, captain?'

Trenchard yelled, 'Mount your vehicles, engines running!'

Murdoch shouted, 'No! No time! Fucking run for it, lads!'

From the curtain of darkness midnight shapes were streaming towards the troops. They coalesced and rippled like streams in a river of malice, but most of the time they looked like an army of people, heavily muscled men, and women. They ran with their mouths open in silent screams and they held long knives, spears, and axes in their fists.

Spelling acted on instinct. He stood his ground and brought his SA80 A2 LSW to bear on the advancing horde. He unleashed a grenade from the underslung launcher before pouring thirty 5.56mm rounds into the melee.

'Run, man, run!' Murdoch yelled at him. 'Spelling, move it. We can't hurt the bastards! Move!'

As if in a dream he watched while Spelling turned to follow him and was instantly cut to ribbons from behind by the nightmare army. They flowed around the vehicles and then were all around the Scotsman, yet not one of them touched him. They parted and passed him as if he was a stone in a black river, and as they passed each one of them thrust their heads towards him and hissed, 'Witness', 'Witness', 'Witness'.

Murdoch collapsed to his knees and covered his head with his hands. His men and officer were behind him. He didn't see what happened, but he heard every slash of the knives and axeblades as they fell on solid meat and bone.

'Stand!'

He looked up and then cowered back like a rabbit before a wolf. The sheer elegant beauty of the shadow woman rearing up before him took his breath away while also turning his bowels to water. She was a weapon shaped like a human. The subtle nuances of her feminine curves were barely hinted at, but they were definitely there. Every line of her body was sleek as a missile, her fingertips sharp as needles.

His body could not resist. He stood, quivering like a rag in the breeze. She spoke without words, but he felt every syllable in his blood. While she spoke she stroked the soft, lined skin under his eyes with her deadly talons.

'I promised I would touch none of His flock. I would take none of His blessed sheep. But you have been chosen as witness and I need you to remember every detail without distraction. What you have seen must not be washed away by later things. You will live, Roman. But your eyes will be forfeit.'

She lifted her right hand and held it steady as a blade ready to strike. She pounced like a cobra and Murdoch's world was rendered a golden white. He flung his hands to his eye sockets, expecting to find bleeding pits where his eyes had been, but they were still in place. He blinked and staggered back.

All around him the nightmare army of shadows was dissolving like mist in the sun. *The Sparkler,* he thought, *it worked!* The answer had been given to him by God and he didn't understand it but there it was. It worked.

'You did this,' the woman's voice shrieked like a banshee. 'You did this, you filthy little worm. You did this. Now you die!'

Agrona flew at him, her hands outstretched like claws to tear his flesh, Murdoch flinched and held up his arms to defend himself. When nothing had happened after a few seconds he dared to look at his attacker.

The shadow woman's form was still dark as pitch, but now behind her there glowed a golden light that blazed up into the night sky. The woman's wrist was held in a delicate yet implacable grip, and her hand was dragged away from the stunned man's face.

The blonde woman who held the shadow's wrist was clothed simply in a shirtdress and tan shoes. Her hair moved around her beautiful features as if tousled by a breeze Murdoch didn't feel. The shadow creature fought and twisted against the grip but was helpless to pull herself free.

In a clear voice the blonde said, 'Enough, noble Agrona. Enough. Your stone gospel is no longer heard here. The henges are places where tourists and children eat ice-cream on hot days. Even the mighty have fallen, and those who once worshipped you are dead. Let them sleep. Let them rest in peace. Have mercy upon your beloved people. Enough.'

Agrona howled and twisted like a mad thing trying to wrench her arm free. Murdoch stepped away from the strange pair and looked around to see what had happened to his fellows. Of the six remaining men in the section three had vanished and the survivors were gazing blankly around them, looking dazed and shocked. Trenchard was one of the living. He stumbled across to the other two and hugged them like a father hugs his children. Murdoch was proud of his friend, he had what it took. *True courage is bone deep,* he thought, *you don't wear it like a badge.*

The strange voice of the shadow woman lashed out, sounding bitter and petulant but also harsh and martial, like steel clashing on stone.

'Who are you to do this to *me*? What are you but the mother of a sacrificed son? How dare you interfere with me? They took my path and I will have it back. And if I must I will destroy you and all His pathetic sheep to get it!'

The blonde smiled, 'No, Agrona, watch.' She pointed to the crest of the hill and the Cathedral Close. Golden fire burned there like a beacon, and then it flooded down the sacred path like boiling lava. The streetlights came on in its wake. The river of light swept across the dual carriageway and then up to the Queen's Mount. When it reached the place where the fort once stood, a mighty gate rose up, outlined by fire. It glowed against the night sky. The gate swung open.

A tall kingly figure walked out, back straight as a spear. He made obeisance to his goddess then held out his arm in invitation to her. The black creature in the blonde's grip stopped struggling. She raised her clawed hand in greeting, and when she did so her body began to wither and change. The inky shadows poured from her like smoke to reveal a raven-haired beauty who glowed in the path's light like a dark flame.

The blonde released her and said, 'It is done. I shall protect your sacred path, Agrona. My Son and His Father will help me keep my promise.'

Then Murdoch saw the shade of a tall bearded man standing at His mother's shoulder, and tears streamed unheeded down his gaunt cheeks. 'My Lord,' he gasped. The man turned his gaze towards Murdoch and smiled, nodding in greeting. The Scotsman smiled back through his tears, his heart so large in his chest he could barely breathe.

The blonde woman whispered, 'Go to him, Agrona. Go home to him, go with our love.'

Like the warrior queen she had once been Agrona walked to her path and climbed it up to the man waiting for her at the gate. They embraced and walked through the gate together, close as man and wife. At the entrance they turned and held up their hands in farewell. Mother and Son waved back. Murdoch smelt a fresh clean scent of roses as if the air had flowed to his nose from heaven itself. His heart swelled to bursting with joy. Then Agrona and the man were gone, the gate collapsed, and the flaming path winked out. The blonde stood alone.

The first threads of a new dawn bleached the sky behind the cathedral. The beautiful woman smiled as the sun arose, and then turned to Murdoch.

She said, 'Every new day is a prayer and a blessing for those who believe.'

'Amen to that, my Lady, amen,' he replied.

And then Rose Platt staggered and blinked, she looked at him in confusion. 'Where am I? What happened here?'

Mohammed and Maryam watched the sun rising over the town with Laurence and his wife Helen. They knew they had witnessed something extraordinary and inexplicable but didn't join in the celebratory carouse that involved passing around heavy jugs of real ale and a liquid they were assured was traditionally made organic mead. At no time did Jerome let go of Mohammed's hand. His warm little fingers pressed against the psychiatrist's palm and touched something deep in the childless man's breast. At that moment Mohammed would have killed to protect the boy who had put such complete trust in him. When the light vanished from the sky around the cathedral and the pearl wash of dawn kissed the sky, Jerome looked up at him.

'Can we go home now, please' he said. 'I'm tired.'

There was a lot of hugging and kissing going on around them, Maryam was fending men off by shaking their hands when they tried to gather her into their arms, but it was only a matter of time before the she started slapping faces. Then she might start throwing punches.

'Yes, Jerome,' said the tall man. 'I think it's time.'

By eleven o'clock, later that morning, Mohammed was in a deep sleep. This time he dreamt he was in the small boat with Jerome and the boy was rocking it trying to lean as far forward as he could to stroke the head of a great white shark. The giant fish was rearing up towards those small fingers, its mouth agape and hunger writ plain in its cold eyes. Mohammed reached out for the oar once more and the shark turned and gripped him in its teeth. He woke up.

'Please, Doctor, Can I go home?'

Jerome was frantically pulling at his wrist with both hands. With difficulty the man shook himself fully awake. He had probably managed almost six hours of sleep, but that would have to do. He put a finger to his lips.

'Give me ten more minutes,' he whispered. 'And stay quiet. Don't wake Maryam up, okay? Go get your stuff.'

He left a note for his wife on the chalkboard in the kitchen, and while he wrote Mohammed wondered how close they would have come to losing everything if Jerome hadn't hustled them out of bed that morning. When he switched on his car's radio the news was full of the night's strange events and focused on the surprisingly large number of sudden natural deaths that had taken place during the hours of the 'power cut', something denied by a spokesperson from the electricity company. The power supply had been uninterrupted all night, they said. There was no outage. It was an event purely local to the town, and nowhere else. They couldn't explain it.

Mohammed glanced across at the silent boy sitting by his side. He suspected there was a lot that had happened recently that was going to remain unexplained.

Rose Platt could remember little of that night. She remembered Flo's cottage erupting like a bomb, or at least she thought she could, and then she woke up standing on the bypass next to a small group of bomb disposal men.

A neat stretch of the road had been excised and somehow replaced by perfectly tended natural grass – studded with a patchwork of established weeds and lichen – that merged seamlessly with the ground around the Queen's Mount. It stretched from the bottom of the sacred path and across to the Mount as if drawn there by a careful hand.

A Scotsman called Murdoch insisted on treating her like a piece of finest Meissen porcelain, while another taller man was shouting into his radio, 'Forget it, yes, abort. Yes, it's over! Just abort, will you, for Chri... Look, just abort, okay! We don't need the *Sparkler* anymore. Okay? Okay, thanks.'

Coombs' disappearance was added to the thick file of unusual events during a long night. It was presumed the policeman had become confused due to his illness and had wondered off. His body was never found.

The vandals who had apparently burned down the circle of yew trees in the Cathedral Close – and erected a reconstruction of the original henge in its place – got less than a minute of air time. No-one questioned how the tricksters had moved and raised several tons of solid stone, of the exact correct type and size, over the course of one evening. On their return from London, Pamela Clarkson and Marcus Williams had visited the Close, and stood holding hands while they examined the miraculous restoration in silence.

When they arrived at Jerome's house Mohammed was surprised to see a workman opening and shutting the front door while locking and unlocking it with a shiny new key. A small VW van sat in the drive with the name *Lockmasters & Safes Ltd* emblazoned on its side. Rose Platt, wearing a bright coloured tee shirt and denim shorts, was chatting with the man while he worked. He was grinning at her with the dazed 'happy puppy' look on his face that Mohammed had grown to recognise. She had that effect on most men.

Jerome took his hand once more while they approached. Mohammed knew he was going to miss that.

'Listen,' said the boy.

'What?'

'The birds are singing again.'

With a sense of wonder Mohammed realised that he was right. The trees and bushes were filled with trills and cascades of joyous birdsong.

'So they are. Isn't it wonderful!'

Rose joined them. 'You listening to the birds? They seem happy to be back, I love the sound. I hadn't realised how much I missed it.'

Mohammed nodded towards the locksmith. 'Break-in or what?'

'What. Stephanie's home from hospital and she's not impressed by the fact that Mike hasn't shown at all over the last few days. He never visited her in St Joseph's and he left Jerome in our, sorry, *your* care. She rang his mobile this morning and a woman answered. She hung up when Stephanie asked where her husband was. Mike rang back five minutes later and tried to convince her that the woman was his secretary.'

'And was she?'

'Today's Saturday. The office is closed.'

'Oh! Oh dear.'

'Oh, very dear, Sharif. When hubby comes home he'll find that the locks have been changed by my friend here and his entire world has been packed in a suitcase and tucked away in the garden shed for him to collect – if he can find his way through the childlock on the gate that is. Ah, here she is.'

A surprisingly fit and determined looking Stephanie came out onto the drive pulling a large suitcase on wheels. She halted when she saw Jerome and threw out her arms in a loving gesture. He ran to her and would have put his arms around her neck in a tight hug, but she held him away defensively.

'Not too hard, little love. Mummy's neck is on the mend, but she's still a little bit sore. We have to be a bit careful.'

Rose indicated the case. 'That Mike's stuff?'

'No, ours. I figured we need a bit of real TLC and I know just where to get it. Mum's waiting for us at her place and then we're going to her caravan down on the Witterings. Be a proper little holiday, and Jerome loves spending time with his Nanny, don't you love? No, Mike's gear's already in the shed. Funny thing, we've been married for nearly nine years but everything he ever brought into our lives can be packed into one case.'

The locksmith picked up his tools and sauntered over. He put four keys in Stephanie's hands.

'There you are, love,' he grumbled in the gravelly voice of a smoker. Mohammed could smell the tobacco leeching from him and his clothes. 'These are for the front door and these for the back. Strongest locks available to the domestic market, you should be all right now.'

'Thank-you, and thanks for being so prompt this morning, Roger. We really appreciate it.'

He coloured, 'Well, you know. Any friend of Rose's an' all that. Here's the invoice, pop into the shop and settle up when you're ready or do it online.'

'If you've got a reader I'll pay you now, I've got my card here.'

'No worries, I trust you. If you can't trust the mate of a copper who *can* you trust?'

He bent down to Jerome and stuck his paw out for a shake. The boy complied, and Roger grinned at him. 'Proper little gent. Your mum brought you up right. See you then.'

He climbed into his van and reversed out onto the road. He tooted a farewell as he drove away and waggled his hand out of the window.

'Seems a nice bloke,' said Mohammed.

'Nice enough,' agreed Rose.

'He smells funny,' said Jerome and the adults laughed.

Stephanie pinned a letter to the door then made sure it was firmly locked. Rose gazed across the road to a parked car and held her thumb up. It flashed its lights at her. She turned to Stephanie, 'Okay, that's it. I think we're ready. You've got my personal phone number. If you need me, call, okay? And look after Jerome, he's special. See you soon, young man.'

She bent and kissed him on the cheek. He replied by pressing his lips against her mouth.

'Bye, bye, Rose. See you soon,' he said. The smiling police officer headed towards town.

Fifteen minutes later Linda Dalmartin opened her door to a smiling blonde woman in a bright tee shirt and shorts.

'Sorry I'm late,' said Rose. 'There was an invitation to breakfast? I got held up.'

'Come in dear,' grinned the old woman. 'No, matter. We can have poached eggs on toast for lunch, just as nice. It is lovely to see you on such a beautiful day. Isn't the day beautiful?'

And her merry blue eyes shone as clear and bright as the sky.

Afterword

Mohammed had finally persuaded a reluctant Stephanie to accept a lift to her mother's house. They had been gone nearly an hour when Talbot's Vauxhall Insignia bounced onto the drive. He stormed to the door and tried to ram his key into the lock. He was confused when it didn't fit, and then he noticed the envelope with his name on it and tore it from its mounting. When he read the brief note that informed him he was an 'unfit father and no longer wanted as a husband' – and learned that his things were in a case in the shed – he went into a rage. He started kicking and pounding at the door, hurling abuse at the all too solid wood.

The sudden, calm voice at his shoulder jolted him. 'Afternoon, sir. Are we having a bit of a problem?'

He turned and found himself confronted by a tall and burly uniformed police officer. He grinned sheepishly, 'My wife changed the locks, the stupid bitch! You wouldn't kick it in for me, would you?'

'I couldn't do that, sir, no. That would be interfering in a domestic situation. We can only do that in cases of violent dispute, sir. You'll have to talk to a lawyer, let the courts sort it out.'

'Lawyers? Courts? What the fuck are you talking about? This is my house! The bitch changed the locks.' He kicked the door again, almost breaking one of his toes, he winced in agony. 'Bitch! I'll smash a fucking window and climb in. She can't keep me out.'

'I wouldn't do that sir. Malicious damage. I'd have to arrest you.'

'Arrest me for breaking into my own house? Don't be so fucking stupid. Anyway, you're trespassing, get off my land!'

The officer leaned forward. 'Have you been drinking, sir?'

Five minutes later an abashed Talbot had been breathalysed and found to be nearly three times the legal limit, the legacy of a drunken binge that hadn't ended until he passed out in the early hours of the morning. His mad dash down the road and into his drive had been filmed by the officers. His car had also been caught on CCTV all the way back to the carpark of his girlfriend's flat on the far side of Chichester. It was considered lucky that the drunken fool hadn't killed himself or anyone else during his fourteen-mile speed fest.

He was cautioned and arrested, the outcome Rose had expected when she had first asked for protective surveillance of the Talbot home. Talbot's case was not helped by his furious assault on the two police officers followed by his limping attempt to run away, which ended with him getting handcuffed in front of his curious neighbours and bundled into the back of the unmarked car before being taken away for an overnight stay in the station's holding cells.

Stephanie and Jerome were alone in the caravan. Her mother had popped out to the local shops to rustle up something for dinner. If there was no joy there she would book a table at the *House at Home*, a child-friendly pub that served good food and was just a short walk from the caravan park. Jerome sat watching the brightly coloured sails of boats seemingly carving a path through fields of wheat, an illusion caused by the canal being just below eye level.

Stephanie thought her son looked vacant and distracted. She felt a knot of fear tighten in her belly. Then Jerome turned to her, his wide eyes fixed on hers.

'Mummy,' he said. 'Can I do some drawing?'

...

Other Works by Derek. E. Pearson

Preacher Spindrift **series**

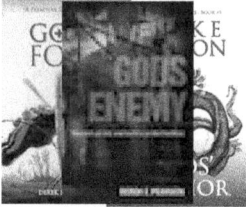

The first two volumes (GODS' Enemy and GODS' Fool) are **Foreword INDIES Book Of The Year Awards FINALISTS** in Fantasy

Soul's Asylum **trilogy**

Star Weaver (book #2)
Foreword INDIES Book Of The Year Awards FINALIST in Science Fiction

Soul's Asylum (book #1)
The Sun ☆☆☆☆ :
"a weird, vivid and creepy book, not for the faint hearted. But its originality and top writing make for a great read."

Body Holiday **trilogy**

T V PRESENTER JULIETTE FOSTER:
"Pearson's galactic-sized imagination delivers, with veiled gallows humour, a compelling image of a chic, high-tech society infused with a toxic strain that feeds on extreme violence."

Lightning Source UK Ltd.
Milton Keynes UK
UKHW01n1352270718
326395UK00001B/10/P